The Village

A Year in Twelve Tales

J.J.Anderson

THE STORY BAZAAR

The Story Bazaar
BM6231
London, United Kingdom, WC1N 3XX
www.thestorybazaar.com

Publisher's Note: This is a work of fiction. Names, characters, places, and incidents are a product of the author's imagination. Locales and public names are sometimes used for atmospheric purposes. Any resemblance to actual people, living or dead, or to businesses, companies, events, institutions, or locales is completely coincidental.

Book Layout © 2014 BookDesignTemplates.com
Cover design; Jorge Lanzi
Photograph; Marc Schlossman

The Village; A Year in Twelve Tales. -- 1st ed.
ISBN 978-0-9932106-0-0

THE VILLAGE

To my parents, Marjorie & Jack

CONTENTS

1.

A New Year

To begin at the beginning. The January days are short and dark and the sparkle of the holiday seems far away. Credit card bills arrive. It is cold and nature hibernates.

In the village people consider the year ahead. Time is passing and certain decisions must now be made. Is this the right time? When are circumstances ever right? Others tidy up and clear out, making room for the new, discarding the past. Or they garner resources already much reduced. Beneath bark and soil regeneration begins.

For some there is relief that the holiday is over, too much enforced idleness in the company of one's nearest and dearest is always salutary. Better to get back to the usual routine, if the usual routine can be endured for another year. There is calculation, for ambition must be furthered and some people must fall if others are to rise.

A man sorts through boxes in his attic, recycling his memories. A woman checks her calendar, as she talks to her cat. The clergyman seals an envelope containing the village entry for a Spring competition, before crossing the graveyard to his church. High above in a window seat, a young woman concentrates on her books, study will determine her future. At a different window in another house curtains are closed against raw winter light and a young woman huddles beneath a duvet, weeping, far from home.

Noisy children dash around the playground, their breath plumes, as a teacher exchanges greetings through the railings with the village policeman. Their voices rise as a delivery lorry passes, its rattling contents awaited at the public houses, where stocks are depleted. Out beyond the by-pass it's a normal day at the hospital, Accident and Emergency is empty. Parked round the back, an undertaker's van collects its cargo.

Nature takes its course. The horse chestnuts around the park stand massive and leafless. Ferns are brown between the thick and twisting roots. The line of trees marches up the hill to meet the ancient woodland, where life is already stirring, though it will not be evident for many weeks to come. The wild wood waits for longer, lighter days, as the turning world continues its course around the heavens, amid the wheeling constellations.

2.

Sunday

Ray almost missed the anonymous opening in the blackthorn hedge. In the passenger seat beside him, twelve year old Paul was navigating with a battered Ordinance Survey map. The sat-nav hadn't recognised 'Old Barton Airfield', but this was the place. Ray hauled hard on the steering wheel to turn the van and drove up the muddy bank onto concrete.

A few vehicles were already parked near a clutch of dilapidated aerodrome buildings beyond the flat expanse of disused runway. Ray drove the 'Marshall & Son' van towards them, bumping across in the dawn half light beneath a dense grey sky. Between the huge slabs, grasses and straggling weeds grew. Paul looked out across the airfield, saying little.

Ray halted a short distance from the others and the organiser, a short man in an outsize windcheater, scurried up to the van.

'Morning,' he called. 'Selling?'

Ray nodded agreement as he jumped out and opened the rear van doors.

'That's a tenner, please.'

'Do you reckon it'll be worth it today?'

'Yeah, should be. You're just early, mate.' The man stamped his feet and blew on his hands. 'It's usually good, the first Sunday sale of the year, as long as it doesn't rain.'

Ray pulled out the tarpaulin and support poles, just in case it did, but didn't erect the cover. He leaned them against the van doors and reached back inside the van, where the tea chests awaited.

'Here, help me get these out,' he called to Paul, who was slumped in the passenger seat playing on his mobile. 'I bet you wish you'd stayed at home in bed, now.'

'No.' Paul said, through a yawn. Ray saw him shiver, zip up his jacket and pull on his gloves before climbing out.

Together they unloaded the van. Paul's pale hair flopped forward as he bent over boxes, young limbs straining. Ray hefted a tea chest, grunting. His grey-flecked chestnut hair curled over his high-zipped coat collar. Father and son had the same broad cheekbones, wide mouth and square jaw.

Paul set up the table. Its bright plastic cloth looked forlorn in the dismal early morning. Soon the counter held a collection of objects, including a toaster, brightly labeled

'Nearly New' in felt tipped pen, a picnic basket set, 'Family Heirloom' and various items and gadgets, brought forth from the loft or the cupboard under the stairs.

'D'you really think we'll sell this stuff, Dad?''

'Why not? "One man's junk is another man's treasure," or something like that. Just because you don't want something doesn't mean that it's not of use to someone else.'

'S'pose so.' Paul thrust his hands into his pockets and surveyed the bleak scene. 'But....'

'It's early, like the man said.' Ray lugged another crate from the van and set it down by the counter. He pulled out a stack of shallow boxes with colourful lids, jigsaw puzzles, 'Fully Complete'. 'Hey, do you remember doing these?'

'Yeah. Well no, not really.'

'Oh.'

They worked in silence for a while.

'Daisy and Mum will be over later. Maybe we could go exploring then, take a look at the old aerodrome buildings? I wanted to be a fighter pilot when I was your age, an air ace. I used to watch war films on TV on Sunday afternoons with my Granddad – The Dam Busters, 633 Squadron. You know, we've watched some of them.'

Quietly at first, Ray began to whine a low drone. His arms stretched out to become aircraft wings and he ran around the stall, dive bombing, chittering machine gun fire and explosion blasts. Paul half-smiled, then glanced around.

'Stop it, Dad. People are looking.'

Ray coughed and returned to stocking the table.

Cars were now arriving at the airfield in a steady stream and lines of stalls formed as the pale globe of winter sun emerged. Stewards carried signs to the lane outside and a sound system growled into life. An 'All Day Breakfast' van and 'Ali's Hot Dogs 'n Burgers' arrived.

'Can I have a sandwich, Dad? Breakfast seems ages ago.'

'All right, watch the stall and I'll go and get us something to eat.'

Walking along the rows of vehicles, Ray spotted the professional traders, but also saw plenty of people like himself, recycling unwanted items. He browsed the merchandise, intrigued to see what others wanted rid of and tried to identify the swiftly discarded Christmas gifts. The recent holiday seemed far away.

Ray spotted the rotund form of Basil de Silva standing behind a stall, the flaps of a knitted hat covering his ears, his hands deep in his pockets. The dark-skinned Sri Lankan looked like he wished himself elsewhere, as a dew drop formed on the end of his nose.

'Morning, Basil.'

'Ray.'

One of Daisy's teachers, Basil was fund-raising for the school and his stall contained a mish-mash of donated items. Amidst the jumble Ray was drawn to an object that seemed familiar to him: a blue and chocolate brown cardboard box, lined with faded silk. It contained a brevet– a fabric insignia– and a metal RAF squadron badge.

'Where'd you get that Basil?'

'I'm not sure. There's supposed to be a number on the bottom.'

Ray turned the box over with care. There was no inscription. 'No.'

'Then I couldn't say. Why?'

'That was my grandfather's squadron. "Corpus non animum ...er... muto"' the motto says, though you can hardly read it, it needs cleaning. I used to have one just like it.' Ray examined the box closely. 'How much d'you want for it?'

'If it means something to you, just take it, please.'

'Thanks, Basil, that's kind, but I'll make a donation anyway.' Ray handed over a fiver. 'See you later.'

Ray sauntered back towards his own stall, removing the badges from the box as he went. He inspected the silk lining. There it was. A smudge of ink on the silk was all that remained of his clumsy childhood attempts to add a label, to write his grandfather's name. These were the very same badges that had been given to Ray more than thirty years before.

Ray halted, frowning and thinking. The badges hadn't been in the attic when he cleared all the boxes out, he was certain. He would have seen them. And there was no way he would part with them. Who else had been up there?

Paul's voice brought him out of his reverie. 'Dad! How much is this?'

There were customers at their table. Hastily, Ray replaced the insignia, closed the box and hurried to the stall. The mystery of how it came to be on Basil's stall would have to wait.

'To you, lady, five pounds.' Ray called to a middle-aged woman in a sheepskin coat, who was holding up a ceramic pineapple ice bucket. 'And a bargain at the price.'

*

The bare light bulb trembled as the earth above the shelter absorbed another shock. The planes and the airfield buildings on the surface were the targets, but a stray bomb could still obliterate them all. No shelter survived a direct hit.

Iris scanned the blanched and frightened faces as the dust settled. All her office girls were there, as well as some uniformed WAAFs, sitting on wooden chairs and bunks beneath the low ceiling. Others had stayed in the control room to keep radio and radar operating. One of the girls handed out tea from the flasks in the emergency hamper. They all clasped the tin mugs for warmth. It was bitterly cold in the shelter, but no-one complained. Ground crewmen played poker on an upturned crate, watched by a flier who hadn't got to his plane. He was the only pilot. How many had managed to get aloft before the bombing began in earnest, no-one knew.

Tom, her beau, was also absent. The warning had sounded during Sunday morning prayers and he and the men, even the padre, had run to the planes. It was standard procedure to launch as many as they could, for the aircraft were safer in the air. Any bombers remaining on the ground were brought inside the blast pens, the huge protective barrows of earth surrounding some of the hangars. On the surface, Tom and the others were exposed, not just to the bombs, but to the strafing fire of the enemy planes.

'There's nothing you can do,' Iris told herself, closing her eyes and silently making promises to gods in whom she did not believe, if only they would keep Tom safe. Some girls had made offerings, sacrifices to buy favour with the Almighty. One had cut off her waist-long hair in a one-sided pact to keep her sweetheart's northern convoy ship free from harm. Iris had dismissed such superstitious nonsense. Now she had nothing to offer.

Iris Everett had known Thomas Marshall, or known of him, since they were young children, the village being too small a place to allow otherwise. But it was working at the aerodrome at RAF Barton that had brought them together. The outbreak of war catapulted Iris from secretarial school assistant to office manager at the airfield, although she was scarcely twelve months older than most of her staff. Each day she arrived, in her mother's altered walking-out suit and brogues, her fair hair pulled back into a tight chignon.

Tom was in the RAF and, as a trained mechanic, was part of the ground staff team. Within a month of joining up, he was driving the aircraft as easily as he drove his old motorcycle. One evening last September, Iris had accepted a pillion ride back to the village on that motorbike and thus their courtship had begun.

The shelter shook, dislodging more dust and dirt and setting the light bulb swinging. That was a close one. One or two of the younger girls began to whimper, but Iris was dry eyed, her thoughts elsewhere. She tried to remember the tales of her childhood and the bargains made by those in need. She couldn't quite recall them.

Iris made a vow. Something, she promised, something of great value to her, in the future, would be given to the gods, if only Tom didn't die.

Now there was nothing to do, but sit and wait.

*

Cars of all varieties filled the area closest to the road and the market was crowded. The Sunday lunchtime request show blared from high metal trumpets, as couples strolled and families wandered, teenagers stretching at their unseen ties. The sale was lively and buzzing. Ray and Paul were kept busy. The little organiser hadn't lied, Ray thought, as he looked around in a brief moment of respite.

'Hello, Dad.' Daisy called out, her long pale hair shining amid the crowd. 'Don't my labels look good?'

Daisy had spent much of the previous evening handwriting the labels. Ray reached out and she came behind the stall into his embrace.

'Hello love. They do, that's why our stuff's selling.'

Paul piped up. 'No it's not. It's my expert sales talk!' and re-arranged some of the items on the stall in proprietorial manner.

Seconds later, Ray's wife arrived. Lynda Marshall pecked her husband's cheek, fair corkscrew curls whipping around her face in the wind.

'This is busier than I thought it'd be.' She handed over a replacement flask and hot sandwiches wrapped in foil. Paul took them, eagerly, and wasn't quick enough to avoid a kiss on the forehead.

'You're doing really well,' said Lynda. 'And you've even got rid of that old picnic hamper set.' She noticed that the jigsaws lay, half-hidden, at the back of the counter.

'Could you take over for a bit?' Ray asked. 'I want to go and have a look at mission control.' He indicated the old buildings, about twenty metres away. Their horizontal lines, wide windows and flat roofing showed their1930s provenance.

'Of course,' Lynda replied. She looked at Paul and Daisy. 'Are you two going with your Dad?'

'I am,' Paul responded quickly, while Daisy hesitated. 'It's man stuff.'

Lynda put a hand on Daisy's shoulder. 'You go if you want to, Daisy, don't you listen to him.'

'It doesn't matter Mum, I'll stay with you.'

Leaving Lynda and Daisy in charge of the stall, Ray took Paul passed the other early-comers' vehicles. They made their way through the throng, towards the nearest block. Rounded at one end and two storeys high, with a much higher control tower at the far end, it would once have been the control centre of the airfield. Now ivy climbed up to the empty metal window frames. Broken bottles and other detritus signalled that it still had occasional human occupation.

On the far side of the building they could hear the wind whistling through the empty rooms. The noise and bustle of the market sounded far away.

'They would have plotted the position of the fighters in there— WAAFs would push markers around maps and listen to radar and radio. Moustachioed officers would be drinking tea and puffing cigarettes.' Ray peopled the ground floor, as they peered in through the windows. 'And identifying the approach of the incoming attack planes.'

'Yeah, we did the Battle of Britain in history,' Paul made his voice deep and rasping. '"Never, in the field of human conflict"... but Dad?'

'Mmm?'

'Didn't that all happen down south, Biggin Hill and Northolt?'

'No. Where'd you get that idea? A lot of the air fields were in the South East, yes, but not all of them. Things happened here too, y'know. We went to RAF Lockeley, remember? That's a World War II airfield.'

'Oh. I didn't think... it was so shiny and new.' Paul looked down at his trainers. 'I liked going there.' He gazed around at the overgrown, crumbling buildings and the emptiness immediately around them.

Ray tried the metal door at the foot of the control tower and, to his surprise, it opened. Inside, a fire had blackened what remained of the ceiling and there was an unpleasant smell. Birds fluttered in the higher storeys, but the structure of the tower was still apparent. Snatches of dialogue from

Angels One Five echoed in Ray's head, as he turned to look at his son.

Paul was staring through the window, towards the far end of the runway, visualising one of the shiny jet fighters he'd seen at Lockeley coming in to land. After a perfect touchdown, the pilot, in an all-in-one, metallic aeronautic suit, descended the cockpit ladder and strode across to the command centre to report. In his head Paul heard the plangent notes of a popular song, as, removing her helmet, the pilot shook out her long, dark hair. She began discussing drag co-efficient and aerodynamics with the engineers and scientists.

Paul felt Ray's hand on his shoulder. It was time to go.

Pigeons burst upwards in a startled spray of feathers, as a mangy cat leapt onto a sill. Paul headed towards the door and Ray followed.

As they retraced their steps, Ray looked back at the control tower, screwing up his face against the icy wind. He imagined the turning grid of the vanished radar antenna, bouncing signals into the ether, while above there was tumult amid the clouds. In his mind's eye planes rolled, dived and spiralled upwards, shot through with ack-ack tracery, against an azure sky.

Paul was forging ahead, back towards the car boot sale. Ray lengthened his stride and caught up with him.

'Hey, how about us going over to Duxford one weekend? It's the Imperial War Museum aerodrome, they've got lots of old planes, fighters and bombers. And the American Air

Museum's there as well. It's only Cambridgeshire, not so far away?'

'Is it near Cambridge Science Park?' Paul's expression brightened. 'We could go round the software engineering firms, they do tours. Their CPUs are in all the best mobiles and Nintendo and Game Boy. You get to try out the new software! Yeah, that'd be good. I'm hungry.'

Paul ran on to their stall and food, while Ray trudged along behind.

*

When the All Clear siren sounded, Iris was first through the shelter doors. She came to an abrupt stop. Behind her, others did the same.

The devastation seemed absolute. Isolated islands of fire were alight across the aerodrome, where aircraft burned. Black smoke plumed from the wreckage of a hangar and already survivors were pulling at the rubble, pushing aside the shards of corrugated iron sheeting, rolling away the heavy concrete bricks. Fire hoses were playing water onto the surviving buildings, directed by columns of men, while others pumped. Bodies lay on the ground.

Two ambulances were fast approaching from the public road, their sirens ringing. Groups hurried towards them, carrying laden stretchers. Further away, a pitiful bleating came from the stalls housing the goats, the squadron's mascots.

Iris stared upwards at what remained of the tower. The main control building had been badly damaged, its windows

14

blown out and its antenna askew. She began to follow the WAAFs who were running towards it, calling out the names of their friends and colleagues.

Where was Tom? He could be anywhere. She turned at the sound of her own name.

'Iris!' one of Tom's workmates called. 'He's over by the blast pens.'

Jubilant, Iris set off at speed.

At the massive berms of earth, people were rushing to preserve what could be saved. There was frantic activity as the planes that hadn't burned were being draped with dampened tarpaulin to prevent them from catching fire. In the second bay Iris saw Tom high up in the cockpit of a Wellington, taxiing the bomber further into the lee of the grassy earthwork. The plane's twin propellers rotated slowly as the giant machine moved forwards.

As she watched, the wind changed. A flurry of sparks blew across the tarmac. Within seconds a thin crescent of flame curled beneath the Wellington's tail fin.

'Fire!' Iris yelled with all her might. 'Tom! Get out!'

But the noise of the engines was too loud. Her voice was lost. She ran towards the plane.

The flames were spreading rapidly to the lower fuselage of the plane, Iris could see the outer covering burning away to reveal the metal skeleton beneath. She knew that the fuel tanks were sealed with layers of rubber, but this would melt if the fire really took hold. The plane would be blown apart.

Tom had only a few minutes.

She was screaming now. She stumbled backwards as someone pulled her away. Then there was shouting and men were all around her as a fire team arrived with their pump. Water spouted from the hose— at first a dribble then a spurt. Up ahead the plane was turning into the wind. She could no longer see Tom's face, the cockpit was obscured by billowing smoke. Everything seemed to slow down.

The water gushed out in a high arc to hit the rear of the plane, which stuttered to a halt. Iris saw the cockpit cover rise. It was almost twenty feet from cockpit to tarmac. If he had to, Tom would jump, Iris told herself. If he was able to.

On the ground a crewman ignored the water and the flames as he rushed his ladder towards the plane. Others ran to hold it steady as a figure appeared from the cockpit. Through the smoke Iris saw him grasp the top of the steps and climb across on to them. Tom clambered down. He and the others ran towards her. Behind them the flames ate up the plane's outer covering, but a steady stream of water kept them away from its fuel tanks.

Iris struggled free and ran to Tom. She buried her face in his shoulder.

'I was so frightened.' She spoke through tears, as his arms held her close. 'I was so afraid that I would lose you.'

'I know, I know. Come away now.'

She felt his face against her hair, as he drew her over to the bay wall. Behind them the flames died, leaving the Wellington's skeleton exposed, a blackened and smoking shell.

*

It was late afternoon and the Marshall family had returned home in the growing dark. In the living room the lights were on and the curtains were drawn against the cold. The flames of a gas fire flickered as Ray relaxed on the sofa. The children were busy in their bedrooms.

Lynda brought over two mugs of tea and settled into the crook of Ray's arm. The newly polished squadron badge sat in his palm and he scrutinised it with a frown.

'Was Paul interested?'

'Not really. He took a look at it, but couldn't wait to go and play his games.' Ray sighed. 'Not so long ago he would have loved to help me clean this up. Not anymore.' He took the mug Lynda handed to him. 'Thanks. He used to like doing things with me.'

'And he will again.' Lynda looked up at him. 'But he needs to find his own way first. You're his father, you can't be his best friend as well. You need to let him go.'

'I know, love, but.....' Ray grimaced.

'Did you ask Daisy to help?'

'No. And before you say it, I should have done, I know. I'll find something else for her to do with me.'

'She's growing up too, so it had better be good.' Lynda shot him a forceful look. 'You mustn't make her feel second best.'

'Second best! How could my mazy-Daisy ever be second best?' Ray looked sideways at his wife and smiled. Lynda harrumphed and sipped her tea.

'I was talking to Basil,' she said. 'I asked him how he got the items for his stall. He told me that all the Priory Road pupils took home a leaflet, asking for donations, last month. Did you see one?'

'No. Did Daisy bring one home?'

'I can't remember, the run-up to Christmas was frantic. And you'd already decided to do the car boot sale yourself.'

'Mmm.'

'When you went through the stuff in the attic, did Paul help you?'

'He came to see if there was anything he wanted, I think. I did wonder... do you think Paul took the badges?'

'I don't know, but I doubt it, they're not his sort of thing.'

'As we've seen,' said Ray with a baleful look.

'Well....' Lynda stroked Ray's cheek. 'Did Daisy help you too?'

'No, you know what she's like about spiders, the attic isn't a good place for her.'

Lynda turned to look at her husband.

'You didn't ask her, did you? You could have brought the boxes down and she could have helped you sort through them. Why are you excluding her?'

'I'm not. Honest.' Ray flushed, then frowned. 'Do you think Daisy could have taken the badges?'

Lynda sighed. 'I don't know. If she did, she knows that she shouldn't have.' She subsided. 'I suppose that would be the point.'

'To get at me? Daisy's not like that.'

'You're right, she's not malicious.' She twisted a strand of hair around her finger and drew her brows together. 'Didn't you let Paul choose something for himself?'

'Yes, but...'

'Did you do the same for Daisy?'

'No, but she didn't help.'

'So? Neither did Paul, not really. And he would have made sure that Daisy knew that he'd been given something and she hadn't.'

Ray shifted his weight on the sofa.

'Okay, maybe you're right,' he said. 'She might feel left out.' He stood up. 'I'm going to talk to my girl.'

Ray took the stairs two at a time.

Daisy looked up from her book and smiled when her father knocked and entered her room. She was curled up in her chair beside the reading lamp, nestling into a bed of brightly patterned cushions. Ray switched on the overhead light.

'Hi Dad.'

'Hello, love.' Ray moved aside the soft toys and sat on her bed. 'Got a minute?'

She closed the book and sat up. 'Yep.'

'D'you know that RAF insignia of great Granddad's?'

'Yes.' Her face grew clouded.

'Was it in any of the boxes brought down from the attic?'

'No.' She shook her head.

'Was it up in the attic?'

She nodded her head in the affirmative.

'Ah.' Ray pursed his lips. 'When did you see it up there?'

'Before you brought everything down.'

'You went up by yourself? Climbing the ladder? Despite the creepy crawlies.'

'Yes, I can do it.' Daisy raised her chin. 'And you always say there aren't any creepy crawlies.'

Ray's hand snaked out and he tapped her nose with his finger. 'You're not so big, you could have fallen.' He smiled.

'Paul goes up by himself.'

'Your brother's older and bigger than you are.'

'It's all right Dad, I'm careful.'

Ray grew serious. 'Is that when you took the badges for the school stall?' He asked.

Daisy was silent.

'They were precious to me, you see....'

'I know. But I didn't know that then. Not then.' Ray could see that she was trying hard not to cry. 'You said Paul could have something.'

Ray wanted to wrap her up in his arms, to make things better. But this was necessary.

'And so could you,' he explained. 'But you shouldn't have taken something without asking. You know that. Why didn't you ask me, love?'

'Because you didn't say... like you did with Paul. And he doesn't even care!' She gulped, then wailed. 'Why does he get you all the time?'

Tears flowed down Daisy's reddened cheeks. She grasped a cushion close, head down, avoiding his eyes.

'I'm sorry, love.' Ray leaned forward. 'I didn't know you wanted to help?'

'You never know. You never think, whatever I say or do.' Her words poured out with more tears.

There was a small silence. Ray realised, to his chagrin, that Lynda had been right. Without knowing it, he had been excluding his daughter. How could he make it up to her?

'You're right, I should've asked you too,' he said. 'I love you just as much as I love Paul.' He tried to catch her eye, looking up at her. 'Though you mustn't take what isn't yours.'

Daisy sniffed resentfully.

Ray decided to take a different tack.

'D'you want to know how I knew the badges were great Granddad's?'

She looked sidelong at her father.

'There's a smudge of ink on the silk lining of the box, underneath the brevet.' Ray produced the box from his pocket to show her. 'See, there?'

Daisy nodded.

'I did that. When I was about Paul's age. Your great Granddad gave the badges to me then, just after my Dad died."

"To cheer you up?" Daisy took the box to look more closely.

"I think so. I was trying to add a label which I'd written, just like you wrote labels for our stall at the car boot sale.'

'What does that mean?' She pointed to the motto.

'It's Latin, it means something like "My body may change, but my spirit lives on". It represents the squadron, those who died and those who joined later.'

'Like a family?'

'Sort of. It's meant to show that the squadron will continue, regardless of losses to the enemy.'

'And where is it now? The squadron?'

'I don't know.' Ray half smiled, then stood. 'That's a good question. Come on.'

Tears already forgotten, Daisy followed her father downstairs to the PC in the corner of the living room. Lynda glanced up from her magazine as they entered and watched him sit on the swivel chair and tap the keys. Daisy pushed him around and clambered to perch on his leg. Ray steadied her, his arm around her waist. Once on-line, he opened the relevant site and both stared at the screen.

'Oh.' He sat back, disappointed. 'It doesn't exist anymore.'

'That's a shame. Let me see.' Lynda was at his shoulder. Taking the mouse she scrolled down the screen. "Look. It's been disbanded before, lots of times, only to be reformed.' There was a long list of dates on screen. 'So it could come back."

'Not the same though.' Ray sighed.

'"My body may change but my spirit lives on,"' Daisy quoted. 'Wasn't that what you said?'

'It was, love.' Ray hugged his daughter and looked up at Lynda, who raised her eyebrows and smiled.

'What's up?' Paul clattered into the room, startled to see the others clustered at the screen. 'What are you lot doing?'

'Finding great Granddad's squadron,' Daisy began.

Paul snorted in derision.

'Yes.' Ray cut in. 'Your sister's been working it all out.'

Daisy's beaming smile was returned by her father, as Paul looked suspiciously from one to the other.

'When's tea?' he demanded.

*

'Iris.' Tom took a deep breath.

Iris and Tom sat on folding chairs under the canvas roof of a temporary mess tent, drinking hot, sweet tea. Iris was thankful for the fierce liquid. She felt wrung out and exhausted, but she knew her job was the easy one. All her girls were alive and well, while other colleagues were injured or dead.

It was a break from the clearing-up operations, which had continued without pause all afternoon and evening. Outside, debris was still being cleared. The buildings, or what remained of them, had been thoroughly searched and everyone was accounted for. Aircraft parts were being salvaged from damaged planes in patches of glaring electric light. Darkness shrouded the outer airfield. Across the concrete a lone figure led a forlorn procession, bells clanking, as the goats were taken to their new home.

Emotion overwhelmed her.

'Tom, I hate this war!' She tried not to cry. 'Everyone in the control tower, all of them...gone!'

'I know.' Tom reached out, but let his hand fall.

'And how many planes did we lose?'

'On the ground, four, though we'll be able to salvage something of them. We'll be on double shifts to get them up again. Two were shot down.'

'I don't know how much more of this I can take. How much longer is it going to go on?'

'I don't know.'

There was a long pause. Outside there were shouts and crashes.

Tom took her hands in his.

'I only know that it's worse, now, isn't it? What I mean is, now we've got each other. Which is a fine thing of course, it's just that....' He stuttered to a halt, then went on at a rush 'Let's not wait for all of this to be over. It could go on for years and we might not live to see the end of it.'

'Oh yes.' Leaning towards him, Iris gripped his fingers. She saw he was leading up to something.

Tom licked his dry lips and swallowed.

'Look, I know we've only been ...well, walking out... for a few months, but we've known each other all our lives.' He sank to one knee. 'Say the word and I'll be round to speak with your father, tonight if need be.'

Iris's fear was replaced by surprise. She looked down at his square face, with its abrupt cheekbones and clean jaw under an unruly brush of chestnut hair.

'Thomas Marshall, are you proposing?'

24

'Yes, of course I am.' He licked his lips again, cast a longing glance at his mug and waited. Iris stared, open-mouthed. Eventually he prompted. 'It's damp down here. How long before I can get up?'

'Get up, you idiot.' Iris's smile belied her words. 'Tonight's fine by me. You can come in when you take me home. Oh, by the way, I want a June wedding.'

With a broad grin Tom clambered to his feet.

'Tonight it is... then June.'

He kissed her forehead and offered her his arm. Iris rose, leaning in close to him. With a new spring in their step they walked, silhouetted against the light, to rejoin the work.

*

Ray and Lynda were settled on the sofa in the soft lamplight, the children now in bed. The box, with its insignia, sat on the sofa arm beside Ray.

'I thought I might do some research, see what I can find out about that old airfield. I'd like to know if my Granddad ever served there.'

'Didn't he say? I thought he liked his war stories.'

'He did, but never about himself. He and Grandma didn't speak about their own younger days. I think it was a hard time. They wanted to shield me from it − there was enough death in my life already. And I think Grandma never got over my father's passing. It was long after the war, but somehow, in her mind, it was all linked. She believed it was her fault, but there was nothing anyone could have done....'

Ray picked up the squadron badge. He gazed into the flames of the fire.

He remembered sunlight streaming down from large, hospital windows on to a group of figures ranged about a heavy iron bed, its wasted occupant imprisoned by starched white cotton. It was his father. At the bedside his mother sat, pinch-faced and wan, already showing signs of the disease that would kill her within a twelve-month.

His grandmother strode back and forth, weeping and berating herself, while his grandfather watched on anxiously.

Never much of a talker, Ray's father had always been a remote figure to his son. He summoned Ray closer, interrupted by a hacking cough. His harsh brusqueness had often grazed and scuffed young Ray, but just then he could hardly be heard.

'Look after your mother,' he whispered, a reprimand in advance. 'And work hard at school.' Perplexed and disappointed, young Ray promised to do both. Bewildered tears flowed soon after. His grandfather took him outside.

'That's when I began to grow up,' Ray murmured, putting the badge in its box

'What?' said Lynda, tired and drowsy.

'Nothing. Just old memories,' Ray replaced the lid. 'Granddad was stationed locally, I think, before going to France.'

'My mother might know. You could ask her − if you can cope with a trip down memory lane. It's one of her favourite thoroughfares.'

'Not so much a day trip, more a holiday fortnight.' Ray grinned. He placed his arm around Lynda.

'What about getting Paul to search on the internet,' she said. 'Aren't all the old records on-line now?'

'Yes, that's how to get him involved. Good idea.' Ray kissed the top of Lynda's head. 'I suggested we might go to Duxford, you know, but all he could think about was Cambridge Science Park.'

'Oh my love, he's just not that engaged by the past. Take him to the Science Park. You could call in at Duxford on the way home. That way each of you does something for the other.'

'Hmm, it might work.' Ray frowned.

'And I'm glad that you spoke with Daisy and sorted things out.' Lynda squeezed Ray's hand. 'You did the right thing.'

'No doubt I'll get my reward in heaven.'

Lynda's mouth twitched.

'Oh, something might be arranged before then.' She got up, taking the box from Ray and placing it in the sideboard drawer. 'I think I'll have an early night.'

'That's... a remarkably good idea,' Ray said, feigning a yawn. 'It's all that fresh air. I think I'll have one too.'

Ray flicked off the lamp switch. Lynda was outlined in the living room doorway by the light beyond, before she disappeared. Turning off the hall light, Ray followed her up the stairs.

3.

The Volunteer

Wednesday was Molly's day for helping at the hospital. Mid-week rarely saw much by way of incident, so she often went into Accident and Emergency for a quiet cup of tea. But today was different.

Ambulance men were just leaving, having made their report at Reception and deposited three individuals in the front row of plastic chairs. A pair of orderlies, one tall, one short, awaited instruction.

'Morning, Molly. Be with you in a minute.' The receptionist turned to the orderlies. 'Can one of you take these two through, please. Their names are Thompson and Beck. Get them into gowns and drop them at X-ray. The nurses will take them from there.'

She indicated two bloody and befuddled teenagers.

'They look like they've been in the wars.' Molly remarked.

'Joy-riders! They crashed a stolen car across the by-pass central reservation.'

Molly inspected the youths. One had a shaven head which was smeared with blood and dirt. The other cradled his lower arm in his other hand, his mouth was bloodied with front teeth missing. Molly tutted.

The receptionist nodded towards the third casualty. 'It gave him a rude awakening.'

A tramp sat, separately, huddled in a greasy black overcoat. He cast furtive glances around the pristine, white room, looking for ways of escape. Molly could detect his unwashed reek even from beside the desk.

'He was living in a shack between the dual carriageways, would you believe? With electricity and everything, even a satellite dish.' Everyone looked at the tramp, who sank further into his stiff coat. 'He'll need checking over, so get him out of those clothes,' she instructed the orderlies. 'And see if you can persuade him into the shower.'

The orderlies looked as if they were going to argue.

The tramp looked horrified.

'I'll just fill the kettle, shall I? A stitch in time waits for no man.' Molly collected the appliance and turned towards the kitchen. She noticed a man, lurking in the back row, writing in a notebook. A reporter from the Herald, no doubt, but, to Molly's surprise, he seemed to be showing more interest in the tramp than the youngsters.

30

On her way to the kitchen she was almost run down by a nurse pushing a trolley. On it lay Alf Harkiss, his weathered face unusually pale. He clutched the large garden fork protruding from his left foot as he was wheeled towards Surgery.

'Oh, Alf, what have you been doing?'

'What's it look like?' Alf glowered at her. 'I was lifting spuds and the ground was 'ard.'

'You shouldn't be gardening at your age.'

'What d'you mean? My age?' He grumbled as he was pushed onwards. 'I don't need no 'elp from nobody, Molly Morgan!'

Molly watched his progress, looking thoughtful. Something, she said to herself, would have to be done.

That afternoon she spoke with an acquaintance from Social Services, who suggested that there might already be a volunteers' gardening scheme. So, on Friday morning, when she helped at the Library, she took the opportunity to slip into the Silver Surfer class where she could access the internet and check. She allowed herself ten minutes to search for charities and voluntary groups.

'Are you looking for anything in particular, may I ask?' A refined-looking gentleman, long past his salad days, enquired.

'Yes, a gardening service for the elderly.' Molly smiled. 'Do you know of anything? I must be quick.' She glanced at the teacher.

'A-ha, you haven't paid,' his voice became conspiratorial. 'Your husband doesn't garden then? Or are you on your own? So many of us are, I'm afraid.'

Molly was busy noting down contact numbers, but she paused and looked across. 'The service isn't for us,' she stated.

'Ah.'

With a nod, she slipped back to the main Library, folding the list of numbers into her jacket pocket. At the desk she glanced at the phone, but hesitated to use it.

'Lunchtime,' she thought. 'When I've got the place to myself - as long as Mrs Dhaliwal isn't prowling around.'

Molly began logging returns into the system. The bar code reader wailed, plaintively.

'Tina, didn't you say this was fixed?' Molly called.

'It is.' The willowy young librarian wheeled the children's trolley from behind the book stacks. She swept her dark hair back behind her ears and pushed her spectacles onto the bridge of her nose. 'You just have to swipe the books more slowly, Molly. You're too quick for the machine.'

'Whatever happened to rubber stamps? More efficient and I could cope with those.' Molly chuckled. 'Did you and Carl go to see that film you told me about?'

Tina coloured slightly.

'No, we went for a Chinese instead.'

'To the Jade Garden?'

'Yes. We like it there.'

Molly's lips compressed.

32

It's cheap, she thought. Carl was between jobs.

The library reception area filled as the eleven o'clock classes ended and people made their way out. She spotted her admirer from earlier, the refined looking gentleman. He was a widower, perhaps, feeling lonely and fishing for information. Molly didn't make eye contact, though she stood a little straighter and smoothed her bright hair. Her husband, Peter, always said that he had first noticed Molly because of her red hair and trim good looks. He told her that she could pass for twenty years younger and it pleased her to think it true. She waged a permanent, not inexpensive, battle with the ravages of time.

Molly realised that someone was talking to her. Tina was pulling on her coat.

'I'll be a bit longer today,' she said. 'I've got to go over to the clinic.'

'That's okay, I'll be here,' Molly replied, with a wave. 'Everything'll be fine.'

The third number she dialled yielded results, a local charity organised cleaning and gardening for people who couldn't do either for themselves.

'Hello, I wonder if you could help me.' Molly explained what was required and answered the young man's questions. 'Mr Alfred Harkiss of Plough Lane Cottage, I don't know what number it is.... A gardening fork through his foot... I saw him in A & E.... No, I'm Mrs Morgan, a family friend.'

Molly waited as the charity official searched for the specific address. 'Yes, that's it.... No, hold on a moment, I've got some questions. Shouldn't you be liaising more closely with Casualty?'

The young man explained a few things. Molly sniffed.

'I don't think it's difficult at all. You just need to establish contact, then maintain it on a regular basis. Someone could easily do that by phone. Yes.... yes. Organisations like yours should be pro-active, not waiting around for people to contact you.'

She held the phone away from her ear.

'There's no need to be so aggressive. You're not the only one who wants to help.'

Molly listened to more.

'Fine. Well, I'll follow up from the hospital end, just to make sure it happens. I'm there every Wednesday, so I'll be checking. I'm Mrs Morgan, remember the name.'

With a nod of satisfaction, she returned the phone to its cradle.

'Now, I've got the Harkiss's number somewhere. Estelle's sure to be at home.' She flicked through her ancient Filofax, but was distracted by urgent movement and clamour in the Library's wide porch.

A group of noisy, jostling children was outside. They wore the uniform of Priory Road School and carried over-sized back-packs and bags. She recognised some of them. They were usually quiet and well behaved, but not today. Molly counted seven of them and no teachers.

'I won't be able to watch them all,' she said to empty space and bit her lip, casting anxious glances around the library. Mr Piestrak, who owned the newsagents across the green, allowed only one child at a time in his shop, because so many items had been stolen. 'But how can I keep some of them out?'

The gaggle of youngsters entered.

'Hello.' A girl with pale plaits walked up to her, leaving the others behind. 'Is it okay to come in? I've been here before.'

'Yes, I've seen you.' The child was self-possessed and well mannered and Molly was impressed. She grew calmer as the others dispersed, quietly, among the bookshelves. 'What's your name?'

'Daisy, Daisy Marshall. I'm ten. I'm in year six. I'll go to big school in the Autumn, my brother's there already.'

'Well, that'll be useful. He can show you how things work.'

'That's what my Mum says, but I'm not sure. Do you have any children?'

'Me? I.... yes, I have a son, but he's much older than you.'

'Oh.' Daisy looked around for her friends. 'Um, I'll...'

'Yes, you go on.' Molly looked at the group of schoolchildren and made a mental note of where each child was. She raised her voice to address them. 'Have you all got your library passes?' There were nods and grunts of assent.

When Tina returned, half an hour later, Daisy was helping Molly re-stock the shelves while the other children were reading at the low table. 'Well, that's what I like to see,' the

35

librarian looked at her watch. 'But shouldn't you all be going back to school?'

There was a noisy exodus as the children gathered up coats and bags and left, waving goodbye to Molly, who was almost sorry to see them go.

'Hasn't Amrita arrived yet?'

'No sign of her,' Molly tidied the table with ill-grace. 'Some people have no idea what committing to volunteering means. They don't understand that people will depend upon them. They can't just come and go as they please. I'll have to go soon...'

'Yes, I know you can't be late.' The librarian followed Molly through to the small rest room behind reception. 'Though, actually, it gives me a chance to tell you my news.' Tina turned to her friend. 'I'm pregnant.'

'That's wonderful news!' Molly hesitated for only a millisecond.

'I did a home test, but wasn't sure,' Tina smiled, shyly. 'Seven weeks.'

'Have you told Carl?'

'No, I wanted to be sure first.' Tina addressed Molly's unspoken concern. 'I'll have to come back to work immediately, of course. Carl can look after the child if he's still at home. If not, I'll bring him or her with me.'

'You'll sort something out,' Molly reassured her. 'But you must take more care of yourself now. No accidents, nothing which could harm the baby. You might want to think... about not working.'

'There's no chance of that.'

'Hello, hello,' trilled Amrita Dhaliwal as she hastened into the rest room, shrugging off her coat and straightening her blouse. 'Sorry I'm late, traffic was a nightmare. There are customers at the counter, I'll deal with them shall I?' Her black hair, piled high upon her head, wobbled as she hurried out.

Molly looked at her watch and pursed her lips.

'I'll drive you,' Tina offered. 'Amrita'll mind the shop, come on. It'll only take half an hour, there and back.'

Fifteen minutes later, Tina turned her car between the hospital gateposts and started up the long drive.

'Listen Molly, someone will have to run the Library while I'm off,' Tina proposed, as they approached the sweeping forecourt. 'You could do it, you'd enjoy it and it would be paid work.'

The facade of the building rose up before them in art deco splendour. Formerly a grand country house, the hospital frontage was little marred by signs of institutional use and the curving lines of bas relief still arched above the new, automatic doors. A clutch of nurses shivered at one side of them, furtively smoking.

'I don't know,'" Molly's mind was elsewhere. "'I don't have the qualifications and what about my other commitments? The guide dogs, Meals on Wheels, my visits here?'

'You know how the Library works and you have the experience.' Tina halted near the main entrance, engine running.

Molly opened the passenger door and swung her legs out.

'Think about it,' said Tina. 'I won't mention anything until next week.'

'Alright, I will.' Molly stood up, waved and slammed the door. Tina's car moved off.

Inside, she nodded to the reception saff and turned along a high arched corridor. At Paediatrics Molly was hailed by a small, white-coated figure. It was Dr Mistry.

"Molly,' she called. 'Thank you for the latest lot of games and toys, the kids love them.'

'No problem, Hari, my pleasure. Just on my way....' Molly didn't stop.

She entered the new wing, all glass walls, low ceilings and rubberised floors. There were fewer echoes here. At the end of the wing was Molly's first destination, Ganymede Ward. Its swing doors opened into a large and bright room, with an atmosphere of quiet contentment, different from the other wards. There were only terminal cases here, the severely disabled whose span, curtailed by faulty genes or childhood misfortune, was coming to an end. Quentin's bed was in the far corner. He'd been on Ganymede for nearly two years.

As Molly approached, she reached inside her holdall for the packet of Jaffa cakes which had always been his favourites.

'He'll be pleased to see those', she thought. 'Even if he doesn't recognise me. I might be lucky, if it's one of his more lucid days we'll be able to chat.' The old pain reared, but Molly was prepared for it.

'Hello there, Sarah.' A nurse was removing Quentin's tray, her spattered plastic apron testament to lunchtime. The nurses used first names, it was easier for those patients able to remember them. 'Sorry I'm late, I got stuck at the Library.'

'S'okay,' Sarah wheeled the bed stand aside. 'He's calm today, but not very communicative. Are you, Quentin?'

Molly kissed her son's forehead and took a bedside chair. Quentin, propped upright against pillows, looked at her vacantly. He was twenty seven years old and for many of those years it had fallen to Molly, or Peter, to tend him, through special school, day care centre and, when they could no longer manage, sanatorium. He had out-lived all predictions.

Molly handed him the biscuits, which raised a smile, and talked to him while he worried at the cardboard to open them. She watched his long fingers work, with their wiry brown hairs and manicured pink nails.

A beaming grin signalled success and Quentin offered the newly opened packet to Molly, who took a biscuit with delicate ceremony and handed it back. As he chewed she told him about her latest plan for Alf. She told him about Tina's pregnancy and the possibility of a job, admitting that she didn't know whether she would be up to it, day after day, but suggesting that she might take it. It would be good for her.

Quentin nodded and stroked her hand, making general noises of encouragement.

It was a successful visit. Quentin was engaged and affectionate and there were no tantrums.

Later, in the hospice, she related it all to Peter, as they sipped tea by the heater in the conservatory. Located in former stables across the gardens of the main hospital building, the hospice sat amidst woodland gardens and was as peaceful a place as the dying could wish for, if peace was what they wanted. Confined to a wheelchair and easily tired, Peter rarely left it these days, even to see his son.

'What do the doctors say?' Peter asked.

'The same,' Molly replied. 'The prognosis hasn't changed.'

'But he's staying on Ganymede?'

'I think so. No one's spoken with me about any changes.'

'Good.'

It was Peter's main preoccupation now that everything would be left for Molly's comfort and support, once he had gone. She knew he was studying her. She knew he'd noticed the dark smudges beneath her eyes and her roots which were showing grey.

'So what's been going on in the village then?' Peter asked. ;What's the latest gossip?'

'I don't listen to gossip.' Molly replied, half smiling. ''Though I do have some news. My friend Tina, the librarian, is having a baby.'

'Oh that is good news.'

'Though hers is the only wage, I don't know how she and Carl will manage.'

'People do, don't they,' Peter gave a gentle smile. 'Others rally round. Don't we still have some things - a pram, a carry-cot? Didn't you keep them?'

'I cleared all that out ages ago. I've told her that she has to be careful, especially if she carries on working.'

'It's normal now,' Peter countered. 'Not like...'

'When I did it.'

Until her early retirement, Molly had ruled over the large accounts department of Kings Electronics. Peter folded Molly's hands in his own, lacing their fingers together.

'You know...'

'Yes, it wasn't my fault. I know. It wasn't anyone's fault.'

'So,' Peter broke the small silence. 'What about the other one? Amrita isn't it?'

'Don't get me started...' Molly began to laugh.

They sat, talking in low voices or keeping a companionable silence, as daylight dimmed. Both were startled when, suddenly, the lights were switched on and someone came to lock the doors. It was already five o'clock. The last bus to the village was at half past.

Molly wheeled her husband into the lounge, where TV news sounded.

'I'll have to go, love,' she held his hand.

'Yes, you mustn't miss the bus,' Peter kissed her fingers. 'And if you do, call for a taxi, don't try to walk, it's too far.'

'All right, I'll be back tomorrow afternoon'" Molly smiled at him and turned away quickly. This pain was newer and harder to bear.

The metal gate squeaked as she stepped into the garden separating hospice from hospital. Dead leaves and withered roses lay on the path and in the dry concrete pond at the garden's heart. She cut through and round to the car park and bus stop.

'Evening, Mrs Morgan,' the bus driver barely looked at her tell-tale pass. The bus was crowded with commuters and the strip lighting was cruel. A man stood and Molly took the seat offered, tentatively. She squared her shoulders and stared out at the passing lights.

'Excuse me.' Someone was addressing her.

'Yes.'

It was a middle-aged woman, unknown to Molly. Her voice was rich with the accent of the Caribbean.

'I'm the daughter of Grace Williams,' she explained. 'I just wanted to thank you for the meals your team brings round to my Mum.'

'Grace...oh yes, Bluebell Road. It's nothing, the least we can do to help. Really...'

'And I'm so sorry to hear about your husband.'

The woman looked pained in sympathy.

'Thank you.' Molly quickly returned her gaze to the window.

She alighted at the crossroads into the village and began to turn away from the well-lit green, when a sudden shout brought her to a standstill.

'Molly! Molly Morgan!'

A tiny figure was heading, bullet-like, across the Green, arms swinging. It was Estelle Harkiss, Alf's wife.

'Hello, Estelle,' Molly ventured. 'How's Alf?'

'Never you mind.'

'What...?' Molly recoiled slightly.

'Just what do you think you've been doing?' Estelle demanded, indignant. 'Meddling with things that don't concern you.'

Estelle planted her feet apart and put her hands on her hips. The stiffness of her heavy overcoat, which had been in her wardrobe since about 1975, and her small stature, gave Estelle the appearance of a fairground marionette. Molly took a step backwards. She saw that the green was busy. People on their way home from work, mothers collecting their pre-schoolers from the community centre and early evening shoppers were all witness to the unfolding scene.

'We've had hoards of folk, charities and the like, round at Plough Lane today. 'Help the Aged', 'Age Concern', watcha-ma-call-it 'Go Geriatrics' – their van chewed up Alf's early bulb display – and they say that you sent 'em!' Estelle's voice rose.

'Yes Estelle, I.....'

'It's got nothing to do with you. I've told them all to bugger off. And I'm going to complain. The man from the charities helpline said I ought to. You've no right to interfere. Mind your own damned business.'

Estelle turned smartly and marched away, leaving Molly gaping after her. Watching eyes were averted and there were sniggers and muffled laughter as people got on with their business.

Molly swallowed hard, her face red. She noticed that she was shaking.

'Molly!'

Molly flinched. But it was Tina, hurrying across the green.

'Come on Molly, come with me. I've locked up now, we can go home.'

'Tina...'

'Yes, come along.'

Molly let herself be guided to Tina's little car. Tina opened the door and Molly collapsed into the passenger seat. Her house was not far and soon they pulled on to the short gravel drive. Molly didn't move.

"Out we get, Tinks'll be waiting for his dinner," Tina cajoled. "Let's go indoors."

Already the cat's plaintive wail sounded from behind the front door.

'Did you hear?' Molly asked abruptly. 'Everyone heard.'

'I heard Estelle Harkiss sounding off, if that's what you mean. Come on. There, let go the seatbelt now.' Gently, Tina released Molly's belt.

She took Molly inside, switching on the lights and turning up the thermostat. Tinks was in the hallway, meowing for his supper.

'Hello lovely boy.' Molly fondled the tabby's ears. 'I only wanted to help.'

'I know you did, Molly. Everyone knows how much you help. Don't worry about it.' Tina drew the curtains against the dark. 'I'm sure Estelle will regret what she said when she comes to her senses. It can't be easy living with Alf at the best of times. It's no wonder she loses it sometimes.'

'Do you think that's it?'

'I'm sure that's all it is.' She ignited the living room fire. 'I bet she'll be ringing later, to apologise.'

Molly stared into the flames. 'Oh, but oughtn't I to apologise to her?'

'Well, perhaps it wasn't the best idea, not telling her what you were arranging. It sounds like she's had a very difficult afternoon. Look Molly, will you be all right now? I have to go and pick Carl up.'

'Out on the town is he?' Molly looked up.

'He's been at a job interview actually.'

'Oh. I do hope he gets it - what with the baby and everything.'

'So do I. I'll pop round tomorrow afternoon, shall I, for a cup of tea?'

'Yes, that would be nice.'

Molly watched Tina's brake lights disappear. She closed the front door and bolted it. Sighing, she opened a tin of cat food, lower lip trembling. 'I'll have to phone her, won't I, Tinks. To apologise?' She dished it out. 'Tomorrow morning. Not tonight.'

Above the fridge the page-a-week calendar was blank for the following day. Molly took it, together with a pen and a newly opened bottle of wine, into the living room and sank into her customary armchair.

'The sun's over the yard-arm, eh Tinks?' She poured herself a glass. The cat leapt on to her lap. 'Even if it does get dark early in February.'

The silence was broken by the shrill ring of the telephone.

Molly sat, motionless.

The flashing light of the answering machine indicated that a message had been left. Molly pressed the button.

'Hello Molly. It's Estelle Harkiss here. I'm phoning to say I'm sorry about my outburst earlier. You meant well. Give me a call, will you? Or I could call round tomorrow afternoon for a cuppa?'

'Tina was right.' Molly snuffled.

Molly picked up the pen and wrote 'Phone Estelle' against the ten o'clock slot. Then, with more purposeful strokes, 'Organise driving lessons' at eleven.

'What do you think about that then, Tinks?' She chucked the cat under the chin. 'It was driving around today that set me thinking. I've already got a licence and there's a car in the garage, 'though it's years since I've driven. But one doesn't completely forget how to drive. It's like falling off a bicycle, or whatever the expression is.'

She took a sip of wine.

'It'll be good to be independent. I can visit Peter whenever I want. It'll make everything easier and I could take on more, like the Library job. Nothing ventured....'

The cat rolled over, rubbed his head upon her knees and looked up at Molly for yet more affection. She stroked him, absent-mindedly.

Book hair appointment' she said aloud as she wrote. 'It's time I went to the salon again. My roots are showing and that won't do at all.'

4.

In Calley Wood

The front door slammed.

His mother's shout was lost on the wind as Paul sprinted away. He had to catch the early bus, he had to. At the corner of Priory Road he saw it coming down the hill, on the other side of the road. There was no way he could dash across to get it. Sure enough, the bus passed him as he waited for a gap in the traffic. Stewie Fisher waved at him, his freckled face pressed close to a downstairs window. Upstairs, the back-seat gang gurned half-heartedly and gave him the finger. His pocket trembled.

Paul texted, he'd join his friend asap. He decided not to wait for the next bus, but walk, cutting through Calley Wood. Paul had never been in there on his own before, it was strictly forbidden. The wood's deeper reaches were the subject of local lore and dark legend, but it was the only way to make up time. He toiled up the hill towards the skeletons of the trees upon its brow. Over the stile, onto the muddy path, he headed into the wood proper.

Birds twittered in the dank cold and wild snowdrops gleamed. Paul pushed aside the stories he'd heard about the place, about strange happenings and ghostly inhabitants. He concentrated on the winding path, ducking beneath trailing branches. In a clearing made by a fallen oak, he wobbled along the giant trunk, arms raised for balance. Carvings etched deep into its bark proclaimed affection or constancy, but Paul ignored them and kept going. The path to school wasn't far now. He clambered down through the twisted tree roots.

'What you doin' 'ere then?'

Paul leapt to the ground and scuttled backwards. In the up-turned base of the oak tree sat a figure, almost entangled in roots and ferns. Stocky and solid, he wore a heavy black overcoat tied at the waist with a piece of twine and a pair of baggy trousers and trainers. His hair, of no colour at all, poked out of a canvas hat and his skin looked grey.

Paul retreated behind a large tree-stump. Peering over it, he saw that the path to school ran close beside the man. Paul fingered his mobile for the emergency key, in case the stump wasn't protection enough.

He gave the man a serious answer.

'I'm going to school,' 'They're expecting me there. What are you doing?'

'Sittin',' the man didn't seem to find the question presumptuous or odd. 'I allus wait for the Spring here.'

'How do you do that?'

'Look around,' the man encompassed the forest with a sweep of his arm.

So Paul did. When he gave it his full attention, he found that he could see the intangible green haze about bushes and trees which indicated readiness to leaf. Glossy red buds of willow bulged, their furry contents not yet revealed. On mossy mounds yellow winter aconites still clustered, spiked through with celandine. The wood felt full of patient life, waiting to explode into being.

'There!' The man's hand shot out. Suddenly he was holding a small, wriggling body.

Paul twitched, but he was curious to see what had been caught so expertly. The man looked over, his red-rimmed eyes a jaundiced yellow. He beckoned the boy closer. Ready to bolt at the first sign of anything untoward, Paul approached with caution.

The man soothed the animal and gently stroked its long velvet ears. It nestled, quaking, in his large hands. It was a young hare, with huge dark eyes and a pounding heart, Paul could see it beating. He'd never seen a hare up close before, although last year he'd watched through his Dad's binoculars as they boxed out in the fields. They were special, his father had told him, an old symbol of the new season. The creature made no attempt to escape.

'You can stroke it if you want.'

'Will you let it go?' Paul was reluctant to get too near.

'Mmmm...they're good eating, hares are.' Brown stained teeth were revealed as the man smiled. 'But I'll not be eating this one. She's bearing.' He ran his finger along the hare's underside and she shivered, before he quietened her again.

'She's... pregnant?'

The man nodded and carefully placed the hare on a hummock of earth. It hesitated, watching for a moment, before loping off into the undergrowth.

'Your school, would it be along that path there?' The man indicated the narrow track. Paul nodded. 'Down past the brook?'

'Furzedown.'

'That's its name, is it? D'you know where that comes from?'

'The common gorse, or European Ulex, also called furze,' Paul recited. This fact was part of every first year's introduction to Furzedown Comprehensive, for the school was built on heath land covered in it. 'It's on our badge.' He pointed to the breast of his pullover, which was just visible beneath his puffy jacket.

'Let me see.' The man leaned out, peering and Paul automatically moved forwards. Seconds later he realised his mistake. He stepped back.

The man's smile was cold as he looked Paul directly in the eye. 'You ought to be more careful, you don't know what I'm like.'

Paul felt the panic rising in his chest. He began to sidle away.

'Well, you don't. Do you?' The man lurched forwards.

Paul took to his heels.

Creaking laughter followed Paul as he shot along the path, ignoring the whipping saplings. He didn't stop until he was almost at the edge of the wood and could see the school buildings beyond the fields. His heart too was pounding, just as the captured hare's had been, but there was no pursuit.

The cows at pasture in the field raised their heads as Paul crossed, then returned to their grazing.

The man was just a tramp, Paul realised, but there was something curious and special about the encounter. He decided to keep it to himself. Besides, it wouldn't be wise to mention that he'd been in the wood alone. Ahead the wide metal school gates stood open. He hurried towards them.

Paul dodged his way through the noisy mass of fellow pupils, milling around enjoying the freedom before the bell sounded. He was headed for the coat racks where Stewie would be waiting.

'What took you so long?' Stewie demanded, pale blue eyes fierce beneath his shock of brown hair. He looked Paul up and down. Paul realised his clothing was dishevelled and pulled his jacket down. He could feel his hair was sweaty.

'What's happened?' Stewie asked.

"Nothing. Come on."

They just had time before assembly to run through to the science labs and check their biology project. Through the glass wall of their soil box, green shoots could clearly be seen. Germination was taking place at different rates, which was what the experiment was designed to show. If the project got a good assessment today they would get the all-important credits needed to go to Wembley on the school trip.

By lunchtime Paul was bursting to tell Stewie about the hare. It was too extraordinary a thing not to share it. This meant he also had to tell him about the tramp, it was unavoidable. They were in the cafeteria swapping the contents of their lunch boxes when Paul broached the subject.

'I saw a hare this morning.'

'They're always in the fields this time of year.' Stewie scrutinised the contents of a sandwich, before taking a bite.

'No. Up close. I could see it's heart beating.'

'Cool. How come?'

'A man caught it. He moved as quick as lightening, but he didn't hurt it.' The more Paul thought about this, the more impressive it became. 'He said it was pregnant.'

'What man?'

'A tramp, in Calley Wood.'

'Did he try anything?'

'No, he just caught the hare, but...'

'Like Paedo Phil?'

This was what everyone called the school's janitor. Paul suspected this was only because the man had made the mistake of letting the kids know his name. Nevertheless, none of his schoolfellows felt comfortable alone with the man.

'No...'

'We should tell someone, a teacher, or at least a prefect.'

'No, it wasn't like that. It was different. And anyway, I'd only get into trouble for going through the wood. I might lose a credit.'

Stewie grunted and chewed his sandwich. 'What was he doing there, then?'

'Dunno, just being a tramp I expect.'

'Do you think he'll be there tomorrow?' Tomorrow was Saturday.

'He might be,' Paul looked at his friend, fear forgotten. 'D'you want to go and look?'

*

There was a roaring in the wind all night and the next day was blustery. The roads looked newly washed and water burbled in the gutters, as cotton wool clouds scudded across the sky and light fractured from sun to shade.

Paul met Stewie at the stile. They planned to follow the same path Paul had taken the day before.

Stewie peered at the lowering wood. 'Isn't it too wet?'

'No.'

'Look. May be this isn't such a good idea.'

'Why?'

'Well..., it's Calley Wood...'

'It's only trees.'

'Yeah, but I'm not supposed...'

'Oh well, if you're not supposed... Come on, we said we'd find the tramp.' Paul climbed over the stile and set off along the path. He heard Stewie scramble over behind him.

55

As they entered, Paul sensed a difference in the wood. The trees snapped and rattled in the wind with gusting agitation. Fierce vortices of twigs and dead leaves formed, swirled and dissolved. The boys became jittery and nervous.

Drawing near to the oak tree clearing they heard voices and laughter. A knot of older youths sat on the huge fallen trunk, smoking. Only one was familiar to them, a sixth former at Furzedown named Matt. His bright red biking leathers were easily recognised, out of place in the woodland setting.

'Look,' one jeered. 'It's the Babes in the Wood.'

Stewie quickly pulled back the hood of his over-sized anorak, his face flushing with embarrassment.

'Let them be,' said Matt. 'Didn't you play here when you were a kid? I used to get up to all sorts.'

The first sniggered. 'And more recently too, I'll bet.'

'Not like what you've been doing, mate.'

Paul and Stewie circled the clearing, for tangled brambles choked the direct way across and the trunk was occupied. Paul set out along the path at the far side, when Stewie spoke.

'Have you guys seen a tramp around here?' He asked.

'What d'you mean a tramp?' An acne-speckled youth jumped down from his perch, throwing his cigarette butt into a puddle. 'Are you being funny?'

'N-no.' Stewie edged away. The youth feinted after him.

'Leave it,' his shaven-headed companion commanded. 'He didn't mean anything and we're in enough trouble as it is.'

'All right, Ian, only playing,' the first answered. 'Shoo!'

He ran at the boys, who hurtled away. After a few minutes, they halted, bent double and panting. No-one was following.

Sorry...' Stewie spluttered, between deep breaths. 'Silly thing to do.'

'Doesn't matter,' Paul said, gasping.

'What were they doing there anyway?' Stewie straightened up. 'Hey, my mobile's out. I can't get a signal.'

'So?'

'What if something happens...?'

'Nothing's going to happen.' Paul turned to go on, chin jutting upwards. Stewie stayed where he was.

'Go home if you want to,' said Paul. 'I'm going on.'

'I don't want to go home! Why makes you think I do?' Stewie countered, face reddening. 'Where do we go next?'

'What about down by the ruins?'

'The ruins!'

But Paul had already started walking along the path.

Stewie's mouth snapped shut and he hurried to catch up.

They moved in single file, heading towards the heart of the wood, a place of shadows. The wind quietened and birdsong sounded. Somewhere a dog-fox barked, as they trekked along the ridge. Here the terrain sloped away from the path into shallow dells and shaded hollows.

In the deepest of these stood an oblong green metal box, about five foot high. Beside it was a concrete blockhouse and a tangle of tumbled transformer wires, all enclosed by iron railings. A rusted metal Danger sign could just be seen beneath the brambles. Long out of use, the old electricity sub-station retained its sense of the forbidden.

Paul led the way, stepping and sliding down the incline. The wood was wilder in the glade, the vegetation denser, despite the evidence of former use. The previous night's rain had hardly penetrated through the tree canopy and it smelled of dry, loamy earth. Inside the railings the ground was completely undisturbed, aside from a well-trodden animal trail, disappearing into a thicket of brambles.

Paul hurried over.

'Come on, give me a bunk up,' he called to his friend.

Stewie drew back. 'What? Over the railings? No-one goes over the railings, it isn't safe.'

'This thing closed down years ago, it's fine.' Paul said. 'I want to follow that trail, look, to see if I can find the hare. That's what we're here for.'

'Is it? What about the tramp...I thought....? Oh, all right, but don't blame me if it all goes wrong.'

Stewie made a stirrup with his hands and Paul put his foot into it.

'Nothing'll go wrong. I promise.'

Paul was boosted upwards and teetered on the cross-rail before vaulting over and half-falling into a patch of nettles.

'Ow!'

'Want some dock weed?' Stewie had spotted some on the precipitous way down into the dell.

"I'm okay," Paul stood up, then crumpled forwards, awkwardly. He held on to the railings, gingerly touching his foot to the ground and wincing. 'No I'm not, I've hurt my foot. I can't stand on it.'

'I told you it was stupid, duh! Now what are we going to do?'

Paul sat down on one side of the railings, with Stewie on the other, handing dock leaves through to soothe Paul's nettle stings.

'How are we going to get you out?' Stewie frowned, his voice cracking.

'We need a ladder, or something.'

'Yeah. I'll just go and get one from behind that tree then, shall I?'

'All right. Keep your hair on.' Paul snapped.

'What we need is some help.'

'Who from?' said Paul. 'Who did you tell about us coming here?'

'Nobody.' Stewie was silent for a moment. 'No way did I tell anyone. If my Dad finds out I've been in here I'll be kept in for weeks.'

'We can't phone our parents anyway,' said Paul. He took out his phone and looked at the display. 'No signal.'

They settled into studied gloom. Paul's leg throbbed and he felt guilty. It was he who had insisted they come to the ruins, he who had climbed over the railings, but Stewie would be punished too. More, even.

'Maybe those others are still by the fallen tree?' Stewie suggested. "I'll bet they're up to something there anyway.'

'Maybe. Will you try and get Matt to help or... the others?'

Stewie stood. He licked his lips and swallowed hard.

'Their bark's probably worse than their bite.' Paul suggested.

'Yeah.' Stewie looked unconvinced. 'Will you be all right on your own?'

'I'm okay, I'm inside the railings.'

"Yeah."

Paul watched Stewie stride up the hill and go over the ridge. He was alone in the dell.

There was no wind in the hollow. Although clouds were racing across the sky, the air around Paul was still. He reached for his mobile, but then pushed it back into his pocket. Somehow, games weren't appropriate here. He shuffled from damp grass onto dry earth, taking care not to jar his foot and ankle. Paul became aware of the sounds of the wood around him and sensed the re-emergence of the wild creatures, ignorant of the presence of the boy in their midst.

Paul manoeuvred so that he could see the mottled grey shell of the blockhouse. The roof was three inches thick and intact, though the single window was a gaping hole. Rusty streaks ran from roof to ground. It didn't look welcoming, but it would provide shelter, if he needed it. The door stood ajar.

Wasn't that closed before?

Could the wind have blown it open? But the air in the dell was still. Paul's skin prickled. He recalled tales about the malevolent and rarely seen inhabitants of Calley Wood, the gypsy child-stealers, the wild hunter. He scanned the undergrowth for hidden watchers. Was that a dark figure, skulking within the trees? A cloud crossed the sun and Paul shivered.

He looked back up to the ridge, to where his friend had disappeared. Stories from early childhood re-surfaced, of evil things – trolls and vampires – hiding deep in the forest. The wayward children were always the ones who were punished, he knew. His heartbeat sounded in his ears.

Swallowing hard, he forced such thoughts away.

'There's no-one here but me!'

He spoke out loud, setting the wood rustling and scuttling. The sound of his own voice gave him courage. And the blockhouse was just an empty blockhouse. A wild thing, a fox or a badger, had opened the door. Nothing else could get inside the railings.

But the only way to be sure was to go and look. Holding on to the bars Paul pulled himself upright and made his way, gritting his teeth against the pain in his ankle, towards the blockhouse. The door hung sideways on one hinge. He took a deep breath and, bracing himself against the doorjamb, he made himself look inside.

At first it was difficult to distinguish anything in the dim light and disorder. There was a pungent smell, of scat or urine. Much of the floor was covered with wire, metal boxes and wood, piling higher up against the far wall. Paul heard a scratching sound from deep within. Something was moving through the debris. Heart thumping, he squatted down low. The sun shone into the building and Paul gasped as light reflected from two eyes within the mound.

He lowered himself further. The reflected lights blinked out.

Then reappeared.

Nearer.

Slowly, very slowly, the eyes came closer towards Paul. First whiskers, then the long twitching nose came into view, into the patch of sunlight. Amber ringed pupils gazed at him as the velvet creature emerged. Paul was transfixed.

The hare sat up, sniffing at the air, smelling his presence. It was wary, but not frightened. A magical creature. The soft fur was flecked and dun-coloured and the long, silky ears lay back against its body.

A twig snapped. The ears flicked upright, translucent in the sunlight.

This was his hare, one he'd found for himself.

A dull growl sounded in the distance. The hare leapt out through the door, vanishing into the weeds. The stuttering rumble grew louder. Paul recognised it as a motor bike engine, coming closer. Soon he caught sight of a red and white blur through the bare tree trunks.

It was Matt, with Stewie clinging on behind, head bent sideways and eyes tightly shut. The bike leapt a fallen trunk with ease and careered to a halt in the hollow. Stewie fell off into the leaves.

'So this is it?' Matt removed his helmet and dismounted, as Paul got to his feet and hobbled over. 'And you're the idiot who's hurt himself.'

'It happens,' Paul's voice squeaked and he grimaced with embarrassment.

Matt strode around the hollow. 'I'll use my bike to climb over,' he said. 'But I'll need something to walk up when I bring you out. Can you find something on that side?'

Paul struggled to push one of the larger metal boxes towards the railings.

'You didn't take long,' he said to Stewie, who paled.

'No, we took the direct route.'

'Yes, I think that'll do,' Matt inspected the box. 'Can you prop it up securely?'

Carefully, Paul set to work, as Matt wheeled his bike over and stripped off his jacket. Within minutes Paul was safely on the ground outside the railings.

'Are you sure you're all right?' Matt asked. 'I think you need to get that ankle looked at. I'll take you to A & E, it isn't far.'

'No.'

'No, there's no need, really.' Stewie echoed.

'Yeah, I've just ricked my ankle, that's all.'

Matt was uneasy. 'Look, I think...'

'We'll be done for if our parents find out we've been in here. In the wood.' Paul said. He and Stewie looked at Matt at the same moment, their eyes beseeching.

Matt sighed. 'Okay, I suppose. Can you find your own way back, or do you want a lift?'

'I'll manage,' Paul replied, quickly. 'But thanks very much for getting me out.'

'No problem,' Matt grinned. Once more in full regalia, he mounted his bike. 'It'll make a good story. No, don't worry,' he added, catching sight of the boys' horrified look. 'I won't tell anyone.'

He pulled on helmet and gauntlets, kicked the stand away and, with a brief salute, roared out of the dell.

'Phew.' Stewie gulped as he watched Matt's exit. 'That was cool. Will you really be able to walk home?"

'Yeah. See if you can find me a strong stick for a crutch. A bit of branch maybe.'

Stewie rootled in the heaps of dead leaves.

'Here.' He handed a piece of broken bough to Paul, who wedged it under his armpit.

'That's it. I'll be fine.' Paul assured his friend. 'I gotta be. Anyway, my Mum'd go mental if I arrived home on a motor bike.'

They set off up the path, Paul managing a lurching walk. Stewie slowed his pace so that Paul could keep up

'So what happened after I went, then? Did anyone come by? Did you see the tramp?'

'No.'

Stewie looked at Paul, expectant and mystified.

'I just waited.'

'Something must've happened.' Stewie exclaimed. 'You ...you seem... different, like. So.. is there a curse of Calley Wood?'

Paul shook his head, observing his friend's confusion. He couldn't precisely explain, even to himself, what had occurred. He didn't have the words. He had just waited in the wood and yet.... something was different. There was no way Stewie would understand.

The pair stomped away, silent. Both were anxious now to get home. At the top of the ridge, Paul looked back into the hollow. Shafts of light slanted through the trees. The blockhouse and the green box were both in sunlight now.

'It is the wood,' Paul said. 'It makes you feel bigger than you are and smaller at the same time.'

'Bigger and smaller at the same time? Yeah, right...' Stewie rolled his eyes.

This was the only explanation Paul could give. Yet Calley Wood had lost its power to terrify. Now charged with possibilities, it would never seem so frightening to Paul again.

The boys turned and disappeared over the ridge.

Behind the concrete blockhouse and beyond the railings, the man in the fraying black overcoat observed their departure. Beside him sat the hare, ears raised and watchful.

'You drew 'im back.' The man commented to the animal. 'A hare's a powerful creature, 'specially this time of year. Mebbe he'll come and visit us agin soon?' He nodded. 'Yes, I think he might.'

Silently and with an ease of movement unlikely in one so old and ragged, the man rose and disappeared into the trees.

5.

Not Even Waving

Tall beeches cast long shadows across the country road. The swirls of the walnut dashboard glowed in the setting sun and there was the satisfying scent of polished leather. The car hummed homeward. There was no reason to feel ill at ease.

A pheasant erupted from the hedgerow and their seat belts tautened as Andrew braked and swerved. Cursing quietly, he manoeuvred back onto their previous course. Diane twisted round, light brown hair swinging, to catch sight of the creature, but all was swallowed up in thickening shadow.

The car plunged between high banks of hawthorn and hazel. The headlight beams grew distinct, painting the frothy hedges with broad strokes of light as the lane turned. There was a faint glow from the dashboard dials and Diane's eye was drawn to the speedometer.

She blinked quickly and looked over at Andrew. The needle was pointing at sixty.

His face was hidden in the gloom. Only his hands were visible. These seemed the hands of a stranger, not the man she knew so intimately. Bony fingers were wrapped around the steering wheel, sinews stretched and veins protruding, a drowning man's hands, as he clung to the last piece of wreckage.

Slices of brightness swept through the dark sky ahead. A car topped the hill and Andrew dimmed their lights and slowed, pulling over as the other car passed. Diane exhaled, a frown forming. Was the speedometer working properly? Headlights up, they started off again and this time she watched the gauge as their speed increased. They accelerated out of corners, the downward force of the heavy vehicle keeping them anchored to the road, but only just. The engine note rose and roared as it echoed between the high sides of the lane.

Diane stared forward, half unbelieving. What on earth was Andrew playing at? She opened her mouth to speak, but did not dare. If she distracted him now....? She pressed her lips closed, in fear of disaster. Her palms grew sweaty and her mouth dry. She kept very still and heard the pounding of her own blood in her ears.

The junction with the main road wasn't far ahead. Diane screwed up her courage, determined to say something even at the risk of crashing, but already the needle was falling. They turned onto the slip road and the high rows of orange lights flanking the carriageway illuminated Andrew's flashing, hawk-like profile. His mouth was stretched into a rictus grin, with his eyes fixed upon the road. Diane looked away, quickly.

The Mercedes slid smoothly into the flow of traffic. Red, white and orange lights moved in a regular dance. Diane began to relax when they reached the outskirts of the town where they lived, the thirty mile an hour zone of Edwardian villas set back behind budding shrubbery. Gravel crunched as Andrew turned up the incline between the rhododendrons and drew around to the porch. Her legs shook as she climbed from the car and he drove on to the garage.

As she poured herself a whisky Diane almost dropped the decanter. Her heart was thumping and all her strength seemed to have leached away, but the fiery liquid and soft lamp light soothed her. Gradually the nightmare drive began to seem unreal.

'That's a good idea,' Andrew placed the car keys on the mantelpiece. He reached for a tumbler, filled it and tossed back its contents. 'Will you be bathing?'

Wordlessly she indicated acquiescence. This was the Sunday evening routine.

Gripping the banister Diane drew herself upwards, eyeing the key in the bathroom door ahead. She entered, locked the door behind her and slumped down onto the lavatory. After a few moments, she forced herself to her feet and began to busy herself with customary ablutions and unguents.

The water was hot and she lay back in the foaming tub, hair scraped up into a top-knot. Memory of the day's events crowded in upon her – the bright morning, the pub at lunch, the terrifying drive. Above all, there was Andrew's strange behaviour. He could have killed them both. Diane slid further down into the warmth. The pain behind her eyes lessened. Her tension began to dissolve. The scented steam was soothing and her eyelids drooped.

She sat up sharply, water sloshing. There had been a rap on the door.

'Hello?'

'It's me. Are you falling asleep in there or something?' Andrew sounded impatient. 'Listen, I'm going to have to work this evening. An emergency instruction, to be prepared for court tomorrow. I'll be in the study. Don't disturb me with supper, I've eaten enough and I need to concentrate."

"I won't disturb you," Diane almost whispered, as the creak of the stair indicated Andrew's withdrawl. She slipped back down into the water, but the tension had returned.

Work, always work. Maybe that's the problem, she thought. We never get to spend any time together.

An hour later she went down to the living room, a silky, yielding creature, still tender with shock. She had puzzled and worried over Andrew's behaviour, to no avail. Why he should endanger them both in that way was beyond her understanding. Glancing over at the study, where Andrew was working behind its closed door, she sighed. Shouldn't she ask him? But when and how? He would, she suspected, simply dismiss the idea of danger, as a fantasy on her part. He often over-ruled her and, she had to admit, he was often right.

Diane pulled her own bulging briefcase onto the dining table, sorting through its haphazard contents. With a school timetable and a shopping list for the next weekend's party beside her, she began to plan the week ahead.

*

'Hello, how lovely to see you.'

Glossy and chic, Diane stood at the front door to welcome guests with a warm smile, before leading them to the kitchen. There Andrew dispensed drinks and ushered people through the double doors into the garden. The early afternoon sun was warm and folk mingled, more than ready to enjoy the Stephens, Smith & Wells Spring garden party.

'Hello, Jane,' she exchanged kisses with the latest arrival. Andrew joined her to welcome Jane and Gus King. The Kings were always invited to the firm's Spring bash, for Kings Electronics was a major client and the couple were part of their social circle.

'Thanks, Gus.' Andrew took the proffered bottle with a practised smile, his out-stretched hand enveloped in Gus's large paw.

'You might want to lay it down.' Gus suggested.

'He means it's too good for the likes of me.' Jane's loose black curls shook as she laughed up at her husband, who grinned, winding an arm around his tall wife's waist. 'Keep it. Stash it in your famous cellar.'

'Infamous, you mean. I never go down there, you know. It's entirely Andrew's domain,' Diane replied with a wry smile.

'What are you keeping down there, Andrew, besides Bordeaux and Beaujolais?' Gus laughed. 'A secret lover?'

'How very Grand Guignol.' Jane feigned horror.

The doorbell rang again and Diane left Jane exclaiming over the canapés.

At the door stood the junior solicitor Yvonne Young and her husband.

'Hello Yvonne. Good to see you again.' Diane smiled. She turned to Yvonne's companion. 'And you must be Steve, I don't believe we've met.' Steve was sandy coloured and athletic looking, a slim, pale counter-point to his wife's rich chestnut colouring and full figure.

Diane and Andrew had dined with Yvonne only the previous Sunday. Steve hadn't joined them, there'd been some excuse. Yvonne's husband was difficult, it was said, and disliked his wife's friends, discouraging her from seeing people.

'Pleased to meet you,' Steve responded.

During the week Diane had beaten down the memory of the nightmare drive. School and the preparations for the party had absorbed all her attention. Andrew had been in unusually good humour all week and surprised her with unexpected sexual passion. She reciprocated with enthusiasm and their dark nights were breathless and fervent. It was almost how it used to be.

Now the arrival of the Youngs brought back all Diane's anxieties and uncertainties.

'Please do come through.' Diane smoothed over any stiffness and led the way.

Yvonne, in rich and velvety plumage, seemed tense and nervy. She hesitated for an instant.

'Well, go on then.' Steve hissed and prodded her, viciously. 'If it's so important to you.'

Diane blinked, eyebrows arching, as Yvonne stepped past her in a haze of patchouli, followed by a thin-lipped Steve.

'Ah, here's Andrew with the booze,' she said. 'This is... Steve. Excuse me, I must go...summoned by bells.'

Diane was a busy and attentive hostess. She chatted with folk whose names she only just remembered and greeted the old stagers with jocular familiarity. It was all going well, although the row of empty wine bottles in the kitchen was growing. She went in search of Andrew, to replenish supplies from the cellar, but couldn't find him. No one had seen him for a while.

'Where on earth can he have got to?' she said, to no-one in particular, and was grateful when Gus offered to look for him, she had so much else to do. Within minutes Andrew stomped into the kitchen.

'Well, what is it? Something so important you had to send out search parties.'

'We're running out of wine,' she kept her voice even. 'You'll need to get some up.'

Andrew went to the heavy cellar door and turned the key. Its hinges creaked as he opened it. Diane heard him thump down the wooden stairs.

After a short while, he came back up and set a case down on the long refectory table. 'Here,' he said. 'I'll get another...'

'May I help?' Yvonne came into the kitchen, carrying empty plates.

Andrew turned and growled at her. 'My wife's more than capable of managing, thank you.' He descended into the cellar again.

Diane smiled, indulgently, and steered Yvonne outside on to the terrace.

'Thanks for offering, but the caterers will take care of things.' She looked around. 'I hope Steve's enjoying himself.' He was no-where to be seen.

"Diane..."

Andrew pushed through the doorway and put an arm around Diane's shoulders, standing between the two women. 'Right! There are another two dozen bottles in the kitchen, don't drink them all at once.' He caught sight of a rotund, dark-skinned figure. A late arrival. 'Hello there, Basil, let me get you a glass.'

Basil de Silva was head-teacher of the village school where Diane taught.

'And some food.' Diane escorted him into the house. 'Before it all disappears!'

When Diane and Basil returned to the terrace, there was no sign of Andrew or Yvonne. In vain Diane scanned the party-goers in the garden.

'Looks like a good party, Diane.' Basil observed. Always dapper, today he wore a pale pink silk cravat that contrasted with his dark skin. 'But a lot of work for you.'

'Oh I don't mind. It's something of a tradition now.' She wondered where Andrew had gone. 'Basil, excuse me, I just need to find my husband.'

Basil followed Diane into the kitchen. The door to the cellar was ajar.

Didn't Andrew close that? Diane crossed the kitchen, but stopped before the rectangle of heavy darkness, which seemed to her to breathe with a life of its own. Was there someone down there still?

'A bit dangerous, leaving that open.' Basil stepped passed her and gently reached around to close the door. He didn't lock it, for the key was absent, but stood before it, awkwardly shifting his considerable weight from foot to foot, as he looked around the kitchen.

Another one behaving strangely, Diane thought, but was distracted by the entrance of Gus and Jane King, laughing.

'Diane, why are you in here?' Jane scolded. 'You should be outside enjoying yourself?'

'The dancing's begun.' Gus offered an arm with elaborate courtesy and Diane noticed the South American rhythms for the first time. 'Allow me to escort you to the dance floor.'

'Do you know, I think I'd rather like that.'

'Come on then.'

Gus drew Diane towards the terrace. Jane and Basil followed. Just as they reached the doors Diane heard the familiar creaking hinge of the cellar door, followed by stifled laughter. She hesitated, about to turn back, but shook her head. 'It's Andrew's precious cellar,' she thought. 'If folk have been down there, let him sort it out.' She stepped out into the garden.

The dancing was popular and people gathered around to watch. Gus was a big man, but he danced well and Diane felt secure enough to trust him. The watching crowd became a blur of colour as they swooped and spun. She was laughing and breathless when the music changed to a slower number and she handed Gus over to Jane.

Diane mingled with the watchers, then noticed Steve standing at the dance floor's edge. Happy and benign, she wandered over to him.

'Hello there. Are you enjoying our little party?'

'Thank you, yes.' Steve gave a thin smile.

Well, his manners seemed to have improved, Diane thought.

'I'm sorry you couldn't join us last Sunday.'

'What?'

'For lunch.'

Steve frowned, he looked baffled, but then his gaze shifted. Andrew and Yvonne had arrived on the dance floor as the salsa began again. The couple moved in perfect unison, the space between their bodies diminishing.

'They dance well together,' Diane said, the buoyant mood beginning to desert her.

Steve did not respond. He was intent upon the dancers. Diane felt bound to continue the conversation.

'I'm always pleasantly surprised by my husband's grace on the dance floor.'

'Mm.' Steve almost grunted. 'I don't dance.'

'Oh. Andrew and I always have. That is to say, we used to.' She paused, watching the couples. 'Dancing is such a pleasure - the sensuousness of synchronised movement and physical closeness.'

Steve turned his head, slowly, to stare at her, his mouth slightly open. 'So why don't you dance then?'

'I do. Didn't you see?'

'With him. Why don't you dance with him?' His face was thrust forward, his expression intense. Diane drew back.

'Well, I've lots to do. I must, um....' Diane made her excuses. Good question, she thought as she headed for the house. Why don't we dance anymore?

Soon coloured lights in the shrubbery began to create small pools of brightness in the evening shadows. Revellers were drawn towards the warmth and light of the house. The party had been a success, people were relaxed and happy and breakages mercifully few. The existing trickle of departures became a flood.

Diane wandered to the front door. Jane and Gus King were taking leave of Andrew.

'Goodbye, Diane'

Diane and Jane exchanged farewell kisses.

'I haven't danced like that in ages, lass,' Gus hugged her with real affection.

'Me neither,' she laughed. 'And I'm a lass no longer, I'll be glad to get my feet up.'

Drive safely!' Andrew called, as they drove away.

'I'll be going too.' It was Basil. 'Now don't spend all tomorrow clearing up, Diane. Have some rest before Monday, spend some time on yourself.'

'He's your boss, not your father.' Andrew commented after Basil had departed. 'Interfering old bugger.'

'He's just being protective. He's a sweetie.' Diane was shocked. 'Everyone adores him."

Yvonne and Steve were almost the last to leave.

'I hope you enjoyed yourselves,' Diane smiled her social smile, anxious now to be rid of them. They reminded her of things she would rather forget.

'It was a good party,' Steve said, tightly. He looked at Andrew and the men strolled over to Steve's car.

'Thank you,' Yvonne clung on to Diane's hands, holding her on the doorstep.

'My – my pleasure,' said Diane, perplexed. She extricated her hands and Yvonne hurried after her husband.

'Well, that was very strange." Diane commented as she closed the door. She followed Andrew through to the lounge and collapsed onto the sofa beside him. 'Andrew? What did you make of the elusive Steve?'

Andrew made a moue of distaste as he swirled the wine around his glass. Diane studied him. She saw the flecking of grey in his dark hair, the lines around his mouth and eyes. But at least he seemed to enjoy himself that afternoon, she thought. She stifled the urge to caress, knowing, instinctively, that it would be unwelcome.

'They're a strange couple, the Youngs, don't you think? Something not quite right, about them?'

She waited in vain for a response. Andrew said nothing, he was sitting very still.

'Well, I'm glad that's all over,' said Diane, finally. 'Shall we lie in tomorrow? Eat breakfast late?'

'I've a case to read up on tomorrow, I'm afraid,' Andrew replied. 'But you go ahead, if you want to. I'm hitting the hay now.' He put down his empty glass.

'There are just a few last things to clear....' But Andrew had gone.

Diane's gaze drifted to the mantelpiece. On it stood the unopened bottle of fine wine from Gus and Jane.

'They're a couple at ease with each other,' Diane thought.

Unaccountably, tears pricked her eyelids. Diane blinked them away, shook herself and stood. She picked up Andrew's glass and collected the bottle of wine on the way to the kitchen.

This wine should go in the cellar, she thought. As she opened the cellar door, a spicy and distinctive perfume hung in the air. She inhaled deeply, her brows drawing together.

She switched on the light. The wooden stairs ran down into the dark.

What could Yvonne have been doing in the cellar?

Teetering under the bare light bulb, Diane took a couple of cautious steps down into the unknown. She felt her way along the rough brickwork of the wall on her left, towards the other light switch at the foot of the steps. To her right was black emptiness. Something ran across her fingers and she snatched back her hand and wobbled. There was a skittering below. With a shiver she shook her head and retreated to the kitchen, but felt dissatisfied. Tomorrow she would venture down, she promised herself. It would be a little adventure, who knows what she might find. She snapped off the light and closed the door.

5.

Open Gardens

Any casual eaves-dropper would have found the conversation very one-sided, one of its two participants being dead, but this didn't signify for the other.

'The competition's for charity,' Winnie Fortune explained as she sat, hands on her substantial knees, on a low marble tomb. It was the hour of rosy twilight. Ancient, lichen covered gravestones were lapped by daisy strewn grass. Clematis climbed up the yew trees, softening the outline of the shadows where bluebells still bloomed.

'We're all supposed to open the gardens to the public at half past ten, 'though I can't imagine there's going to be many folk coming to see our little patch.' She brushed a midge away from lacquered grey curls. 'The Vicar's coming round with the judging panel. There's a science teacher from Furzedown and the Head of Priory Road School, de Silva from Ceylon. I don't know what they'll make of it.'

In the distance, a car passed along the lane.

'The winner is to be announced after Evensong tomorrow.'

The liquid song of a blackbird song floated on the air. Winnie pondered.

'Sylvia Luck's entered too, so ours isn't the only garden from the estate.' She paused. 'Personally, I think she's overdone things, that memorial stone is just attention seeking. She always was a drama queen – it's as if I'd buried you underneath the dahlias. Oh my giddy aunt!'

A loud blast of music escaped from an opened door in The Lion nearby. It was Saturday night.

'They should never have been allowed to develop that stable block,' she said. 'It's enough....'

The church clock struck eight.

'Ah well, best be on my way.'

She patted the monument upon which she had been sitting as she clambered to her feet. Its occupant had deceased sometime late in the eighteenth century, but Winnie was punctilious in her courtesy.

'I'll tell you all about it tomorrow.' She tidied the flowers in the vase on Frank's last resting place, where she had placed him eighteen months before. 'Goodnight now.'

Winnie walked through the lych-gate, across the green and along Hawthorn Lane. Deep in thought, she was surprised, fifteen minutes later, to find herself in Lower Cowslip Lane, it wasn't on her usual route home. The solid, pebbledashed,1930s semis were the same all over the Flowers Estate, many of them sprouting new porches and sky-light windows, but Winnie's feet knew their way to her home in Marigold Road, even if her mind wasn't engaged. Somewhere a dog was yapping.

'Now, why'd I come here?' she muttered to herself, perplexed. She shook her head and turned for home, but stopped, drawn to number twenty two. This was Sylvia Luck's garden and Winnie couldn't resist a little look.

'Evening, Winnie.'

Winnie leaped several inches into the air.

Sylvia emerged from behind the front privet, holding a small white-grey terrier.

'You're out of your way. Come to check out the competition, have you?' Sylvia smiled the wide smile, which had won her so many admirers in her younger days. She still wore her hair long, held back by an Alice band that matched the cornflower blue of her eyes.

'Are you all ready for tomorrow? My grandson, Matt, has been working hard here all week and my Vince's got an urn from the Park House, so that we can give folk their cup of tea. It's a pity you don't have any menfolk to help you now that Frank has passed.'

Winnie gave a light laugh. 'I've got help enough thank you. Good luck for tomorrow!'

'Likewise, I'm sure.' Sylvia watched Winnie tramp off towards Marigold Road.

'Bloody woman!' Winnie grumbled. 'Don't have any men indeed. I seem to remember that her problem was always the other way about.'

Winnie was soon at her gate. The picket fence was newly painted, courtesy of her son-in-law, and the paths were weed-free and tidy, cleared, for a small consideration, by her grandson, Paul. Nearest the house was the cottage garden, with traditional perennials, climbing roses and espaliered fruit trees. Further away, on the edges of the large plot, were a series of smaller, intimate spaces, each separated from the other by flowering hedges. These were planted simply and their tiny lawns were sown with herbs, so visitors released perfumes, of camomile, oregano or thyme, as they trod.

Winnie was calmed by the aromas. In the little garden furthest from the road, night stocks were opening in the near darkness, adding their scent. Frank always said that he planted night stocks....

'So that it'll be beautiful by candle-light.'

Winnie gasped. It was as if he was right there beside her again and she could almost touch him, stroke his sinewy forearm or hold his long fingers, mottled by age and soil.

She shook her head and wiped her eyes. "I shouldn't have entered the compeition," she said and headed for the house. "He never would have."

Much later, long after Winnie had retired to bed, two teenagers passed by the picket fence in the brazen lamplight. One supported the other.

'Leggo! I'm oar rye I tell you!'

'Ssshh! You'll wake everybody up!'

'So?' The tousle haired youth pulled himself free of his helper and shouted. 'Wakey wakey!'

In the front bedroom, Winnie stirred.

'Shut up Matt!' His tall, skinny companion stepped sharply in front of him and Matt fell to the ground, only his biking leathers saving him from the asphalt. 'Or I'll leave you. The cops can find you again. Then you'll be in real trouble.'

'Urgh, don care.'

'You will tomorrow. And you've got the competition, come on. You can't let your Gran down.'

Winnie drew back a curtain and peered out. She watched as the youth pulled Matt to his feet and they proceeded, haltingly, into Bluebell Road. At number fifteen an oblong of light illuminated them as a front door opened.

'We heard you coming.' The man's gruff voice was low, but the sound carried in the silence. 'Let me take him.'

'I can't believe he keeps doing this!' The smaller figure of a woman peered out, hands fluttering about her face. 'As if it's not bad enough....'

Matthew was man-handled into the house.

'It's the anniversary....' said his friend.

'Yeah, we know.' Matt's father responded. 'But he's got to get a grip.'

'Well, I'd best be off. I'll be skinned alive as it is.'

'Thanks Dev.' The woman nodded as he made his exit. 'Your mother was looking for you earlier. You'd best get yourself home.'

'Yes, Mrs Hare.'

'Goodnight.'

The door closed. Winnie watched Dev walk off into orange-lit blackness, footsteps echoing. Awake now, she returned to her bed.

*

In bright Spring sunshine the Reverend Jim Gardener chatted with his Sunday morning flock outside St Agnes church. He disliked hurrying away, for the informal mingling after service always offered a useful opportunity to find out what was really going on in his parish. Yet, at the edge of his vision, the members of the competition judging panel hovered, their stance impatient, beside Basil de Silva's Land Rover.

There was Howard Goodman, fifty year old biology teacher, lounging casually against the bonnet in his brown corduroys and pullover. Though he had lived in the village for a decade or more, Howard had been brought up in the back streets of Manchester, where he had escaped a future on his father's market stall through a university education. Now he helped others to make their escape too.

Basil himself leaned on the open car door, mopping his dark and shining pate with a voluminous yellow handkerchief.

Jim made his excuses and hurried across, cassock flowing. His close-cut fair hair and eyebrows almost disappeared in the brilliant morning light.

'Sorry to keep you waiting. Think of these as my working clothes, it is the Sabbath,' he said and climbed aboard.

'Not for me, it isn't,' Howard chortled as he followed suit. Jim nodded.

'I thought we'd take the Flowers Estate gardens first, if that's okay?' Basil suggested as he put the land rover into gear.

'The estate has the late Frank Fortune's garden in Marigold Road, entered by his widow, Winnie, and the garden belonging to Sylvia Luck in Lower Cowslip Lane. Both are my parishioners, so we must be diplomatic,' said Jim. 'They're as territorial as a pair of tigresses.'

'Let's hope they don't sniff out our weaknesses,' Howard replied.

'You mean me...' Jim sighed. The only thing horticultural about him was his name. A child of inner city tower blocks, he was more comfortable with concrete. 'I really shouldn't be adjudicating this competition...I'm not qualified.'

'The village thinks you should.' Basil countered. 'You started the whole thing and anyway, people instinctively connect this role with your being the vicar. Something to do with passing judgement, I'd say, or being fair and reasonable.'

'Thanks a lot.' Jim pursed his lips. 'I blame the King James Bible, myself. It's got too many agricultural metaphors.'

'Right, pop quiz,' Howard said. 'What are those?' He gestured towards a bank of tall pink flower-spikes, coming up on their left.

'Er, hollyhocks,' Jim replied.

'Try again.'

Jim turned to keep them in view.

'Lupins?'

'Very good.'

'I was staring at Linneaus Plant Taxonomy until two this morning. I got some very strange glances during service, I must look as if I've been out on the tiles.' Jim stretched to look in the wing mirror. There were dark rings beneath his eyes. 'I wish I'd never started this.'

'So you've said.' Basil answered as they crossed Canal Road. 'Perhaps you should stick to asking general questions. Howard and I'll do the details.'

'Speaking of details...you both know about the memorial in the Luck garden?' Jim checked. 'It'll be hard to ignore. Young Matt Hare, who maintains the garden, has been very cut up about it all and got himself into some trouble.'

The tiny memorial was to Matt's elder brother, John, who had been on patrol in Helmand when an afghan cadet had blown himself and the other members of the squad to kingdom come.

'But that's not a reason, in itself, to favour his grand-mother's garden.' Basil insisted on impartiality. 'Remember, we judge each garden purely on its own merits.'

The Land Rover turned onto the Flowers Estate, where wide grass verges lined the curving roads, which were set out in geometric patterns.

*

Over in Marigold Road, tucked away behind her house, Winnie reclined in an ancient deck chair on her back step, enjoying the spring sunshine. She fanned herself with an 'Open Gardens Catalogue', a village publication of dubious accuracy but good entertainment value. Her daughter, Lynda Marshall, was at the garden gate, dispensing tickets and taking entrance money.

Winnie could hear people arriving. Since the previous evening her unease about entering the competition had grown.

'I dunno, Frank.' Winnie riffled the pamphlet's pages. 'There's a string quartet over at The Elms, with tea or champagne on the lawn and the hospital garden is open, I saw Molly Morgan driving round with plants for it. It somehow doesn't seem right that our little garden's in the same competition, 'though there's plenty of folk coming round.'

Winnie cocked an ear, trying, without success, to distinguish specific comments in the low murmur of sound generated by the visitors to her garden.

'I bet all the gardens are busy, even Sylvia's. She isn't backward in pushing herself forward, but then she never was. You remember.'

Winnie felt a sour taste in her mouth.

'You were quite keen on her at one time, I seem to recall.'

Her wounded silence was interrupted by strident voices rapidly approaching, which she recognised instantly. It was a delegation from the Ladies Society. Winnie struggled frantically to get up from the deckchair.

By the time the little group opened the wooden gate a neat, if red-cheeked, Winnie as ready to escort them around her plot. She pointed out the highlights and handed round

Darjeeling in the second best china, with Garibaldi biscuits, reserving the end of the packet for the judges later.

*

In Lower Cowslip Lane, Jim climbed from the Land Rover. Sylvia Luck was at her gate to greet him. By her side, Matt was red-eyed and stupefied and towered over Sylvia. Their garden was a formal parterre, in which bright primulas sat within privet and box.

Jim's eye was drawn to the small memorial, a simple raised stone, inscribed with the deceased's name and dates. John Hare had been only twenty two. It was set in a carpet of purple aubretia and half-circled by daffodils.

'Very sad,' Basil remarked and Jim remembered that he had lost relatives in the conflict in Sri Lanka, from whence he and his family had fled to find sanctuary in the village.

Matt appeared at Jim's elbow. Jim offered his hand to the tall youth and drew him away from the others.

'It's Matt, isn't it? I understand that you do all the spade work around here.'

Matt laughed politely. 'I keep it tidy and put the bedding plants in...' Half his attention seemed to be elsewhere.

'Matt.'

The youth stopped gazing into the distance and focussed on Jim.

'You look almost as bad as I feel. Were you hitting the bottle again last night?'

Matt stared at his feet. There was a small silence.

'John wouldn't want this you know. He'd be angry at you.'

'Well, I'm angry at him.'

'People often feel anger towards loved ones who've died." Jim said. 'It's normal. But you have to set that aside, otherwise you can't heal.'

'I'm not sure I want to. Heal that is.' Matt looked at the memorial. His voice wavered. 'It would be like forgetting him.'

'Of course you've got to heal. It's self-indulgence not to.' Jim glanced across at Matt. 'What I mean is....'

'I understand what you mean.'

'It isn't forgetting him at all.'

'It's been...'

'A year, I know. And you've done your mourning. It's time for you to think about what you're going to do with your life.'

Matt looked anywhere but at Jim.

'Do you think you're the only one touched by death? It's part of life. It's hard, but people get over it. Your grandmother didn't give up when your grandfather died, 'though she must have felt lonely and sad, knowing that he would never be with her again. And think about your parents. They loved John just as much as you did. Think what it's like for your mother, to lose a son.'

Matt shuffled his feet.

'Does it go away? The hurt?' He asked.

'Not really, it just becomes a part of you. But it lessens, gets pushed aside by other things, by life.' Jim gestured to the garden with a sweep of his arm 'Things like this garden.'

Matt nodded, looking around the brightly coloured patch. He took a deep breath.

'I'll lift those violas next week,' he said. 'It's time for some summer blooms. Aster amellus, I think. Michealmas daisies.'

'Good.'

'Reverend?'

'Yes.'

'You haven't mentioned ...like....God, heaven... or anything.'

'Nope. Did you want me to?'

'Er, no, I suppose not.'

'Right then. So, which ones are the bedding plants?'

The Luck garden was small, even if it was perfectly formed, and in less than an hour the judges prepared to make their way to Marigold Road and Winnie.

'Thank you, Mrs Luck. You have a lovely garden.' Basil made his farewells. 'And you have a real flair for plants, Matt.'

'You ought to consider it as a career,' Howard added.

Matt flushed and mumbled a response.

'Are you off to Frank Fortune's garden?' Sylvia asked, pleasantly. 'Why Winnie has entered, I don't know. It's hardly the sort of thing Frank would approve of, I'm sure.'

'Now, now, Sylvia,' Jim admonished, gently, as he left. 'That's up to Winnie.' He climbed into the Land Rover.

*

Minutes later Basil parked in Marigold Road and Jim stepped out to be greeted by Winnie herself.

'Good afternoon, Vicar. Let me show you around.'

Winnie ushered the judges through the gate and restarted the tour she had so recently given to the Ladies Society, but with added improvements.

'Would you like a cup of tea? Proper tea, made in a teapot,' she said, pointedly. She made her voice louder and called over her shoulder. 'Lynda! Bring the tray out please!'

Jim and the others proceeded around the garden, making notes and asking questions, while daintily carrying the china cups and (to Winnie's ill-concealed dismay) dunking their Garibaldi biscuits.

There was more liquid refreshment as they moved on. At The Elms Gus and Jane King insisted that they have some champagne and at Plough Lane Cottage some much admired Harkiss home brew was produced, all gratefully consumed, to Basil's disappointment, by Howard and Jim. Its effects could be detected in their enthusiasm for chatting with the nurses beneath the cherry blossom at the hospital and their delight in the wild meadow garden on the Green. It was almost four when they started back to the Vicarage.

Discussion began on the way. All agreed that the wild meadow garden should receive a coveted 'Special Mention' as would the hospital garden. The private gardens prompted considerably more discussion. The Kings had raised large sums for charity, but no one believed that the prize award should go to The Elms, or to any of the similarly grand gardens. As the tower of St Agnes came into view, it became clear that the front runners were the two gardens on the Flowers Estate.

'The planting at Cowslip Lane is well designed,' Howard said as he clambered from the vehicle. 'Matt Hare has a real talent, but the design at Marigold Road is exceptional. The work of the late Mr Fortune, I assume.'

'Yes, Winnie's kept it the way Frank wanted it.' Jim answered, opening the vicarage door. 'In its way, that garden is as much a memorial as the stone in the Luck garden. Now...I suggest that we eat and concentrate on judging. We need to make a decision and, whichever way we decide, it's not going to be easy on the loser.'

It took the whole of a leisurely high tea, but consensus was finally reached in time for Jim to prepare for Evensong. He hurried to change into his Sunday evening finery, while the other two members of the judging panel repaired to the pub, just across the churchyard.

One of the Flowers Estate gardeners was about to be disappointed.

*

In Marigold Road Winnie closed the gate behind the last of her visitors with a contented sigh, but then was startled by a clattering noise further inside the garden.

'Hello? Is someone there?'

Had she'd missed a stray garden-goer, someone still lurking around? She followed the sounds into the night-stocks garden, where a stone seat stood against the wall, flanked by urns planted with stocks.

'What! My giddy aunt!'

The grass was strewn with soil and greenery, the gorgeous blooms ripped and shredded. Around the grassy space a small white short-haired terrier grubbed at plants, grasping stalks in his mouth and threading a way through the legs of the garden seat.

'Bloody thing! You bloody, bloody thing!' Winnie subsided onto the seat, crushing her hands into fists, trying not to weep. The dog jumped up, dropping blossoms onto Winnie's lap. Its tail wagged as it waited for approval.

'Damn you!' Winnie hurled the flowers down. 'Did she put you up to this?'

The dog sat on the bench, looking less hopeful. Minutes passed and still it did not move.

'Oh, all right.' Winnie stroked his head. 'I know you only wanted to play.'

The terrier barked, jumped into Winnie's lap and nuzzled her face.

'You're a good dog really.' He gazed at her adoringly as she caressed his ears. 'I wouldn't mind a little dog like you.'

Frank would never countenance a dog, she thought. A dog would present too great a risk to his precious plants. But then......

'Well, come on, you can help me clear up this mess.'

Winnie stood. The dog jumped down and leapt about her ankles, barking.

'Then we'll get ready for church. Sylvia's sure to be at the announcement, so I can hand you back then.'

*

An hour later, as the sound of distant voices raised in song filtered out from the church, a growing band of villagers, including Sylvia Luck and Matt Hare, converged upon the lych-gate, accompanied by a photographer from the Herald. There was a general air of expectation and some little excitement as they waited for the announcement. Jim arrived, with much of his congregation. They were muttering and excited. He leapt up onto a low stone pedestal and produced a note from within the folds of his surplice.

'Good evening, everyone,' he began. 'As you know, my colleagues and I have today been visiting all the gardens in the village Open Gardens competition. The standard has been incredibly high.' There was applause. 'It was very, very difficult to decide upon the winners and we reflected long and hard.'

'And full of 'ome brew,' came a disembodied voice from the back. There was laughter and reproof in equal measure.

'We have, however, arrived at our decision.' Silence fell. 'Special Mention awards go to.....' Jim paused dramatically, in the manner of television competition hosts. 'High Acres Hospital.' There was unsurprised applause. 'And the Village Green Committee for the Wildflower Meadow.' This was a popular choice.

'And finally, the Open Gardens award for the best private garden goes to.... pause for effect..... 13, Marigold Road and its owner, Mrs Winnie Fortune. Where are you Winnie, I saw you in your usual place a few minutes ago?'

Winnie was shepherded through the applauding crowd and Jim jumped down to shake her hand as cameras flashed.

'Speech!' Someone called and Winnie looked round in dismay. Jim and Basil helped her up on to a step so that she could be seen.

'I don't have much to say,' she began, as she wiped a tear from her eye. 'Most of you know that my garden is really Frank's, so the credit belongs to him.' She motioned towards the churchyard, prompting a scattering of muted, uncertain applause. 'It's been hard carrying it on, and carrying on in general, if I'm honest, since he passed. But he wouldn't have wanted me to give up and go gently into my dotage.' She smiled, eyes filled with mischief. 'Even when I do things I know he might not approve of.., like entering this competition. But still, I think he would be very proud today. Thank you from both of us.'

Winnie stepped, solidly, to the floor and people began making their way through the churchyard to the pub, where a buffet awaited, in honour of the occasion. Matt lingered at his grandmother's side. Throughout Winnie's speech he had been very still.

'Never mind, love,' Sylvia patted Matt's arm. 'There's always next year.'

'I don't mind, Gran.'

Dev was waving at Matt to join him.

'You go on, Dev's waiting. I'm away home' The terrier had already read Sylvia's thoughts and was pulling at her on the end of a lead. 'Don't stay too long, mind and soft drinks only.'

Matt went to join his friend.

Jim, Basil and Howard strolled over to the pub, following the crowd.

'I think that went quite well,' Jim said. 'All my fears proved groundless. And that was a nice dedication from Winnie.'

'Yes,' Basil replied. 'And everyone will expect you to do it all again next year.'

Jim smiled, broadly. I might just do that.'

Bells rang out from the ivy-mantled tower. Folk paused and turned. The pealing triples, usually saved for weddings and festivals, were being rung in celebration.

Basil paused. '"The curfew tolls the knell of parting day',' he declaimed. 'My brother and I had to learn 'Gray's Elegy'. We used to recite it on the way home from school.'

Basil remembered wind-blown palm trees and the sound of surf on the sand, as he and his brother walked through tropical shrubbery, sweltering in their stiff school blazers. Silent, he resumed his path towards The Lion.

In the pub's cobbled courtyard, the landlord approached the Reverend. 'There's food, Vicar, if you're hungry. And here's something to keep you going.' He handed Jim a glass of old-fashioned stout.

'Ah, that's good,' Jim smacked his lips. 'What's that you've got?'

'The postman's been confusing the sacred with the profane, again. These were delivered here by mistake.' He handed over a sheaf of envelopes, one of which was marked 'HMRC'. Jim's eyebrows rose.

'It's judgement day indeed,' he murmured. 'Publicans, tax-gatherers....'

In the churchyard Winnie had co-opted a tomb that was less visible than her usual perch.

'So, we won.' She didn't know what else to say.

The low hum of conversation, shot through with laughter, spread from the Lion.

'It'll be in the national magazine. I thought I might call it The Frank Fortune Garden.'

A blackbird alighted on the tomb's stone angel.

'Well, I don't have to, if you'd rather not.' She looked askance at the headstone. 'Anyway, Ray and Lynda will do all the arranging, it won't be any bother for me.'

A bee droned by.

'I thought...umm.... I'd get Sylvia Luck involved too, bury the hatchet, like. It all seems a bit daft now, my love. And her garden was runner-up after all. Tell young John if you happen to see him.' She paused. 'The family's suffering, especially little Matt. It's hard, I know. John was so young.'

The blackbird took flight, wheeling above the yew trees, to catch the last rays of the sun, high up on St Agnes' tower.

'Now, what else have I got to tell you? The Summer Fete's the next big event and it seems there might be some sort of contest with that too. It's all a bit too competitive if you ask me. As for gossip, well that Yvonne Young from down on the Bridge Road is carrying on with the school teacher's husband. The scandal! And her with three young children.'

Winnie shook her head in disbelief.

'And there's just one other thing. I was thinking... I was thinking that I might get myself a little dog. I know you never liked them, because of all the damage they could do but a dog would be company for me.'

Winnie paused.

'A cat's all very well, but it's not the same........'

Winnie's voice merged with the sounds of the evening. This conversation would continue for some time to come.

7.

Mixed Doubles

Lynda heaved shopping bags into the kitchen as the front door closed behind her.

'Hello! I'm back! What?'

Drawers were half-open, with items strewn over the surfaces and the floor. Cupboard doors were ajar. The room looked like it had been ransacked.

'Ray?'

The house was silent.

'Ray, are you home?'

There was a noise. It came from the garden. She picked up a heavy frying pan and tiptoed towards the back door.

Beyond the windows the garden stretched away from the house, down a slight incline to the shed, where a fence divided it from the bank that led down to the canal. It was an obvious exit route for any intruder. The noise came again, a metallic clattering.

Quietly, Lynda crept along the path, passing bean pole wig-wams and raspberry canes, edging nearer to the sound. As she neared the shed she saw tools, boxes and other articles, strewn across the grass. And the noise was coming from within the shed. She straightened up and sighed.

'Ray.' She called again, lightly.

'Yes. Lynda, is that you? Are you back already?'

'Yes. What are you doing?'

'Doing?' Ray's head appeared around the shed door. 'Just clearing out.'

He looked at Lynda and at the frying pan in her hands.

'What are you doing?'

'Planning to wallop a non-existent burglar. The kitchen looks like a bomb's hit it.'

'Oh, that was me. Why'd you think we were being burgled? You knew I was here.'

Lynda opened her mouth to reply then closed it again.

'I've been searching for my Granddad's tool box. Yes, I know, raking through the past again.' Ray gestured at the chaos. 'It's here somewhere, I know it is.'

'I'll go and make us some coffee.'

Minutes later she placed Ray's mug upon the sill and leaned back against the open door. Lynda liked the shed. It had a distinct creosote-laden smell that reminded her of childhood. Ray was kneeling on the floor, surrounded by containers and drawers. He looked up.

'What time am I picking them up? When does football practice finish?'

'Twelve o'clock at the school for Paul. Daisy's being brought home from dancing class by Amrita.'

Ray nodded and sat back on his heels.

'Speaking of your Granddad...' Lynda continued. 'Did you ask my Ma about him?'

'I did, but she didn't know anything, said she was too young.' Ray flashed a crooked grin.

'Well, she would only have been a child...'

'I know.' He stopped rootling. 'Though she's not getting any younger, love. She looked a bit unwell to me last time I saw her. Very pale.'

'Pale?' Lynda's eyebrows rose, then she began to smile. 'Do you think so? Are you sure it isn't the hair dye.'

'Hair dye?' Ray's mouth dropped open. 'Now you come to mention it, her hair is darker. What does she want with dying her hair?'

'She's doing all sorts of new things. It's since she took up with Sylvia Luck. It's good for her, a new lease of life.'

'Mm, Vince mentioned something. I thought Ma and Sylvia always disliked one another.'

'They did, from way back. But since she won the garden competition she's often round at Cowslip Lane and Sylvia's grandson and his friend have been doing some of the heavy gardening work for her.'

'I thought she'd not been asking me to do so much.'

'The other day she was after loose black clothing.' Lynda smiled at Ray's quizzical look. 'She and Sylvia are joining a T'ai Chi class.'

'T'ai chi. That's a bit experimental for Winnie, isn't it?'

'That's what I said. But you know how she is, she just sniffed and muttered something about my being behind the times.'

'The return of Kung Fu Granny.' Ray chuckled and reached for his mug. 'Well, good luck to her, but I hope this doesn't mean trouble.'

'No reason why it should. So, are you staying in here for the rest of the morning?'

'No. I give up. I can't find it. I'll put everything back. Then I'll mow the lawn.'

'Well, you could....or you could do something else.' Lynda gave Ray a sultry look and a slow smile. 'Take advantage of a Saturday morning without the kids, perhaps.

Ray looked Lynda up and down appreciatively. '"Something else" might interest me. Use up some of that excess, burglar-hunting adrenalin maybe.'

He put his mug on the workbench and took hers from her with a playful smile. Treading over the detritus, Lynda began to laugh. She wound her arms around his neck.

'Twelve o'clock you said.' Ray walked her backwards until her thighs touched the dusty work surface.

'Twelve o'clock.'

'Lots of time, for all sorts of things, then.'

Ray lifted her on to the work bench and slid his hand beneath her T-shirt, tracing the corrugations of her spine. Lynda kicked the shed door closed.

At the front door, Daisy turned her key in the lock and waved goodbye to Mrs Dhaliwal as she drove away. Patka Dhaliwal, Daisy's friend, had been taken ill and their ballroom dancing class had been abandoned. Checking her mobile, Daisy went straight to her bedroom and dumped her rucksack, then ventured out again in search of juice.

Still mobile focussed, she opened the fridge door and reached for a small carton, barely noticing the chaos around her. Then she spotted the shopping bags on the work surface.

'Mum? I'm back early! Mum!'

Noticing that the garden door was ajar, she trotted out, piercing the carton and sucking as she wandered down the path in the sunshine. Distracted, she watched the bees on the lavender and looked for the tiny fruits already forming on the apple tree.

There was a muffled crash from the shed. Her head turned sharply. Then she recognised her parents' laughter.

'Mum?' Her voice was quiet.

Curious, Daisy maneuvered through the scattered boxes towards the shed door and listened. The noises were different now. Growls and snufflings, regular staccato mewing sounds. She reached up for the handle.

A metallic click came from her pocket and the ringtone music sounded loud above the birdsong. Daisy reached for her mobile and turned back up the path.

"Hello? Oh, hi Pat, how are you feeling now? Yeah, I think so, tomorrow morning. Shall I come round, or do you want to come here?"

Daisy glanced back at the shed again, but all was now silent.

*

Beyond the garden fence, at the foot of a nettle-covered bank, a cuckoo called. Willows leant into their own reflection in the canal. The dark water was stippled with the progress of insects upon its surface and rippled by the predatory fish below.

A towpath ran alongside, at the boundaries of gardens and shops. A hundred yards hence were the crumbling steps and trodden earth pathway up to Canal Road. The path ran beneath the echoing underside of the bridge, occasional haunt of amorous youth and the itinerant. Thereafter the buildings thinned and the canal crossed fields and copses as it progressed towards its junction with a larger version of itself, a once-mighty waterway.

A tinny rhythm escaped from the headset of a solitary jogger. Andrew Wells' powerful legs pounded the towpath towards The Lockkeepers, an isolated old inn and useful trysting place. Today a gaggle of youngsters were sitting on the picnic benches by the lock itself. Andrew glanced over at the boy-men and girls enjoying that brief period of freedom, after school, but before work and college began. He wiped the sheen of sweat from the dark curls at his temples and stooped beneath the heavy lintel into the building.

Standing at the bar, Andrew observed the little group in the bright sunshine outside, sniggering and muttering. Were they talking about him? He pressed his lips tightly together.

Andrew saw a blue Fiat pull onto the car park. He hurried through the front door.

Yvonne stepped out of the car. She wore a tight little cotton blouse and pale jeans. Both accentuated her shapeliness. Her hair fell about her shoulders.

Andrew drew her into the shadow of the whitewashed wall, out of sight of the picnic benches and kissed and stroked her face. 'My darling.'

'My love.'

'Let's go. Let's not stay here. I want to be alone with you.'

'Andrew, really.' Yvonne laughed, tossing back her hair.

He took her arm and led her back to the car.

"Well..."

Raucous shouts came from pub garden. Beer glasses were raised towards them, to hoots of laughter and cat-calls.

'What!'

'We're leaving. Just get in the car.'

'Wey-hey!'

'Good God. Are they shouting as us?'

They climbed hurriedly into the Fiat. Yvonne turned the ignition key and it swerved slightly as they turned on to the lane.

'Well, we can't meet here again!' Yvonne flushed as she pulled away.

'Don't worry about it, it isn't worth it.' Andrew stared forward, fixedly. 'Bloody kids!'

Andrew had already been aroused in anticipation of their love making and the scent of Yvonne's skin had only increased his ardour. But now consummation would have to be deferred, while he calmed and soothed her.

'Anyway, soon we won't have to do this, he said. He saw her bite her lip. 'Will we?'

'Steve's being difficult. He refuses to move out.' Yvonne flicked a glance his way.

'So? It's inconvenient, but I'll buy somewhere for us, in the village or just outside. We'll be together soon.'

'Oh, Andrew, I do hope so.' She sounded reassured.

'You shouldn't let him set the agenda, you know. You should be more forceful.'

'I know, but it's difficult. The children....' Yvonne shook her head.

He slid his hand beneath her long chestnut hair and caressed her neck.

"Things will work out." He stroked her. "Here. Turn into that lane there. We'll go to the old airfield. At least we'll get some privacy there."

*

Ray and Lynda relaxed on the sofa after lunch, the gentle 'pock, pock' of televised tennis provided a regular undercurrent of sound beneath their voices. The children were happily occupied in their respective bedrooms.

'Will you be working in the village on Tuesday?' Lynda asked.

'Yeah, the Reverend wants the Vicarage gabling done. Why?'

'It's Daisy's end of term parents evening at Priory Road. Some of the Furzedown teachers are going to be there too, doing a bit of induction for next term.'

'Okay, what time?'

'Six o'clock.'

'Hang on. Haven't you got that training thing on Tuesday? In town?'

'Yeah, that's why I'm asking. It doesn't finish until six and these things tend to run on.'

'Is it mandatory?'

''Fraid so. Professional skills development."

Lynda worked as a social worker, based in the nearby town.

'Even for part-timers?'

'Yes. Astonishingly, even part-timers are professionals and need to keep up to date.'

'Okay, okay, I'll make sure I'm there for six. And you'll just get there when you get there.'

'Thanks.' Lynda took a deep breath. 'Actually, I've been thinking....'

'Oh-oh.'

She cuffed Ray with a cushion.

'Once Daisy settles in at Furzedown and we've established a routine, I could expand my hours. Not go full-time just yet maybe, but do another day a week. That was always what we agreed and we could certainly do with the money. What do you think?'

'Good idea, but 'family comes first' remember. It's what we've always said.'

'Every member of the family,' Lynda squirmed around to face Ray. 'Including me. I love my job.'

'I know. And we agreed that you'd go back full-time eventually. Let's do the sums shall we? See how it pans out. I could work shorter days, but that could have a financial impact. I might have to employ someone.'

Lynda fixed her gaze inwards, her mouth a thin line. Minutes passed.

'It wasn't just me who wanted a family,' she said.

'Yes, but, you were the one giving birth...'

'I could have gone straight back, lots of women do. I agreed to stay at home for a while, but I was always going to go back.'

'And you can...I'm just saying...' Ray sounded more placatory.

'What exactly?' Lynda's voice was hard and flat.

'That we'll have to do the sums. What's got into you?'

'I sense a reluctance on your part...you seem to like things how they are now.'

Ray sighed.

'Isn't there an open day at Furzedown before the Autumn term starts?'

'Yes.'

'We'll have to take Daisy.'

'Yes.'

'And Paul, he needs to show her around. I'll have a chat with him, about Daisy going to Furzedown,' Ray said. 'He should take some responsibility for helping his sister in her new school. That will be good for both of them and may be of some practical help.'

'Mmm.' Lynda looked sceptical.

'Come on, love.' Ray burrowed into the sofa, put his arms around her waist and drew her to him. 'Look. I'm not going to go back on what we agreed. We just need to do the maths, make sure it doesn't make too much of a dent in our finances and work out the practicalities.'

Lynda looked up into his face and half-smiled, grudgingly.

'Okay,' she said. 'But we do it soon.'

*

Two skeins of smoke curled upwards from the long grass until they were dissipated by the breeze. Andrew and Yvonne lay, half-clad, in each other's arms, lazy with sex and sunshine, smoking forbidden cigarettes.

'I could stay here with you forever.' Andrew leaned over and kissed her closed eyelids.

'Or until you have to go home.' Yvonne's smile was tender. 'As must I.'

'Why don't you move in with me, at least temporarily? Diane's staying with the Kings.'

'You know why. It's hard, but it's even harder for the children. At least they should be in their own home, go to school as usual, meet their friends as normal.'

Andrew opened his mouth to reply, then thought better of it. He sat up and stubbed out his cigarette in one of the plastic glasses they'd bought with them. An empty champagne bottle lay next to it. He looked down at Yvonne, lying back in an abandoned pose, her long, thick hair emphasising the whiteness of her flesh. The thin fabric of her shirt still covered one of her upper arms and Andrew felt the urgent desire to remove it, to tear it away and reveal her bare shoulder, before making love to her again. As he reached over he heard the approaching splutter of an engine.

"What the hell?" Andrew struggled into his track-suit trousers, while Yvonne cast about, anxiously searching for items of clothing.

Some fifty metres away a motorcycle circled on the old runway, halting before the crumbling buildings. Its two riders dismounted. The first, a young man, took their helmets and hung them on the handle bars. He reached his arm around the girl's waist, slinging his jacket over his shoulder. The girl, slim and straight with fair hair, leant into him as they walked towards the tower.

Andrew watched from behind a tree. Yvonne crept up to his shoulder.

'So we're not the only ones.'

'No.' Andrew pulled on his sweatshirt. 'I'll bet this place has seen some things over the years. Though I'm surprised those are still standing.' He gestured at the control tower buildings. 'Why someone hasn't developed the site is beyond me.'

'Andrew, this is a lovers' assignation, not a business opportunity.' Yvonne stood in front of him, blocking his view of the airfield. Her hands reached under the sweatshirt and encircled his waist against his skin. She looked up into his eyes.

'Prove it to me.'

'Not if you can't manage a better line than that. Anyway, I thought I already had.'

'Hmmm.'

Their embrace grew passionate, but Yvonne pulled away.

'Later, my love. We must go now. I have to pick up the children at three thirty."

Reluctantly Andrew let her go. Clenching his teeth he shook out the blanket and Yvonne threw their rubbish into a plastic carrier. As they returned to the car he glanced back, an almost wistful look on his face, towards the young couple.

On the other side of the tower Ellen Fisher turned her face towards the sun as she and Matt Hare walked, hand in hand.

'D'you know, I've never been here before,' she said, looking around. 'What was this place, an airport?'

'An RAF base, I think,' Matt replied. 'No-one comes here any more.'

'So how'd you know about it?'

'A young kid told me about it. He came here to a car boot sale. I got him out of a spot of bother and his Gran's friendly with my Gran. So I looked for it, when I was riding round. It seems the sort of place where important things happened.'

'And did they?'

'Dunno.'

'You're just a romantic.'

They laughed and walked on.

'Are you going to do work experience, before the long holiday?' Ellen asked.

'I'm going to the agricultural college, I've got to re-take biology.'

'What about the rest of the gang?'

'Colin's at Boots, Dev's at the council...'

'His Mum got him the place?'

'Yep. She'll have called in a few favours for that one. I don't think Dev had much to say about it.'

'Has she chosen his degree course yet?'

They smiled and lapsed into a companionable silence which stretched on for a little too long. Matt halted.

'What about you?'

'I've decided. I'm not doing work experience. I've got an apprenticeship and a job.' She turned her face away and continued walking. 'At the Salon in Priory Road.'

'Hair-dressing.' Matt's voice was studiedly neutral.

'What's wrong with hair-dressing?' Ellen stood still. 'It's a useful, transferable skill – like accountancy. Or embalming.'

'I didn't say there was-'

'It's obvious what you think.'

Another silence.

'So you're definitely staying then?'

'Yep.' She kicked at a loose stone. 'I start work next month. Maybe I'll leave eventually, I like the idea of travelling, seeing the world, but that costs money. For now, I'm staying here and I need to bring in a wage. I'm lucky to have the job, there's plenty who haven't.' Ellen looked Matt in the eyes. 'But you're definitely going, aren't you. You've made up your mind.'

'As long as I get biology, I've got a place and, well, I seem to have wasted enough time, you know. We could still keep in touch. We could write. It doesn't have to be the end for us.'

'We could, but why draw things out?' Ellen smiled a grim little smile. 'Better to make a new start.'

'Maybe I don't want to.'

'Matt, I don't think you'll know what you want until you get to uni.'

'I probably won't get the grades I need anyway.'

'No, but you have to try.' Ellen reached up and gave him an affectionate kiss.

Wound around each other, they resumed their course. Neither spoke as they circled the end of the building. A small, blue Fiat sped across the deserted runway. Matt grinned as his jaw dropped.

'Them again!'

Ellen gurgled with laughter.

*

The light and airy training room held three small groups of social workers, each puzzling over a different problem.

'Excuse me,' the young woman apologised for interrupting. 'Lynda, you've got an urgent phone call.'

'A phone call?' Lynda rose from her place, reaching into her pocket for her mobile. Switched off for the training session, it registered three missed calls. Today she was dressed for work, in a neat black business suit, her curls constrained in a pony tail.

'On the desk there.' The woman explained as Lynda followed her out of the room.

Lynda picked up the telephone receiver indicated. 'Hello? It's Lynda Marshall.'

'Hello Mum.'

'Daisy?' Lynda lowered her voice. 'What is it? Why are you phoning me here?'

'It's Dad, Mum. He hasn't come. I had tennis after school, so I stayed to wait, but there's no sign of him. All my teachers asked if you're coming. I told them you were.'

'And we are, love. He's probably just been delayed, that's all.' Her watch said a quarter past six. 'And I'll be coming soon. Is Patka's mum there?'

'Yes.'

'Well, you go and join her until your Dad or I get there. Okay?'

'Okay. But Mum...'

'Yes love.'

'Don't be long. Everyone else's parents are here, even Terry Beck's and his Dad's only just come out of jail.'

'All right love. I'll speak to your Dad now.'

'Okay. Bye.'

It was a while before Ray's mobile was answered.

'Hello? Ray Marshall's telephone, Jim Gardener speaking.'

'Hello Reverend. It's Lynda. Is Ray there?

'Oh, hello Lynda. Yes. He's just up a ladder. I'll get him.'

Lynda heard a door being opened and the sounds of outside. There were indistinct voices, then...

'Hello? What's the emergency? I was up on the roof.'

'The emergency is your daughter, who is, at this very moment, hanging about Priory Road School looking helpless because her father's not turned up for parents' evening.'

'Shit! Sorry, Reverend.'

'Don't tell me you've forgotten your own daughter! Or is this some sort of point you're trying to prove?'

'Eh'

'The one time I'm not there, you decide to go AWOL.'

'No, it's not...I'm on my way. I'm going now'

Lynda waited for the line to go dead. Instead of the 'click' she heard one half of a distant conversation. Only Ray's faint voice was distinguishable.

'I'm sorry Vicar. I'm going to have to go.'

Something was said in reply.

'No, it's just the wife, throwing a wobbler. You're lucky you're a bachelor.'

By the time the phone went dead Lynda was half way to her car.

*

'Just forgot! How could you just forget?'

'I don't know, I just... did!'

They glared at each other across the living room. The children were in their rooms.

'When I think of that child, our child, just standing there, waiting!'

'She was all right, she was with Amrita and Pat.'

'But she should have been with you!'

'Keep your voice down.'

The evening had been strained. When Lynda arrived at Priory Road Ray and Daisy were in discussions with Daisy's form teacher. Lynda gave Daisy a very big hug. Everyone was polite. Daisy was doing well, though, as ever, her teachers identified her shyness and reluctance to speak up as a potential obstacle to progress.

'You've got to be more confident, love,' Ray explained as Lynda drove the short journey home. He'd left his van at the Vicarage. 'Put your hand up more. You know the answers and are just as clever as your classmates. Cleverer even.'

'Yes Dad, but....'

'What love?'

'If I'm wrong they'll all laugh at me.'

'Does everyone else always get everything right?'

'No.'

'And do people laugh at them when they get things wrong?'

'Not really.'

'Well, there you are. Being wrong occasionally is all part of learning.'

Their late supper had been a subdued and tense affair, the children eating and going, unbidden, to their rooms afterwards. Ray wiped as Lynda washed.

'You see, she's fine.'

Lynda clattered the plates into the sink.

'Careful.'

Ray followed her through into the living room and perched on the edge of the sofa, channel surfing. Lynda sat in an armchair, flicking through her course notes.

'Was it good, your course?'

'It was okay, before I had to leave.'

Ray took a deep breath.

'I'm sorry, I just forgot.'

Both were bristling now.

'And don't think I don't know what's going on, either.' Lynda hissed.

'Nothing's going on! I was trying to finish a job and I didn't realise the time.'

'Oh yeah?'

'Yes.'

'On the exact night you happen to have responsibilities elsewhere.'

'I forgot!'

Lynda returned to her notes. Ray watched the changes on the silent screen.

'It's no wonder she's reluctant to come forward. She's even invisible to her own father!'

'That's not true.' Ray was on his feet, but he lowered his voice. 'I love my children.'

'I thought you'd rather be a bachelor.'

'Eh? Oh. You heard that.'

'Yes, I did.'

'I was annoyed at the time. Annoyed at myself, before you jump down my throat.'

'How could you leave her standing there?' Lynda gasped, her voice rising an octave. She wiped the back of her hand across her eyes.

'I don't know, but I'm sorry.' Swiftly, Ray knelt at Lynda's feet and put his arms around her waist and his head in her lap, ignoring the papers with which she beat him. 'I'm sorry.'

Eventually she stopped and swallowed hard. She moved over as Ray joined her in the armchair and put his arm around her.

'I'm sorry, love. I didn't do it on purpose.'

Lynda sniffed and raised her chin. 'Okay.' She turned to him.

In his bedroom Paul gave a small cheer. He had just got to Level Three of Tomb Raider. Stewie was still on Level Two.

In her bedroom Daisy was nodding along to her current favourite playlist. She admired the latest badge on her jacket, which she had just sewn on. Reaching for her mobile she began to text.

*

'The point is to maintain balance and improve breathing,' Winnie explained.

Clad in a black smock and loose trousers, she set her right foot firmly down to one side of the garden path and put her weight upon it. Ray and Lynda sat in garden chairs in the sunshine, amused spectators to Winnie's demonstration. On the hour the bells of St Agnes rang out, as they had the whole of that day, to signal yet another summer wedding.

'By the way,' said Winnie. 'Young Matt's bringing Sylvia over on that motor bike of his. So as you can take us both to class.' She nodded at Ray, then she began the slow and elegant circling arm movements. 'This will improve my chi.'

'Your chi?' Lynda asked. She glared pointedly at her son in disapproval.

Further down the garden, Paul was mimicking his grandmother's every movement, in somewhat wobbly fashion. Ray stared hard at the nearest wall.

'It means life energy.' Winnie spoke without interrupting her flow. 'People do exhibitions and compete, you know.'

'Really? Well, be sure and tell me where you're making an exhibition of yourself and I'll come and watch.'

'It might be included in the Olympic Games.' Winnie focussed on her slow posturing, as did Paul. He was now crossing his eyes and sticking out his tongue in a parody of deep concentration. Lynda and Ray exchanged sly smiles.

'I'll just - um...,' Ray put the tea things on to the tray and took them inside.

'Are you two all right now?' Winnie asked.

Lynda shaded her eyes and looked up at Winnie. 'Yes, we're fine.'

''Cause I wondered...'

'We're fine.'

There was a small silence as mother looked at daughter.

Winnie returned to her explanation. 'T'ai chi started out as a martial art. I just haven't got to the weapons stage yet.'

'Weapons?' Paul stopped, mid-gesture. He trotted up to Winnie. 'What weapons?'

'All sorts - swords, spears, staffs and whips - the better to beat naughty children with.'

On the balls of her feet, Winnie swung around rapidly and Paul narrowly avoided a blow to the head.

'Hey, you nearly hit me!'

'Really? Oh dear. Now what were you doing there?'

Paul screwed up his face and opened his mouth to argue.

'Yes, what were you doing there, Paul?' Lynda repeated, sharply.

Paul pulled a face as his grand-mother elegantly reversed her move and began the circling exercise again.

'I'm going inside to play,' he announced and stalked off.

'He spends far too much time on that machine.' Winnie shifted her weight to her other foot. 'It's not healthy and it gives him ideas.'

'Heaven forbid that he should have ideas! I notice that your new inner harmony doesn't prevent you from unrequested criticism.'

'You may mock, but you'll regret giving him so much freedom in the end.'

'Yes, what he needs is a mother's constant attention.' Ray returned and sat at Lynda's feet. She narrowed her eyes and prodded him with her foot.

'What do you want with working full-time anyway?' Winnie stepped elaborately from side to side.

'Self-fulfilment, intellectual stimulation, diverting colleagues, need I go on? Especially now both the children will be at Furzedown.'

'I always had plenty to occupy me when you were at school.'

Above them a window opened and a light voice sounded.

'So do Mum and Dad, especially when they think Daisy and me aren't around.' It was Paul. 'In the shed on a Saturday morning.'

Lynda gaped. She looked at Ray in astonishment. 'How?' she mouthed.

Ray shrugged and shook his head. He reddened as he caught sight of Winnie.

'You shouldn't be shouting out of the window,' he said. 'Come down here and say that.'

'No chance.' Paul laughed. 'Daisy didn't understand, but I do.' The window closed.

'What will the neighbours think?' Lynda muttered, flushing pink.

'They won't know what he's talking about,' Ray looked her in the eye. 'Though they might be envious,' he added, sotto voce.

'Well, well.... What have you two been up to?' Winnie's eyes widened in mock disapproval, as she launched into her exercises again.

'Wait till I get hold of him.' Lynda fulminated, but her mouth twitched.

'What did I tell you? Too much freedom.' Winnie was imperious. 'Though what you two thought you were about...? I never -.'

'Oh, I'll bet you did.' Ray was on his feet, but he was laughing.

'Not in a garden shed.'

When Daisy showed Matt Hare into the garden a short time later tears were rolling down Winnie's cheeks, while Lynda was bent with laughter. Ray lay prone on the grass.

'Er, hello Mr and Mrs Marshall, Mrs Fortune.' Matt gripped his motorcycle helmet, looking from one to another. 'Gran says that she'll see you at the Community Centre, she's just got caught up in something, clearing out the shed.'

He half-smiled in response to the renewed gales of laughter.

What's so funny?'

'Nothing, nothing Matt.' Winnie brought herself under control. 'We're just having a silly half hour. Oh, my... never you mind us.'

'I'll put some shoes on, then I'll drive you round, Winnie.' Ray brushed grass off his trousers. He walked inside, accompanied by a bemused Matt.

Winnie collected up her over-sized handbag and prepared to depart.

'Oh, by the way, I almost forgot. Ray was asking me about his grand-parents the other day. Well, I happened to mention it to Sylvia. It turns out that her older cousin used to work at RAF Barton, during the war. Guess who she worked for?'

'Thomas?'

'No, Iris.' Winnie smirked. 'There, that's surprised you.'

'It certainly has. What was Iris doing there?'

'She was in charge of the office girls. That's where Thomas and Iris started courting, he was stationed there, on the ground staff.'

'Really? Mum, that's amazing. We didn't know. Ray!' Lynda called.

'You should speak with Sylvia, she'll tell you all about it. Her cousin even attended Tom and Iris's wedding.'

'Their wedding....' Lynda sat up, Ray was returning. 'Listen, it's about your grand-parents. Go on, Mum. We don't know anything about the wedding. There weren't any photographs or anything. We think it's because it was wartime.'

Ray was all attention. 'I've got the photographs of my parents wedding, all flares and kipper ties, but I know nothing about how my grandparents got together. They were the people who really raised me.' In the church the bells pealed out once more.

'Is the cousin...does she live round here? Can we talk to her?'

'I don't think she lives in the village, but she's still alive. Though you'd better get a move on, if you want to speak with her, there aren't that many folk left now who can remember that far back.'

'We will, Winnie, we will. So, we've got a lead at last!' Ray kissed Winnie's dry cheek. 'And we'll talk with Sylvia too. We'll take you both out. How about tomorrow? Sunday lunch at The Lockkeepers, they've got a new cook who's supposed to be good.'

Lynda gave him a look.

'Well why not, we can afford it, especially if you're going back to work.'

*

A blizzard of home-made confetti fluttered down as the couple walked through the tunnel of arching sabres.

'Hurray!'

'Long life and many children!'

RAF friends supplied the sabres and farming friends and neighbours the air rifles, mattocks and hoes which augmented to the arch. There was a mix of uniforms and civilian clothes, accompanied by good natured rivalry.

Iris wore a dress of lace and satin, a mongrel creation made using fabric from her mother's wedding gown. Her hair was newly curled and held up by a borrowed diamante pin, she wore a blue garter over precious new silk stockings. Tom wore his RAF battle dress uniform, his winged brevet upon his chest and his squadron badge prominent on the peaked cap borrowed from his sergeant. On a sunny, warm June Saturday, Iris Everett became Mrs Thomas Marshall.

Bride and groom looked back at St Agnes. Jasmine bloomed against the dark yews and buttercups littered the grass. The bell tower was silent, but hand bells were rung with much gusto by the local bell ringers.

A growing rumble heralded the arrival overhead of a Wellington, its bomb doors opening to cascade more hand-made petals on the newly-weds. Everyone waved and shouted, even the Wing Commander. The impromptu fly past was against all regulations.

Iris and Tom smiled into each others' eyes. The local doctor's car was waiting beyond the lych-gate, to take them to a small hotel in Bridge, for their first night as a married couple. It had taken three weeks hoarded petrol coupons and a side of bacon to arrange. Iris tossed her bouquet of wild flowers towards the onlookers. Not waiting to see who caught it, she and Tom ran down the wide path and through the lych-gate, pursued by well-wishers. With a clattering cacophony the Morris pulled away.

8.

The Summer Fete

Dr Harinda Mistry picked a path across grass strewn with litter, the stale smell of the night before hung heavy in the clear morning air. Funfair workers raked rubbish into bin bags, while others dismantled stalls and rides. By the large wooden gates she spotted the familiar, bear-like figure of Gus King, overseeing the removal of the heavy equipment. Hari tucked her slim fingers into the pockets of her jeans.

'Morning, Gus.'

'Hello Hari. How'd you feel this morning?'

'All right,' Hari grimaced. 'A bit shaky.'

'Yesterday was very strange.' Gus ran a hand through his greying curls with a frown. 'I don't understand exactly what happened –'

'Nor do I.'

Gus turned his attention to directing a lorry through the gates. Hari looked back over the park's expanse. Everything was as it had been early the previous morning. The football pitches and tennis courts, the bowling green, the white-painted, wooden pavilion and the venerable Park House, the red brick, Victorian villa where the Village Fete Committee held its meetings. Noisy young children played on the swings nearby.

It had all begun so innocently.

*

On a tranquil summer's evening Hari climbed the shallow steps through dusty shrubbery to the Park House. Its crumbling gingerbread gables frowned down at her. Formerly the permanent home of the park-keeper, the building and its garden retained a genteel aura of days gone by.

Inside Hari found used tea bags mouldering in the kitchen sink and ants on sugar encrusted work surfaces. Vince Luck, the Park Partnership Manager, was supposed to sort out cleaning and maintenance, but he probably wouldn't even attend the evening's Fete Committee meeting. Vince was always busy somewhere else. Angry and tired after a long day at the hospital, Hari picked up a cloth.

'You're a glutton for punishment.' Beth Castle breezed in, tucking back her perfectly cut and coloured hair. Beth owned a beautician's salon near the Cross, 'though it was run by a manager, as Beth considered herself a business woman with wider horizons than simply keeping shop. 'Are we in the parlour tonight?' Without waiting for a reply, Beth went through, high heels clicking on the tiled floor. 'I'll have a coffee if there's one going,' she called. 'Scott too. He's just parking the Jag.'

Scott Castle ducked beneath the lintel, brushing an invisible fleck from his well-tailored Italian suit. Craggily handsome with thick black hair untouched by grey, he flashed Hari a lop-sided grin. Scott was senior executive of a large department store in a nearby town. The Castles were youngish, intelligent and full of energy, but were still regarded as newcomers by the locals, having lived in the village for only four years.

'Hello there!' Gus King filled the doorway as he entered. Chairman of the King Electronics Group, a Rotarian and a member of all the right clubs, Gus had chaired the Summer Fete Committee for the last five years. 'I'll have a coffee too, Hari, there's a love.'

With lips compressed, Hari made coffees and carried them through to the small parlour. A round wooden dining table in the centre of the room had seen better days, its surface ringed by coffee mugs past. Dust motes floated in shafts of late evening sunlight. Gus King and the Castles sat at the table.

'I have apologies from our Park Partnership Manager,' Gus began.

The others groaned.

'Now, now, everyone. Vince is a busy man.'

'Too busy to get the Park House kitchen cleaned,' Hari commented, sharply. Beth Castle gave her a sympathetic glance.

'What's our agenda for tonight?' Gus donned half-moon specs and opened the minutes binder on the table. 'Competitions, fancy dress, a fun-fair. The RAF has offered a fly-past – the base Commander is a pal of mine, so...'

'That's sorted.' Scott Castle nodded.

'Oughtn't we first to deal with the parade and who is going to open the fete?' Beth suggested. 'That so-called celebrity we hired last year was quite simply unacceptable.'

The fete parade was a major item on the agenda. Every year it wound through the village to the park, a jubilant phalanx of marching bands, floats, clowns and, until recently, a Fete Princess, who had then opened the Summer Fete.

'He was, I think we can agree, a mistake,' said Scott and everyone nodded. 'So I propose that, this year, someone from the village performs the honours. Not a princess, perhaps, but an elderly resident, or a promising young student, someone chosen by the community.'

'The Fete Princess role attracted as many objections as applicants.' Gus reminded everyone. 'Surely we don't want to resurrect it?'

'Certainly not,' Hari responded. 'These days little girls have better things to aspire to than being a princess.'

Gus glanced over his spectacles at the doctor. Hari had been a village resident for almost a decade. Her family originated in the Punjab, but Hari had arrived in the village by way of several generations of Yorkshire folk. She was a plain speaker and a thoroughly modern woman.

'This would be different,' said Scott. 'We could run a competition and get everyone in the village involved. Get a discussion going about civic contributions to village life and individual achievements.'

'And it would also save money,' Beth added. 'We wouldn't have to pay them.'

'Wouldn't contributions and achievements be different?' Hari asked. 'How would we compare them?'

'What worries me is the dissent it may cause,' said Gus, frowning. 'We don't want to set people against each other.'

'What's wrong with a little healthy competition?' Scott responded. 'The gardening contest was a success.'

'How would we run such a thing, anyway?' asked Hari.

'It would have to be easy for people to participate.' Beth explained. 'We would have a free phone number, and take votes electronically, by text or e-mail. It's not difficult to arrange.'

'I'm not convinced.' Gus put up a big hand. 'Be careful what you wish for.'

Beth and Scott exchanged glances. Beth spoke.

'I understand that there may have been some wishful thinking in the past and some inappropriate strings pulled. Wasn't that one of the reasons why the Fete Princess role was abandoned?'

'What do you mean...?' Gus bridled.

Scott interrupted him. 'What about you, Hari? Which way do you vote?'

'Couldn't we ask what people in the village think? See if there's an appetite for this sort of thing, consult with pensioners' groups, the Legion, faith groups?'

'Let the community have its say?' Gus wavered. He looked around the assembled faces. Hari looked tired and conciliatory, Scott square-jawed and determined and Beth bright-eyed, with a superior air. 'Okay, we can do that.'

*

'Can I have more chips, Mum?' Daisy sat, hair braided into two long, pale plaits, with knife and fork held upright in her small fists.

'Hold on, I haven't served up yet.' Lynda distributed food between three plates. 'You're asking for more before you know what you've got.'

'She's just greedy.' Paul looked sidelong at his sister.

'Why're we so early tonight, Mum?' Daisy pounded her fists on the table.

Lynda brought dinner over and the children began to devour the food. 'I have my Pilates class on Wednesday evenings, you know that. Grandma will sit with you until Dad gets home from work.'

As if by magic, the doorbell rang.

Lynda went to answer it, then ushered Winnie's short and stocky form into the kitchen. 'We're in here. We're just having tea.'

'Have you brought us anything, Nan?' Daisy raised her face for her Grandma's kiss.

Paul waited, expectant, but safely out of reach.

'Spoiled children.' Winnie pursed her lips. 'Always wanting treats.'

Lynda cleared away her own plate, so that Winnie could take her place at the table. Daisy brought the rest of the dirty crockery and cutlery to the sink.

'Thanks, love. Are you going to watch your programme? It starts in a couple of minutes.'

The children decamped to the living room and began fighting over the remote.

'Mine, mine!'

'Give it –'

'It's my programme!'

'Now don't misbehave in front of Grandma,' Lynda called through gritted teeth.

Winnie stood and picked up a tea towel. She started to dry.

'Have you heard about the Summer Fete?' she asked.

'What about it?'

'Dr Hari came to Ladies Society yesterday. There's going to be a competition, to find someone to open it. I'm not surprised, after what's-'is-name was so drunk he could hardly stand upright last year.'

'Another competition? What sort?'

'Well, a vote really, like on the telly. They want a child from the village who's won or achieved something. I thought about our Daisy's dancing. I was thinking I might nominate her?'

'Hmmm.' Lynda wasn't listening, her eyes were glazed over.

'By the way, why isn't Paul going to Sunday School any more?'

'Paul has decided he's an atheist.'

'My giddy aunt! What shall I tell the Reverend?'

'Tell him the truth.'

Daisy came to the doorway, face screwed up. 'Nana, Paul says that you don't love us anymore.'

'Don't be a silly. Come here.' Knees cracking, Winnie crouched to envelop Daisy in her arms.

'I didn't.' Paul appeared. 'She just wants to get me into trouble.'

'And why would she want to do that? Godless child.'

Unsteadily, Winnie rose and bundled Daisy back into the living room. Lynda heard her begin to wheedle. '"I know you bought sweets, Nan.'

'Here.' Winnie emptied her pockets. 'But save some for your brother.' She and Daisy settled on to the sofa. 'Now, what have you done with the remote?'

Lynda hurried upstairs to change, almost colliding on the landing with a sulky Paul.

'Is Nan going to enter Daisy in the Summer Fete competition?' His face crumpled up. 'She's Nana's little creep!' He slammed his bedroom door behind him.

Lynda shook her head and opened the door again.

'Paul.' He lay on the bed, sprawled on his tummy with his pale fringe falling into his eyes. She sat beside him. 'It might sometimes seem as if your Grandma favours your sister, but I know that she loves you both equally. It's just that she sometimes finds Daisy easier to deal with. Your grandmother's getting old and old people are sometimes stuck in their ways. When she was young...'

'Children would be seen and not heard.'

Lynda tried to suppress a smile. 'You know that your father and I don't think that. You have a say in this family.'

'I know.' Paul acknowledged, reluctantly.

'It isn't always Daisy's fault either. You have been known to provoke your sister.'

'It wasn't me this time.'

'Maybe not, but remember, you're older than Daisy. You're her big brother. You should be looking after her, not trying to do her down. I thought that you and your father talked about this?'

'We did.' Paul sat up. 'Man to man.' He smiled. 'I know I should be helping her.' He paused, looking at his laptop. 'And I will.'

'Good.' Lynda hugged him. He showed only token resistance. 'Now, I must be off.'

'When will Ray be back, Lynda?' Winnie called.

'Soon, Mum. You children be good for your Grandma. 'Bye.'

Lynda slammed the door behind her as she escaped in search of relaxation through exercise.

*

Friday evening was well advanced and the drinkers in the Lion were jolly. In the lounge bar a collection of sepia-toned daguerreotypes showed a more rural Lion, with the tower of

St Agnes beyond it. That the lion lay down with the lamb was a time-worn village saying.

Ray paid for two pints at the bar and manoeuvred his way through the crowd to his table, just beside the archway to the snug. At the far end of the snug a meeting was in progress, in full view of the pub's customers, although they were not encouraged to join it. The Summer Fete Committee was in public session.

'Ta, Ray.' Vince Luck took his pint and drank with enthusiasm. 'I can't stay long, I'm supposed to be in the meeting next door. Ah, that's good.' He wiped away a frothy moustache with the back of his hand.

'Why is the meeting here anyway?'

'We're adjudicating the competition,' said Vince. 'There's been so much interest that we've got to reduce the numbers for the final round and the chairman thought it should be done somewhere public, so that people could observe. Like with the united nations.' Vince snorted, derisively. He loosened the necktie beneath his overalls and returned to his pint.

'What does that mean, exactly?'

'We're putting together the short list,' Vince replied. 'Then the village will vote.'

'How do you decide who's on the list?'

'Erm.. by taking various things into account. Number of nominations, range and so on.' Vince put down his empty glass and stood up, flexing his shoulders . 'Your little girl's one of the leaders Ray. What do you think of that?'

'Oh no.' Ray's shoulders sagged. 'Winnie.'

'Winnie Fortune and her fortunate grand-daughter. Ah well, I'd best go in. Oh, nearly forgot.' Vince turned back. 'I've had complaints about the state of the Park House. It needs cleaning up. My Ma said she'd do it, but not on her own. She suggested asking Winnie. Do you think she'd help?'

'If Sylvia's suggested it, I suspect Winnie's already agreed.' Ray took a swig from his drink. 'Those two have become as thick as thieves lately.'

'It's an improvement over them being at loggerheads all the time. I'll tell Ma.'

'Vince, when will the meeting finish? Are you coming back?' Ray asked, but Vince had already passed beyond the arch and was out of earshot.

In the snug Gus cleared his throat. 'Ah, Vince. You've finally decided to join us. As I was saying, the competition has proved more popular than we had imagined.'

'Which is good news.' Beth interrupted, cheerfully.

'Indeed. However, one child seems to have attracted rather more votes than there are people in the village,' Gus continued.

'How did that happen?' Hari chuckled.

'An over enthusiastic hacker, we think,' Scott replied.

'Our task tonight is to agree ten names to go forward. The list of nominees is on page two.' Gus glared at Vince. "Our Park Partnership Manager may not have seen them -'

Scott stepped in. 'Beth, would you read them through?'

Beth smiled at him. 'Of course, darling. First, a successful young mountaineer, who attends St Jerome's College...' Beth read aloud the list of candidates and their achievements. 'And finally, the youngest nominee is the winner of a series of ballroom dancing medals. It is she who has attracted the large number of on-line votes.'

Vince pricked up his ears.

'Is that Ray's lass?' He studied the photograph submitted. 'Young Daisy, pretty as a picture. My mother told me all about it. She was nominated by her grandmother, who's been canvassing for support across the village.'

Gus wasn't impressed. 'I'm not sure about dancing medals. They're not exceptional. It's like taking swimming badges, something lots of children do.'

'In pure terms perhaps,' Scott argued 'But the girl's much younger than the others and we shouldn't automatically disregard popular activities.'

'She's the only nominee still at primary school,' Hari pointed out. 'And her family's one of the oldest in the village.' As paediatrician at the local hospital, Hari had treated most of the individuals on the list. She broached the difficult question. 'Daisy Marshall is probably the only representative of those villagers who couldn't afford to send their off-spring to St Jerome's. Other candidates have more privileged backgrounds.'

'There's nothing wrong with her background,' Vince muttered.

'Hari didn't say there was.' Gus kept the peace. 'It's just that other nominees come from families with more money.

But I'm not sure that's relevant, this is about quality of achievement.'

'Which may be relative-‘ Scott interjected. 'In different circumstances.'

'I knew there'd be problems with this.' Hari sighed.

'She is much younger,' Gus continued doggedly. 'Ten is very young for public events. How do we know she's capable? It could be worse than last year.'

'I really don't think we should discard Daisy,' said Scott. 'We need a range of finalists and including her gives us a good spread in terms of age and social class, not to put too fine a point on it.' He winked at Beth.

'I agree.' Hari put her list down on the table amidst the glasses. 'Although Gus is right – it would be a lot to ask of a ten year old.'

'I think we need to include her too.' Vince's freckled face flushed up to his sandy hairline. 'You might find it funny,' he shot Scott a malevolent look, 'that some people don't have as much money as you do, or speak as fancy, but I'd watch where you park that Jag next time you come to the Park House.'

'Look, that's not what I meant!' Scott kept his voice even. 'And there's no need to be so aggressive and unpleasant....' His eyes were flinty and his mouth a thin line.

'Now, now... let's be civilised.' Gus intervened. He leaned forward, palms outward, looking around the table at each of them in turn.

'I agree too.' Beth chipped in. 'And that's four votes to one, so Daisy Marshall goes into the last ten.'

Out voted and out maneuvered, Gus glowered. 'If you insist.'

A roar of laughter from the lounge bar distracted them all.

Gus moved on to the next agenda item. 'Now, what about publicity? We usually do pieces about the Fete in the Parish magazine.'

'We've suggested lots of other things,' Hari commented. 'And Reverend Jim's tried all manner of innovations, but most folk are wedded to their old ways.'

Beth blinked and Scott looked at the ceiling.

'How about getting The Herald involved?' Scott proposed. The Herald was the closest to a local newspaper the village had, though it was produced in a nearby town. 'We already have a community email list, so we can circulate material online and text everyone as the day approaches. It might be useful to have a Twitter account, too.'

'I'd be happy to make contact with The Herald.' Beth said, as, assuming agreement, she began to collect up the meeting papers.

'Speak with the editor, mention my name,' Gus agreed with as much grace as he could muster.

Vince was on his feet. 'Business concluded?

'Yes, Mr Luck,' Gus replied. 'But everyone please remember, we absolutely must not divulge the names of the finalists to anyone.' He looked especially hard at Vince.

Vince turned and passed through the arch.

Beyond the archway Ray looked up expectantly.

'Oh. All right.' Vince stopped, legs braced. 'Same again is it?'

*

Beth sat alone in the parlour window of the Park House. The low sunlight picked out the auburn highlights in her caramel coloured hair. She examined, with close attention, a press release which read 'Summer Fete Fraud and Corruption. Chairman's family perks'. The accompanying article alleged that fete contracts had been awarded, unfairly, to friends and business partners of King Electronics. She smirked at the photographs of Gus and of his grand-daughter on the Fete Princess float years earlier.

Looking into the middle distance, she spoke to herself.

'If we're going to do this, it'll have to be done tonight. Gus will resign rather than risk this coming out.' She looked up at the sound of a car, folding the piece of paper.

It was Scott. He walked in and leaned over her to kiss the top of her head. 'Have you written it? Will the Editor run it?'

'He won't need to,' Beth said, 'if we do what's necessary.' She gave Scott's chest an affectionate pat. 'Chair of the Summer Fete Committee is an important and influential position in this village and you deserve it. Look at the improvements that have been made since we joined up.'

'"We" is right.' Scott folded himself around his wife.

'Tush, someone might come in.'

'So what if they do?' Scott nuzzled her neck.

'Hallo, hallo –' Vince appeared in the doorway, still wearing his overalls after organising a rubbish collection. 'You'd best move your car, Scott. We've got deliveries for the fete and those drivers aren't over careful.'

'Thanks.' Scott detached himself from Beth. 'I'll just go and do that.' He hurried out of the room.

Hari Mistry was the first arrival to notice that the kitchen was sparkling clean. A tray, laden with cups and a bowl of sugar cubes, sat ready for use. Vince had been as good as his word. With care, she carried the tray into the parlour.

Gus was standing at the parlour table, flanked by Beth and Vince, both seated. 'If we're all here?' He waited as Scott returned. 'Now, next Saturday's final arrangements.'

A large scale map of the village and environs lay opened before him.

'The Parade will start here.' Gus stabbed his finger on the starting point and began to trace the route. 'On the edge of the village at midday. It should arrive at the park at about one thirty, when the fete will formally be opened by the chosen child. At three o'clock the Great Stupendo will escape from a strait jacket while suspended, upside down, from a burning rope. The RAF fly past is at four. If the escape goes wrong, that'll take everyone's mind off it. Canvas tents and trestles are ready behind the pavilion and the fun fair will open this Thursday.' Gus sat down. 'Everything seems in order.'

'Yes, well done, everyone.' Hari applauded lightly. Vince gave her a grateful look.

'Now, the ceremonial. Where are we with the votes?'

'Almost all counted,' Scott replied. 'Subject to votes received in the last few days, our Summer Fete opener is likely to be Daisy Marshall.'

'If she's capable.' Gus was quick to respond. 'Well, there's nothing we can do about it now. We'll just have to tutor the girl.' He harrumphed and brought his papers together. 'Any other business?'

Beth nudged Scott. 'Now, darling,' she whispered.

As the others dispersed Scott moved closer to Gus. 'A quick word? I've something to show you.' He steered Gus into a corner and handed him the press release.

'What?' Gus paused to read and stepped backwards. 'This is preposterous! Favours and corruption! The Herald wouldn't run this without talking to me first.' Gus reached for his mobile. 'I'll speak to the editor, he'll sort this out.'

'He already knows,' Beth said icily. Only Gus and the Castles remained in the parlour. 'He thinks we need some new blood on the committee, younger, more in touch with the times.'

Gus ceased punching the number into his phone. He looked at Beth and then Scott. 'I see. I should've guessed.' His face compressed. 'But there's no proof in this story. The Herald wouldn't risk a law suit.... unless the Editor thinks there's evidence. What have you said to him?'

'Me. Nothing,' said Scott. 'I didn't have to. The Herald's been digging on its own account.'

'So what do you want? That I stand down after the fete?'

'Before, don't you think?' Beth's eyes glittered. 'To avoid bad publicity.'

Gus's mouth fell open at the audacity, but he wasn't done yet. 'Let them publish, I'll sue! If anything it'll increase interest in the Fete.'

'Not for your grand-daughter.' Scott placed a restraining hand on Gus's arm. 'She's how old now? It's some years since you arranged for her little treat. Surely you don't want her associated with this story, all over the press?'

'You wouldn't.'

'Try me.'

Gus seemed to deflate. 'Very well.' He gave Scott a haunted look. 'How are we going to do this?'

'A letter of resignation would be usual –' Beth began.

'I'm surprised you haven't written one for me.' Gus rounded on her.

'Now, now,' said Scott. 'Let's not be bitter. We thought we'd stage a presentation, at the opening ceremony, to thank you.'

'And to announce my successor, I suppose.' Gus gave a mirthless laugh.

Scott inclined his head, graciously. 'I will stand in, temporarily, of course.'

Gus put a hand to his throat, as if he was finding it hard to breathe. He pushed his way between the Castles and out of the parlour, slamming the door.

Scott and Beth smiled at each other in shared triumph.

Outside the parlour doorway a figure moved, unseen, in the shadowy corner of the high wooden settle. Toiling all that afternoon, Winnie had sat, just for a moment, to get her breath and ease her legs, but had fallen into a doze, hidden from view. Startled awake by Beth's arrival, she had overheard everything. And no-one needed to tell Winnie that information was power.

*

The day of the Summer Fete dawned clear and sunny, with the promise of heat later. Anticipation hung in the air like early morning mist.

In the Marshall's neat modern semi, Ray and Lynda sat at the kitchen table, pretending that they weren't uncomfortable with all the attention which would be paid to Daisy that afternoon.

'Stop that!' Lynda caught Paul's hand as he flicked a sodden cornflake at his sister. 'Ray, speak to him.'

Ray lowered The Trader, he'd been reading the small ads. 'There's no need to behave like that. It's a special day for your sister. You should be pleased for her, not trying to spoil it.'

'I'm not trying to spoil it.' Paul kicked the table leg. 'It was me who –' he stopped himself. 'Dad, are hackers sent to jail?'

'Computer hackers?' Ray lifted The Trader again. 'Sometimes. I don't advise it as a career option. We don't have the resources for bail.'

'Are you coming with us to the start of the parade?' Lynda wiped spilled milk from the table around his bowl. 'Paul?'

'Do I have to?'

'Please yourself.' Lynda pulled back his chair. 'You can get down now.'

*

In an older part of the village, Winnie had already cleared breakfast away. Vince Luck had told his mother that Gus King had tried to exclude Daisy from the competition. Sylvia had told Winnie. So Winnie wasn't about to do Gus any favours. Not that she liked the Castles, so glossy and self-regarding, but she wanted the day of the Fete and Daisy's triumph, to be untouched by scandal. She went out to water her garden before the sun grew too high in the sky.

*

At the Castle house, Beth sipped a smoothie and read newspapers in a kimono, while Scott ran through his acceptance speech. The conservatory doors stood ajar, birds were singing and the air was already warm. Beth stretched across the table towards her husband and Scott, absent-mindedly, caught her hand and nuzzled it. Beth looked up at him from beneath her eye lashes and raised an eyebrow, catching her husband's eye.

*

Just outside the village, at The Elms, Jane King watched Gus eat his morning egg, knowing that he was stolidly ignoring her anxious scrutiny. He had told her nothing of the goings-on at the committee, but she knew that something was awry. She

148

vacillated between trusting him to tell her about it when he was ready and asking him outright what had occurred. She suspected a coup and her money was on the Castles as the usurpers.

*

In the park Vince and his small army of volunteers, seduced by the offer of free beer later, had already staked and raised the larger marquees. A platform was being erected, from which the Summer Fete would be opened at the end of the parade. A disembodied voice was testing for sound. Competitors in the vegetable show were already arriving, to perfect their displays of carrots or onions.

The travelling-fair folk were clearing up the previous night's litter in their corner of the park. It had been a good night, with lots of punters and only two arrests, but Fete day was always better. Just over the wall, in Hawthorn Lane, a convoy of twelve articulated lorries headed towards the starting point of the Fete parade where they would be transformed into parade floats and tableaux. Armed with the 'agreed running order' the lead driver envisaged getting all set up within the hour. This was his first time on the Summer Fete parade.

*

By the time Lynda and Ray arrived, the parade start point was thronging with marchers, serenaded by snatches of music as bands tuned and practiced. On Daisy's float, an embarrassed youth in climbing gear stood beside a cardboard Matterhorn while a sour-faced girl clutched a ping-pong bat beside a miniature table. Ray lifted Daisy, gossamer-light in her dancing dress, on to the float, where she gazed at the scene around her.

'Go on love,' urged Lynda. 'Sit on your throne.'

From the large, decorated velvet and gold chair, a relic of Princess days, Daisy gazed down at Lynda and Ray, her golden curls falling about her shoulders.

Then the parade leader put his Land-rover into gear, the large 'Summer Fete' sign on its roof wobbling alarmingly. Immediately behind, the band of the RAF struck up "The Liberty Bell". Stuttering at first, the column of floats and marchers snaked away, between lines of applauding parents and friends. Ray ran alongside Daisy's float until he was out of breath, while Lynda and Paul stood, hand-in-hand, waving until it disappeared from sight.

*

The park too was full of activity. Hari supervised the floral decorations from high on a ladder in front of the main marquee, where she was fixing garlands. She wore a fine salwar khameez in honour of the occasion, which accentuated her delicate form. Vince and his helpers had erected tables and benches, within and around the marquee.

'I notice that our new chair, Mr Castle, hasn't bothered to turn up and help with the heavy lifting.' He called up to her.

Before she could respond Hari spotted Gus and Jane King arriving. She climbed down to welcome them.

'Hello, Hari.' Jane called. 'This all looks tremendous.' Hari watched Jane admire everything with febrile brightness and an air of distracted condescension.

'Hallo, hallo.' Vince joined them and everyone looked slightly uncomfortable as they exchanged glances.

'The artics were due to be delivered first thing this morning, so the parade should be underway by now.' Gus filled the silence as Jane smiled, anxiously. 'Will we be able to open on time?'

'Should be,' Vince answered. 'There's already a crowd outside and the car parks are full to bursting. It could be a bumper year. Do you want to do the usual?'

As chair, Gus had always done the rounds to check everything before the gates opened. He hesitated only momentarily.

'Lead on.'

Gus and Vince started their circuit.

Around a central display area stood canvas tents and wooden stands, gaudy games and stalls. Signs directed pet owners to the tennis courts, where showing classes would commence at two thirty. The pavilion was the 'Fancy Dress Changing Rooms', with temporary lavatories added. The brightly-coloured children's play area blazed alongside the richly painted swing-boats of the fun fair. A warm breeze rustled the horse chestnuts as empty walzters eddied and the music of the fairground competed against the testing of microphones on the platform stage.

Just then the gleaming Jaguar slid to a halt beside the Park House. Scott Castle emerged from behind the wheel, smooth and handsome, and Beth, elegant in a dress of deepest crimson, slipped from the passenger seat in textbook manner.

'At least it won't show the blood,' said one of Vince's helpers, to no-one in particular.

*

The parade, meanwhile, had wound its way through the outlying parts of the village. As it neared the centre the crowds got denser. The roads were closed and many cars were parked at the road-side, not a few of which would be clamped by evening when their owners returned.

Towards the rear of the cavalcade Daisy sat on her over-sized throne, the sunlight shining in her golden hair. She'd waved with enthusiasm to school-friends and acquaintances as they'd meandered through the housing estates at the edge of the village. Now there were more people. She kept waving politely, occasionally casting flowers from the huge basket at her feet, as she had been told. The crowd cooed and sighed.

At the Cross Lynda and Ray stood, with Paul and Winnie, in the car park of the Lion. Daisy jumped up, standing on the throne so as to keep them in sight as she was swept on. It wasn't far to the park and the roadside verges were thick with people cheering and clapping in time to the music. Others fell in behind the parade, which slowed as it swung between the wrought-iron gates and climbed the curving drive. The gates were closed behind it.

Ticket-sellers at the entrances were soon hard pressed. The Marshall party arrived, with an impatient Winnie

'The Ladies Society has a stall,' Winnie explained, shouting over the noise.

'And she's keen to criticise what's on it,' Ray murmured, catching Lynda's eye.

The gate-keeper ushered the whole group through and they made their way towards the stage. Paul joined in the polite applause and peered around, fretfully, to locate his sister. He pushed his way to the very front, Winnie following in his wake.

On the platform, Scott Castle straightened his silk tie and stepped to the microphone.

'Ladies and gentlemen. Thank you all for coming this afternoon and making our Summer Fete another great success! This year we have the honour of congratulating chairman Gus King on five years of service. Gus.' Scott gestured gracefully.

'Thank you Scott.' Gus' face was rosy in the glare of the afternoon sun. 'I'm not as inebriated as last year's guest was, though I might not be as entertaining either. I will, however, keep this brief. We've had a fruitful five years, in spite of ourselves.....'

On the platform behind Scott, Beth's face grew pinched as Gus's speech was received with laughter and applause. She tapped a foot in irritation. Annoyance and bile distorted her pleasant smile.

'Which is why I'm now announcing my resignation from the Summer Fete Committee.' The spectators fell quiet. 'I am stepping aside to make room for new, and considerably younger, blood.' Gus grasped Scott's hand and raised it above his head. 'Scott Castle will act as my replacement as chairman of the Fete Committee.'

Cries of 'Shame!' echoed from the throng.

'Now, now,' Gus remonstrated. 'Hold your horses. He'll be a fine chairman.' Gus stepped back. 'So let the man do his job.'

There was scattered laughter and the commotion subsided.

Scott took the microphone and began to call the Fete competition runners-up to the front of the stage and present them with their medals, each on a golden ribbon.

'And, finally,' called Scott. 'Let us congratulate the winner of our Summer Fete Competition – Daisy Marshall!" There was a loud burst of cheering and applause.

Daisy didn't move. Her float had parked next to the platform. Now Daisy stood, rooted beside her throne, her dress shimmering.

'Our winner –' Scott tried again 'Daisy Marshall!'

Daisy stared at him, eyes saucers, skirt crumpled in her small fists.

'What's the matter?' Lynda gripped Ray's hand. 'Why isn't she coming forward?'

'I knew something would happen!' Ray ricked his neck trying to see better.

Beth climbed up onto Daisy's float and hauled her forward, roughly. 'We don't have time for this.'

'Ow!' Daisy rubbed her arm and dropped the bouquet which had been thrust into her hands.

Spectators at the front began to mutter, while those further back grew restive, impatient to go and have fun. There were isolated catcalls.

Gus stepped in and glared at Beth. 'Steady on!' He lited Daisy on to the platform, retrieved the bouquet and spoke gently. 'Now, can you remember what to do next?' He smiled in encouragement.

Daisy nodded, hesitantly. She turned and smiled. A sound like the falling of a soft wave rippled through the crowd.

Gus held the microphone out for her.

Behind them Beth hissed 'Just get on with it'

Daisy leaned forward into Gus's arm and whispered, "I declare the Summer Fete open!"

Cheers and applause erupted from the crowd, before the funfair music resumed, louder than before and people turned away.

'Well, I'm glad that's over,' Ray muttered. He put his arm around Lynda's shoulders and hugged her

'Who does that Beth Castle think she is?' Winnie bustled up, angrily. 'Laying her hands on our Daisy. I'll not let that pass.'

Ray looked askance at his mother-in-law, but instantly forgot her words as Daisy ran towards him, skirts billowing. He swung her high up into the air.

'How's my lovely girl?' Ray placed her gently on her feet. 'All okay?'

'What was it like?' Paul demanded. 'Could you see everyone?'

'Yes. I saw you at the Lion.' Daisy was flushed and bright-eyed. 'We went all around and I saw lots of people from school. Is there anything to eat?'

'Right, time for food.' Lynda ordered and they started towards the tea tent. She noticed a mark on Daisy's arm. 'Are you bruised, love? How did you manage to do that?'

'It was that horrible woman, Mum.'

Winnie watched Lynda, Ray and Daisy thread through the crowd, but didn't follow. She was working herself up into a lather. 'That Beth needs taking down a peg or two,' she muttered. 'And that smarmy husband of hers.'

Paul was still standing beside her. 'So what are you going to do about it, Nana?'

'Never you mind what I'm going to do. I'm going to...,' she glanced around her. 'Go and have a look at the pets.'

'You're going to the pet show?' Paul paused, then grinned in understanding. That wasn't where Nana was going. 'There are reptiles this year,' he added anyway.

'Any I know?' Winnie snapped. 'Newts, frogs..?'

She began to stomp away, but looked back at Paul. 'Well, you coming then?'

Paul ran after her, a wide smile on his face. Food could wait. Nana was on the warpath. He wasn't going to miss this.

*

The late afternoon was hot and the distinctive fairground smell of grease overlaid with burnt sugar added to the metallic taste of electricity in the air. Vince Luck was patrolling the tents and sideshows, his Park Partnership Manager badge prominent on his lapel. He looked in at the tea tent, but spied Hari Mistry and Gus King talking, animatedly, in the corner. Vince wasn't sure why Gus had stepped down as chair, but he suspected that there was something not quite right about it and he wanted to keep clear. Castle was in charge now.

In the tea tent Hari leaned across the table and fixed Gus with a concerned look. 'Jane is upset and worried about you. I think you really ought to talk to her about your decision to step down.'

'I didn't really make a decision.' Gus huffed. 'It was the Castles. They dug up dirt about Fete sponsors and my businesses. They wrote it up for The Herald and presented it as if I'd been giving contracts for favours.'

'But surely you could have denied it?'

'That was my first reaction, even if...' Gus pressed on. 'But I couldn't involve my grand-daughter. She was Fete Princess that year and it's true that I encouraged her appointment. That was The Herald's proposed headline. I couldn't let her be involved.'

'But Gus, that's blackmail.'

'Yes and they've got away with it too. At least so far.....'

Hari stood. 'I'm sorry, Gus, I must go. I have to check-in with the St John Ambulance. Speak with Jane, eh?'

'Okay, Hari. Thanks for listening. You go on.'

Hari ducked out of the tent. Queues for ices and cold drinks were long in the afternoon sun and tempers were short.

Families passed her with arms full of trophies, while teenagers strutted or fretted in coveys of youth at the funfair or pavilion. The afternoon was ending but the night had not yet begun.

At the Ambulance stand the uniformed group leader handed her the accident list, comprising several faintings and rather more cases of dehydration, most of them involving alcohol. She was complimenting the group when Vince stormed up, his face purple with outrage.

'He's gone! Castle's done a runner! And he's driven that bloody Jag all over the Centenary border. We'll have to replant the lot!' He spluttered. "I don't suppose you've seen Winnie Fortune? There's trouble brewing there, I can tell you."

Hari was too astonished to reply, but Vince hurried away, without waiting for a response.

Hari's pocket quivered. A message. She reached for her mobile, it was probably a message from the hospital.

No, it was an email from the Summer Fete address. 'BLACKMAIL at Summer Fete', it read, 'King stabbed in the back by Scott + Beth Castle'. With a sinking feeling Hari realised that the email had been sent to everyone on the community address list.

This explained Scott's precipitate departure, but had he told his wife? And did Gus know about any of this? Hari wondered who had sent the email. Only people involved with the fete had access to that email account, unless someone had hacked into their system. A faint bell of recollection jangled, but she couldn't quite pin it down. Things were spiralling out of control. She needed to find Beth.

Hari set off towards the children's play area, where the Castles had been scheduled to give an interview to local television. She seemed to see people all around her looking at their mobile phones. Swiftly, she lengthened her stride.

*

Licking her ice cream, Daisy tugged at Ray's arm. "Look, Dad, there's Dr Mistry. She's in a hurry. Where's she going?"

Ray turned to see Hari striding purposefully in the direction of the children's play area, her gauzy tunic flowing behind her.

'Dunno, love. Uncle Vince went that way too, as if his trousers were on fire, only a minute ago. Shall we see?'

Ray scooped Daisy on to his shoulders.

'Lynda,' he called. 'We're off to see what's up.'

He and Daisy went in pursuit, leaving Lynda to follow behind.

Thus, in the early evening sunshine the opener of the Summer Fete and most of its committee, though not the absent chair, began converging upon the children's play area.

Beth Castle stood on the playground safety surface in her crimson finery, talking to a local TV news crew. Nearby children played on a bouncy castle. People were gathering to watch the interview.

'Look this way, please?' The reporter called out and Beth twirled and smiled, before re-directing the cameraman — her left side was her best.

Beyond the camera, just visible in the middle distance, a wheezing, hatchet-faced old woman hove into view, followed closely by a pale-haired boy. Short of breath, Winnie paused and placed her hands upon her knees. Beside her Paul hovered, protectively placing a hand upon her shoulder. Winnie looked up, shaking her head, as Hari strode past her.

'Come along.' Winnie resumed her course towards Beth.

Well ahead of her, Hari reached the journalists. 'Excuse me. I need to speak with you Beth.'

'Can't it wait?' Beth was dismissive.

'No it can't I'm afraid.' Hari stepped in front of the cameras and took Beth's arm, firmly drawing her away. 'Your husband has gone, Beth, Scott's left you to face the music alone.'

'What are you talking about?' Beth stared down her nose and shook herself free. She waved at the news cameras 'One moment. I'll be right with you.' She turned on Hari. 'What on earth do you want?'

Hari pulled her phone out of her pocket. All over the park the gesture was being repeated, as people were notified that they had incoming mail. Foul whisperings were abroad and the message had gone viral.

'Look at your phone,' Hari said.

The reporter pushed forward and thrust his microphone at Beth. 'Would you care to comment on the accusations now circulating about why Gus King stepped down as chairman of the Fete committee? What part did you and your husband play in the affair, Mrs Castle?'

Heads lifted in the crowd and there were cries of 'Speak up!'

'I don't know what you're insinuating.' Beth almost spat at the reporter. 'How dare you! Don't you bandy such accusations about us around without proof. It could be very costly for your station.'

'I heard her, I heard them both, with my own ears!'

Winnie, the true spectre at the feast, pulled back her shoulders. Her cracked voice rang out to seal the Castle's fate. 'I heard them discussing it after one of the meetings. Beth and Scott forced Gus King to step down. They threatened to send a story to the press, accusing him of corruption. It was the year his little grand-daughter was the Fete Princess. They said she would be smeared all over the newspapers.'

There was a collective sharp intake of breath, faintly echoed as Winnie's words were relayed to those at the back. Seeing that attention was focussed elsewhere, Beth began to slip away.

'Oh, no you don't!' The diminutive but determined Hari stepped into Beth's path.

A piping cry floated overhead, from where Daisy sat, high above the hurly burly, on Ray's shoulders. 'Hooray for Dr Mistry! That's the nasty woman who hurt my arm. Hooray for Dr Hari!' Daisy shouted as loudly as she could. 'What's Nana doing there, Dad?'

Winnie was gesturing theatrically to a knot of enthralled, if elderly, spectators as the television reporter interviewed her. 'I heard them,' she re-iterated, melodramatically. 'They didn't know I was sat outside the parlour, but I heard the whole thing.'

Meanwhile, a white-faced Vince skirted around the children's play area speaking rapidly into a walkie-talkie, desperately scanning the horizon for the arrival of PC William Ford and his colleagues.

'This is ridiculous!" Beth cried. She kept a physical obstacle between herself and Hari at all times, as she backed away. Circling behind the children's roundabout, she ducked under the plastic slide. One of her tall red heels snapped and Beth staggered. There were one or two jeers, as a crowd began to form around the play area. Beth's eyes slid sideways, searching for a way out.

A large figure, a head taller than most, pushed through the throng. Gently but firmly, Gus took the bedraggled Beth by her elbow and escorted her from the fray. The crowd fell back as they passed and tension dissipated, as people sought diversion elsewhere.

Hari crossed to a swing and collapsed.

'What's going on?' Lynda, a late arrival, asked.

'You wouldn't believe it. I don't believe it myself!' Hari looked up at her and laughed.

'Come along, Nana.' Paul pulled Winnie away from the camera crew and over to the climbing frame. 'You've done the job. You need a cup of tea now. Look at all my new Twitter followers.' He held up his phone to show her. 'On-line, Nan, you know. I might be able to make some money out of this,' he confided. 'I'll go halves with you.'

Winnie hugged him roughly to her. 'You're your Nana's boy and no mistake.'

'I'll take that!' Lynda relieved Paul of his mobile. 'You might get it back one day, if you're good and once we've had a little chat. I want to know everything you've been up to, young man, chapter and verse.' She pocketed the phone.

Paul narrowed his eyes and looked as if he might fight for the phone, but, at a stern look from Ray, he exhaled and fell into line behind, sulking, as the Marshalls and Winnie headed home.

*

A car horn tooted.

Jane King waved from the driving seat of the four by four drawn up just beyond the wooden park gates. Gus acknowledged his wife's arrival with a smile.

'I'll be off now, Hari,' he said, starting away. 'Are you hanging around here? Or can we give you a lift?'

'No thanks,' Hari replied. 'The walk home will be good for me. But Gus...?'

He stopped and turned, raising his eyebrows.

'What'll happen now? Are you the Committee chair again?'

'Let's discuss it at the next meeting, eh?' Gus made to resume his course, but hesitated. 'By the way, I had that chat with Jane.'

'Good.'

'But she doesn't know that you and I discussed it.' Gus looked sheepish. 'I'd be grateful if you didn't mention it.'

'Of course not.' Hari smiled, looking beyond the tall man to wave at Jane. Then, as Gus continued onwards, she walked away.

9.

The Lion

A burst of laughter snagged at Len's attention, his head swivelling towards the sound. In the public bar some Friday lunchtime regulars were sharing a joke, sitting at a table laden with glasses.

'Calm down,' he told himself. 'It's only people enjoying themselves.'

A former soldier, who had toured in Belfast and Iraq, Len made himself relax as he patrolled the rooms of The Lion. Just as a motionless pike could feel tremors in the surface tension of the water around him, Len could sense changes in the atmosphere of his pub. But now he was on edge, like the rest of the village, after the violence out on the Flowers estate only the previous weekend.

Len had taken on The Lion when he was invalided out. The ancient inn had seen better days, but it gave Len pleasure to restore the fabric of the black and white Tudor building. It was well positioned and in the years which followed, both it, and Len, had thrived. His hair, still short and neat, had become grizzled, but his jaw-line remained clean-cut and he carried little extra flesh. The name 'Leonard Pendleton' written on the brass plaque above the heavy black door was still a source of pride to him.

The sound of hammering came from the snug, where Ray Marshall was kneeling to repair the old wooden panelling, surrounded by tools. Len stood in the snug doorway.

'Hello Ray, how's that little girl of yours? And young Paul?'

'They're both well thanks, Len, but growing up too fast, the pair of them. Sometimes I struggle to keep up. It won't be long before they'll be partying with the rest of them.' Ray nodded toward the courtyard where preparations for that evening's eighteenth birthday party were already under way. 'How's your Susan? Settling in at university is she?'

'I think so. She couldn't wait to go, she's gone early for the summer school, but she doesn't tell us much.' Len scrutinized the snug's late lunchtime drinkers as he spoke, then turned to the younger man. 'You've got it all yet to come, you know.'

'Well, yes, maybe.' Ray didn't look ready to contemplate either of his children leaving home. 'Did she see what happened then?'

'Would've been difficult not to.'

'There was some nasty footage on Youtube, I'm told.'

'Yep, I think that affected Sue more than anything else. She was in a state when last she phoned. It took her mother half an hour to calm her down.' Indeed, his wife, Carol had been very upset afterwards.

'And do you think that it's over?' Ray downed tools and sat on a low stool. 'I'm not so sure. There's a lot of resentment − folk round here think fruit picking is their own private job creation scheme.'

'A season in the Vale has seen the start of more than one village family in the past,' Len said. 'Young people out in the fields all day and getting together afterwards.'

'Not this year. There are coach-loads of pickers arriving from outside, sleeping out on the farms.'

'I've seen them around the village.' As he, too, sat, Len picked up a copy of The Herald, which lay upon the table. '"Rural communities swamped by migrants",' he read aloud and threw it down. 'Pickers have always come here for the fruit harvest.'

'I know, but there seems to be more of them this year, and that,' Ray indicated the newspaper, 'feeds peoples' fears. What I don't understand is the level of violence, it was brutal. They found a machete and knives, I heard. This is vicious.'

Both men puzzled over how this could happen, in their sleepy village.

'More than a handful of those arrested have been released, you know?' Ray shook his head. 'Problems with identification, apparently.'

Len harrumphed.

'And I think whoever's behind it won't be satisfied until there's more trouble.' Ray waved his screwdriver in emphasis. 'Just wait.'

'I agree. I'll be keeping a close watch, in here at least.' Len stood, as the small, strawberry blonde figure of Carol Pendleton arrived suddenly at his shoulder. Her blue eyes twinkled and she fizzed with excitement.

'Good news!' She clapped her hands in delight. 'Guess who's coming home today?'

'Our Susan?' Len's face softened, then he laughed. 'What is it with kids? They can't wait to strike out on their own, but they expect what they leave behind to stay the same. Then they get in a state when it doesn't.'

'Don't be a curmudgeon! You'll be pleased to see her.' Carol poked Len in the ribs, then confided to Ray. 'Someone misses her more than he's prepared to admit.'

'Yes, I'm glad she's coming home.' Susan had been only six years old when Len arrived in the village, with his short back and sides and his Army pay-out. 'I got myself a ready-made family as well as a pub, all those years ago,' Len chuckled as he put his arm around his wife's shoulders. Carol had been a barmaid at the old inn and unmarried, but with one daughter. 'Not bad for an old squaddie.'

Carol raised her face to her husband and they exchanged warm smiles, then she extricated herself. 'Well, I'd best get on, lots to do.'

She bustled off into the courtyard, where several tall young men from the catering supply company were waiting with box loads of crockery and glassware. They gazed at her, mute and ready to hang upon her every word.

Nodding to Ray, Len resumed his rounds. With Susan coming home, it was even more important that there should be no trouble.

From the lounge bar doorway he watched another barmaid clearing tables, chatting and smiling with customers. This was Valentina, a much more recent arrival. He observed the confident young woman and recalled the awkward Romanian girl they had first met. The long stringy hair was now glossy and black, swept up into a high pony tail, the dull eyes were bright and she had put on weight, though she was still thin. Arriving at the right moment, just after Susan's departure, Valentina had slotted in, seamlessly taking on all Susan's tasks. Len wondered if his wife had mentioned Val when she spoke with Susan.

Valentina noticed Len's scrutiny. She waved and returned his smile, but Len was distracted as shrieks of delight signalled Susan's early arrival. He strode through to the pub's kitchen and found Susan swooping into her mother's embrace. Carol clasped her daughter close.

'How's my girl?' Len engulfed Susan from the other side. 'Can't keep away, can you?'

'Yes Dad, the place has got so exciting since I left,' Susan hugged him.

'Come on upstairs,' Carol led the way up to the flat and into the cosy living room, where a pair of sofas flanked the large chimney breast and horse brasses hung from the huge wooden beams.

'So, how long are you staying for then?' Len asked eagerly, once they were seated.

'I thought I'd go back on Monday, if that's all right. I don't want to miss much.'

'But that's hardly worth...'

'We could do with some help tonight, if you don't have plans,' Carol cut in quickly. 'We've an eighteenth in the St Agnes Room as well as the usual Friday night crowd.'

'Yeah, okay. I haven't contacted any of the old gang.'

'Well, it'd be good if you could help in the Lounge, love?'

'Sure, no problem.'

'Come on then,' Len sat forward. 'Tell us what it's like at uni.'

'It's fine - it's good,' Susan replied, hesitating. 'It was empty when I first got there, Summer School only, but there are more people now.'

'Made any friends yet?'

'I'm just getting to know people,' Susan demurred. 'I don't want to fall in with the first crowd I happen to meet.'

There was a tremendous crash from downstairs.

'Those lads from the caterers, I can't leave them alone for a minute.' Carol rose. 'Sorry, love, I'd better go and sort them out.' She hurried out.

'She's still keeping things running round here then,' Susan turned back to her father.

'You know what she's like,' Len smiled. 'You really don't mind helping?'

'Really.' Susan nodded, smiling in return.

'You'll have to meet Val, our new barmaid and general helper. She's a real find – a Romanian. I don't know how we'd have managed without her... in the pub.... after you left.'

'Romanian. Is that the same as some of the trouble—makers?' Susan tilted her head to one side and looked wary.

'Yes, but Valentina's not with them.' Len assured her.

'I met some journalists on the train, coming to follow up the coverage of the trouble last weekend. It's August – I guess there isn't a lot of other news.'

'I hope you told them all where they could find a fine hostelry.'

'I did. One promised to look in, once her photographer arrived from London.'

Len leaned over and kissed his daughter's brow. 'I'm glad you're home, Sue, even if it's only for a bit.'

Susan flung her arms around him, blinking back tears.

'Let's go see what your mother's doing to those poor lads,' Len disentangled himself. 'Put your stuff in your room, it hasn't changed.'

Len waited as Susan dropped her rucksack on the window seat. She glanced out at St Agnes' bell tower and the churchyard and he watched her look around at those possessions not deemed important or portable enough to be taken to college.

'It all looks exactly the same,' she said, noticing his scrutiny and smiling awkwardly. 'It feels...strange. It's hard to explain. When I arrived at the halls of residence, it was a bit... the corridors echoed and the noises of the night were different. Now it feels like home, at least for a while and this is... '

'Like going backwards?' Len suggested, quietly. 'Or into a safe place.'

Susan didn't reply at first. 'I – I don't know. I'm split in two, it's weird.'

Downstairs, the courtyard was being cleared of broken glass and Carol was speaking, in a voice which brooked no denial, to the catering supply company.

'Come on, I'll introduce you to Val.'

Len and Susan followed the sound of vacuuming. A young woman was cleaning in the lounge. The large room had a long polished bar along one side. Comfortable banquette seating hugged the walls, which were decorated with hunting prints and sepia-tinted photographs. Cottage style wooden chairs and tables filled the central space. It was empty.

'Val,' Len shouted and the machine stopped. 'This is Susan.'

'Hello,' Susan spoke into the silence.

'I've heard a lot about you.' Valentina held out a hand. 'Very pleased to meet you.'

'Oh. Yes.' Susan shook hands formally. 'Likewise, I'm sure.'

Each stood, looking the other over. Len watched them, sensing potential trouble.

They were physically unlike. Susan was slim and long-boned, much taller than her mother, though she had the same strawberry blonde colouring. Valentina was shorter, with pale skin and dark, liquid eyes, which met Susan's brilliant blue gaze without flinching.

'Dad's been telling me how helpful you've been.' Susan gestured towards Len. 'They really need someone round here, now that I've gone. Just as well that you came along.'

'That's kind of them, but it's really the other way around. Len and Carol have been very kind to me.' Valentina bobbed her head in Len's direction.

Carol's voice could be heard, out in the courtyard, haranguing the young men.

'You're from Romania? I don't know much about the country, I'm afraid.'

'Not many westerners do. My parents' home is in the Carpathian mountains, part of Transylvania.'

'Ah, that's... nice.'

'It's very beautiful,' Valentina responded, coolly. 'But the tourist industry prefers to concentrate on Dracula.'

Len laughed, moving his weight from foot to foot, and both young women smiled.

'Your English is very good.'

'I studied, I have a diploma.' Len knew Valentina was proud of her qualification, she had worked hard for it, but now she spoke as if it was nothing.

173

'I'm afraid the best I can do is a bit of French.'

'Susan's studying French at University,' Len interjected. Far more than 'a bit of French'. What were these girls playing at?

'You're lucky.' Valentina's eyebrows arched.

'I know, I'm lucky in lots of ways.' Susan gave a thin smile.

'In my village at this time of year the river is low and children can play in the water. Families picnic on the bank among the wild flowers. I remember,' Valentina shrugged. 'But it's very poor. People scrape a living from the land.'

'So people travel to look for work where ever they can find it,' Len said, sombrely. 'It's a courageous thing to do, all on your own.'

'But sometimes they're in groups, aren't they, like the fruit pickers?' Susan countered.

'Yes,' Valentina responded. 'People are recruited, promised all sorts of things when they sign up, not knowing what they're coming to. It's far from home, but they have little choice, it's money.'

Len cleared his throat.

'Now, tonight you'll both behind the bar in here, while Mum – Carol,' Len added quickly, 'is out in the St Agnes.' Both young women looked at him and he felt his cheeks flushing. 'I don't think there's anything new, Sue.'

'We have a new cash machine.' Valentina reminded him. 'I can show Susan how to use it.'

'Yes, of course, I forgot. Thanks Val.'

'I'm sure I'll pick it up easily enough.'

'Yes, well Val, you'd best be off. It's nearly four and you're back on at seven. Get a bit of rest. We'll be busy tonight. And you,' he put an arm around Susan's waist, 'can come and have a chat with your Mum. Catch up. It'll be the last chance you'll get today.'

Len started away, but Susan hesitated for an instant. Her eyes followed the departing Valentina.

'I've only been away a month, but, yes, there's a lot to catch up on.'

Susan strode passed her father, chin tilting upwards. Len sighed and went after her.

*

The Lion was never really silent during the day, though late afternoon was a quiet time. At six Len re-opened the Lounge, Susan taking station behind the long wooden bar, while, in the St Agnes Rooms, temporary staff set out the buffet and the DJ unloaded his equipment.

The early Friday evening regulars filtered in, greeting Susan cheerily. Len bade them good evening and Susan gave each a resigned smile. Keeping up his patrol, Len never tarried too long in one place, though he knew he was gravitating towards the Lounge rather more frequently than was necessary. Valentina arrived an hour later and Len noted how each of the two young women took half of the bar, working efficiently and well.

That's what I like to see, he thought.

A gaggle of people entered the lounge. Their sharp jackets and quick-fire speech marked them out as metropolitan, their gadgetry and conversation as media. He assumed they must be the journalists Susan had met on the train and saw Susan brighten at their arrival. They were, he supposed, a reminder of the world outside the village.

'You got pressed into service quickly,' a young journalist said as she came to the bar.

'There's a lot to do tonight.' Susan answered.' What can I get you?'

Having ordered a round of drinks, the journalist introduced her companion. 'This is Greg, my photographer.'

'Greg Layton.' He offered his hand. A tall man with longish, greying hair, a camera was slung around his neck. 'Travelling picture-man.'

'Susan Pendleton. That'll be ten forty five please.' She laughed at the look on their faces. 'We don't have London prices here.'

'Too right,' the reporter took her change. 'Do you know a decent place to eat? Where we wouldn't need a reservation.'

'Normally I'd suggest here, but we're not cooking tonight. Try the Jade Garden over by the park.'

'Thanks.' Greg carried drinks away.

'Your photographer looks familiar, has he been on TV or something? I seem to recognise him.' Susan shook her head in irritation.

'No, Greg's strictly behind the camera. Though he knows this village, he said he's been here before, a long time ago.' The reporter told her.

'Yes, about twenty years ago,' Greg returned to collect more, smiling. He raised his eyebrows. 'There was a pretty barmaid here then too.'

'And I'll bet that you flirted with her as well.' Susan admonished, but smiled.

'As it happens....,' he leaned forwards.

Not liking the man's demeanour, Len decided to join the conversation.

'Everything all right here, love?' He leaned on the wooden bar, directing a level and constant gaze at Greg.

'Yes Dad, fine.' Susan pursed her lips.

'C'mon Greg,' the journalist nudged her colleague and they moved away.

'What was that about?' Susan glared at her father.

'Well, he's at least forty. Is this what you do at University then, flirt with men old enough to be your father?'

Susan stared at Len. Her mouth dropped open and she took a step back. Then her expression altered. She whirled around and hurried away.

'Sue! Hey! Look, I'm just....'

Len walked through to the snug, but there was no sign of Susan. The public bar was full, but she wasn't there either. He'd offended her, he suspected, though he wasn't entirely sure how – things hadn't seemed right since she'd arrived. He wandered into the courtyard.

Outside, youngsters loitered in the twilight, smoking and getting some air, for the party in the stable block was crowded and noisy. A booming bass note sounded beneath the beery hub-bub. Len strolled along by the church railings, in search of his daughter. Then he pulled up short.

Beyond the buildings Carol stood close to a man, gesticulating and arguing. They were too far away for him to hear what was being said, but Len saw that she was angry and weeping. Then the man briefly took her in his arms.

It was the photographer from the lounge bar − the man who'd been flirting with Susan only minutes before.

Len straightened his back and relaxed his shoulder muscles, letting his arms swing loose at his sides. He flexed his hands as he strode forward. The photographer, oblivious to Len's approach, turned on his heel. Carol stood immobile, staring after him.

Len was with her in an instant. Gently he held her shoulders and looked into her face.

'What is it love?' he asked. 'Who was that upsetting you?'

'Oh Len,' Carol buried her head on his chest. 'Now, of all times.'

When Susan rounded the corner, her parents were embracing.

'Mum? Dad?'

'It's all right, love,' Carol sniffed and smiled as Len relaxed his grip.

'I knew I'd seen him somewhere before.' Susan held out a tattered photograph of a young, bubble-haired Carol and a tall,

178

skinny young man, arm in arm on an English seaside promenade.

'I didn't know you still had that,' Carol took the photograph. 'Yes, this man was here just now, though he's a lot older.'

Len examined the image. He hadn't seen it before.

'Is he....who I think he is?' Susan asked. 'Is he my biological father?'

Len's vision swam. He'd been out-flanked, ambushed and side-swiped. He felt very, very stupid. He thumped a fist into his open palm in annoyance, then raised his chin to look at Susan. The resemblance was there, in the long nose and pointed chin.

'You look like him, love,' he said in a husky voice. 'He's tall too.'

Susan contemplated her father, eyes unwavering.

'But you're my Dad.'

Len blinked, he didn't trust himself to speak, but stretched out an arm. Susan sidled into Len's half embrace and the Pendletons walked back towards The Lion together.

'I'll come through with you,' Len reassured her. 'He might still be there.'

He would be there, Len was certain. And he would be there in future, the man whose genes Susan carried. There was no getting away from him.

Len puffed out his cheeks, realising that he would have to adapt and the quicker he did it the better things would be.

'You might want to speak to him.' Carol gave a bashful smile. 'He wants to meet you. He was angry at first, he didn't know, you see.'

'Know about me? Why?'

'I didn't get the chance to tell him, he was only here for a while, then he was off to some war-zone or other.'

'Is he famous then?'

A famous photographer, that was all he needed, Len thought. He would woo Susan away to the bright lights. Then he silently up-braided himself, he should be thinking about Susan not about himself. How must she be feeling?

'Hey,' Len gripped his daughter's shoulder. 'After a famous Dad now are you?'

'Maybe,' Susan replied, smiling. 'It's handy to have a replacement.'

'I'll just go and wash my face, sort myself out.' Carol disappeared up the stairs, Len watching her. He and Sue walked through to the lounge bar.

The big room was filling rapidly and drinkers were two deep at the bar. Valentina gestured in relief at the sight of Len and Susan, who, immediately, began to serve.

Len scanned the crowded room as he pulled pints, checking on new arrivals. There were the Friday night regulars, those media folk who hadn't yet left for the Jade Garden and a group of young men. There was a swagger about these, a bravado born of their having to establish their right to be there. Their voices were a little too loud and they spoke in an abrasive, but fluid foreign tongue. Regular customers watched their progress. Their leader, a tall, dark-haired young man in a leather jacket, sauntered up to the bar.

'Six pints of lager,' he demanded of Valentina.

'Six pints of lager, please,' she responded in English, as she began to pull the drinks.

The young man's eyes narrowed.

'Don't play silly games with me little gadgi,' he spoke a Carpathian dialect. 'I know where you come from, just like me.' His smile revealed sharp, wolf-like incisors.

'Not like you,' Valentina replied, her eyes fierce.

He proffered a folded twenty pound note, but held on to it when Valentina reached to take it. Eventually he smirked and let go, but caught her wrist. Valentina winced. She began to remonstrate in a low voice in her native tongue.

At the other end of the bar Len stiffened. There were half a dozen of them, he counted, and already a space was forming around them, as, instinctively, other drinkers moved away. He couldn't deal with all six of them, especially as some might have weapons. Better to contain the situation.

'Dad!' Susan hissed in his ear and he half-turned. 'I've called the police. I recognise the one in the leather jacket. He was one of the leaders of the riot.'

'Good. Are you sure?'

'I watched the footage a dozen times,' Susan was certain. 'He had a scarf around his face, but it was him. He was carrying a machete.'

'A machete.' Len looked at the man more closely. He couldn't be hiding a machete under that jacket, but he might have a knife.

'Okay. Tell the police as soon as they arrive.'

Throughout this exchange Len's gaze had been fixed on Valentina and the young man. Now he began to move along behind the bar towards her, jovially greeting many of the customers, the consummate landlord.

Susan trailed in his wake. 'What are you going to do, Dad?' she whispered. 'Dad!'

'Be with you in a moment,' he said to the waiting crowd of drinkers. There was a collective groan as he stepped away from the pumps and turned to Susan. 'Wait outside for Bill Ford, or whoever comes, tell them what's happening then go upstairs to your mother,' he said. 'Go on.'

Once sure that she was going, Len turned back to the bar. 'Val, can you serve some of these people please!' he called, peremptorily.

Valentina pulled her arm away from the young man, who loosened his grip with a knowing smile. She hurried to Len.

'Go upstairs,' he instructed her, in a level voice.

'But I can talk to them...' she began to argue.

'They won't want to talk.' Len's face was closed, expressionless. 'Go now.'

From the corner of his eye Len saw the leader was watching them, but then he was distracted by his companions, who wanted to sit. As they moved away from the bar they were swiftly replaced by customers demanding service. The

182

clamour grew and Len was busy, when PC Ford found him, minutes later. Drinkers gave the landlord and the policeman room.

'Yes, I've seen some of them before,' PC Ford observed them in the mirror behind the optics. 'And your Susan's correct, the rangy one looks like the ringleader we're after.'

'So what happens now?'

'I'll ask him to step aside and speak with me. Either he'll agree to do so, in which case I'll take him outside and arrest him, or he'll object and start trouble. That's when we need to prevent others from being hurt.' PC Ford was quiet and controlled. Len nodded.

'How will we do that?'

'I've got two support officers by the hatch, do you see?' Len nodded a reluctant affirmative. 'The exits are covered too.'

'But Bill, they're only support officers. Have they had any experience....?'

'All that's available....'

Len was unconvinced, but William Ford prepared to deal with the thugs. 'Wish me luck,' he grinned and turned away. Too late, Len remembered that there were media people present and the PC should know. Besides, he couldn't let Bill face the gang alone.

Len stepped out from behind the bar, concentrating on the gang's leader, who was sitting amongst his cronies. The leader, he saw, had noticed PC Ford. The young man's eyes flicked around the room and it was clear that he had identified the other officers, for his lip curled into a small smile. His right hand slipped inside his jacket and he began to stand. A weapon, Len judged. Probably a large knife, a hunting knife maybe. It wouldn't be long now.

The leader's mood transmitted to his companions and they too were standing. How stubborn would they prove if their leader was down? Len sensed that the support officers were moving too, ready to back-up the constable. The atmosphere in the Lounge grew tense, heads began to turn and people grew quiet. Len quickened his step.

The leader watched PC Ford approach, but his eyes also scanned the people in the pub. Then they met Len's iron stare as Len moved forward, weaving smartly through the tables. For an instant Len smiled and the leader recoiled. There was a flash of a blade.

*

The brief altercation in The Lion hardly merited the national press coverage that followed. Once their leader was floored and disarmed, the rest of the gang didn't give much trouble. It had all happened so quickly that some of the Lion's regular drinkers didn't realise what was going on until it was all over.

One photograph became quite famous. It showed an attractive young woman swabbing the bruised forehead of the clean cut, doe-eyed young policeman who had made the arrest. The Lion's trade increased, although Len discouraged questions, mindful of Valentina's position. Her gratitude was matched only by the affection in which she held the Pendletons, an affection which was freely returned.

The new photographs hung alongside those of older vintage on the walls of the lounge bar, where, for a while, they attracted much attention. In the weeks which followed these events, and the 'Flowers Estate Riot', were absorbed into village lore, its first true disturbance since Tudor times.

Len was viewing the pictures again before opening the lounge bar when he was joined by Ray.

'At least things have settled down,' Ray sipped his pint.

'I guess everyone feels safer now that gang of ringleaders has been deported. They were the ones stirring up the trouble.'

There was a pause.

'Susan's gone back, then?'

'Yes.' Once more Len was adjusting to her absence. 'Vali's going to visit her soon.'

'You've got yourself an extra daughter there.'

'Extra daughters, natural fathers, this is getting too much like a soap opera," Len chuntered.

Len's subsequent meeting with Greg Layton had been a strained affair, but Susan wanted so much for them to get along that Len had tried hard to do so and he could see that Greg, to his credit, was doing the same. Wary respect and a shared desire for what was the best for Susan had mutated into a kind of kinship.

'Sue's been down to London too, having a great time. Greg's showing her off and I can't blame him. It'll be good for her, she'll see a whole different world.'

'Our Paul thinks London is the centre of the universe,' Ray said. 'If there is a centre and not something virtual in cyberspace. I tell him about the history here, but he's not interested.'

'There's not enough goes on here for the young, I suppose,' Len corrected himself. 'Usually, I mean. There's always something better elsewhere.' He rallied. 'Talking of cyberspace, tell your Paul that The Lion's got a Twitter account now, thanks to Sue and Vali, and a Facebook page. You should have seen Bill Ford's face when he found out about #hotcopper. I blame that photograph.'

'I'll tell Paul.' Ray said, laughing. 'He can look once he's allowed internet access again.'

'Oh, been up to no good has he?'

'Something like that.' Ray nodded, as he reached for his mobile and gazed at the splendid array of icons, including the bird and the Facebook letterform. 'Though I might have a little chat with our Daisy about all this first. Cheers.'

10.

Harvest

The compact modern kitchen was tidy and spotlessly clean, Molly noted with approval. Yet it felt crowded with only two people in it, one of whom was heavily pregnant.

'Let's get some air.' Preceded by her enormous belly, Tina carried her tea into the garden, where honeysuckle and buddleia filled the space with perfume and butterflies.

'This'll be a fine place for the baby,' Molly inspected the neat pots and patch of lawn as she followed. 'So when's it due?'

'The twenty seventh, so they say, but it could be earlier.' With care Tina lowered herself onto a shaded garden seat. 'I can't wait. I'll be so glad to get back to my normal self. It's so uncomfortable and I feel out of place and clumsy everywhere but the hospital.'

'Have you and Carl decided on names?' Molly joined her.

'Neil, if it's a boy, for Carl's father.'

'That's a nice, sensible name. And if it's a girl? I assume that you don't know?'

'We decided not to...if it's a girl, Enid, for my mother.'

'It's good to carry on family names.' Molly said, after a moment's hesitation.

'Anyway, how are you? Still doing well at the library, I hear.'

'How'd you hear that then?'

'Neighbours, people in the village,' Tina extemporised. 'Tell me how... efficient it all is.'

'Good, it's nice to be appreciated.' Molly looked at her watch. 'Though I can't stay long, my lunch break's almost over. I don't like leaving Amrita. I'm rather worried about her, she looked very red-eyed when she arrived the other day.'

'Oh?'

'Yes, I saw her just at the end of your road. Had she been... oh, are you all right?'

Tina winced, her hands on her belly. 'Yes, just a twinge. So you're busy then?'

'We're certainly are.' Molly confirmed, with enthusiasm. 'More people are coming in to use the internet. I'm going to have to allocate time slots, apportion access.'

'Well, that should help, but remember, the idea is to encourage people to come in,' Tina suggested, gently. 'It's not like your old accounts department, is it? People don't have to clock in and out.'

'Yes. No, but it's good to be in control.' Molly sipped her tea. 'If you can be.'

Molly was aware of her friend's eyes upon her.

'Is everything okay? How's Peter?'

'Fine.'

Tina turned towards her. 'You mightn't feel like talking about it right now, Molly, but at some point... well, I'm here if you need me.'

Molly watched a yellow admiral alight upon a buddleia spike.

'Maybe I ought to look for someone else for the library? Then you could spend more time at the hospice.'

'No.' Molly said, quickly. 'I promised. And the council are paying me.'

'I'm sure they'd understand. We didn't know that... this was going to happen. I'll find some volunteers for the library, especially when the time comes.'

'The time....The time!' Molly stood, brisk and bright, brushing a few stray petals from the back of her skirt. 'Well, I'll be over next week, if you're still here.'

She took Tina's half-full mug away, too quickly for Tina to object and hurried into the kitchen.

'Must go now,' she called, poking her head back around the door. She waved to a bemused Tina. 'Bye!'

On the driveway Molly fumbled with her car keys. Her eyes were watery. It was the sunlight, she told herself, so strong after the quiet cool of the house. She effected repairs to her make-up in the driving mirror.

'People would only misunderstand, circumstances being as they are,' she muttered to herself before driving away. 'And we can't have that.'

When she entered the Library Amrita was logging in returns with the bar code reader, helped, for the last time, by Daisy Marshall. Autumn term was about to start and Daisy would begin at Furzedown School, on the edge of the village and too far away to allow her to visit the Library at lunchtimes.

'Hello,' Molly called, breezily. 'I'm back.'

'How was Tina?'

'Very well, though I wouldn't be surprised if that baby arrives long before the end of the month. She's huge.'

'She'll be anxious, it being her first.' Amrita had a trio. 'Early mightn't be a bad thing. I remember being so clumsy during the final weeks, I felt gross. And the labour.....well.'

'Oh, I know.....' Molly began to reciprocate with tales of her own, then noticed Daisy listening and instead asked 'did you sort out the books from the old stockroom?'

'Yes. They're in a box in the restroom.'

'Good. We're going to miss you, Daisy, I don't know how we managed without you. You'll still come and visit us, I hope?'

'Of course.' Daisy smiled.

'And I'll take the books out to the hospital later, someone might like to read them.'

'Why don't you go on over now, Molly? It is library business.' Amrita suggested. 'Daisy's here to help me and our Pat's coming down later.'

'Yes, Mrs Morgan, we can manage,' the girl added.

'Want rid of me, do you?' Molly was almost willing to be persuaded. 'No, I'm getting paid for this now, I'll just leave a bit earlier, that's all.'

Molly left for the hospital with her box of books after she had closed the library. She went first to Paediatrics where she put most of the volumes in the nurses' room. Retaining a stain-mottled book of poems she set out to visit Quentin, planning to read to him, as he liked the regularity of rhythm and the certainty of rhyme, but he was sleeping.

Molly sat at his bedside, watching the rise and fall of his breathing. In sleep Quentin resembled other young men of his age, mouth open and vulnerable. It was only when he was awake that the differences showed.

'It'll be like it was before,' she thought. 'You'll be the main reason for my visits here. Only soon it'll just be me, your last protector and shield.'

For a while her mind was white and formless. She felt numb. When she bestirred herself, half an hour had passed. She hurried on to the hospice.

Peter was sitting by the window in his wheelchair, muffled as if it was winter, gazing out into the woodland. The late afternoon sun lit his fine, white hair, spun into a cloud above speckled pink flesh. A splinter of memory worked into Molly's heart, a vision of their walking hand in hand up on the moors, his thick curls blowing back from his powerful, tanned face.

Her slight noise roused him, so she hastened in, all brightness.

'Hello my dear.' She bent and kissed his lips, entwining his hands in her own.

'Hello chick.' He gripped them, weakly. 'I've been watching the season changing. Look, you can already see the berries on the hawthorn.'

Molly saw only a froth of orange red as she stared outwards.

'What's that you've got?' He indicated the volume she still held, The Children's Compendium of Poetry.

'We've been sorting out old books at the library,' she answered cheerily. 'I left some in Paediatrics and took this for Quentin. It's a bit mouldy, but the pictures are beautiful.'

Together they studied the jewelled colours of the illustrations and the exquisitely drawn marginalia. The book had not been borrowed since July 1973.

'We're getting some new stock, for the young reader...'

'Yes. Molly, I...'

'Though some of the old books are still popular.'

'Molly...'

'Yes my love.'

'Mr Al-Khalil came around today.'

'Really, what did he say?' Molly pointed to a sinuous line drawing. 'Isn't that fine?'

'It is.' Molly felt Peter's unwavering gaze upon her. 'Very soon, he says, only a matter of days.' He paused. 'I think..., I think that I knew, I've known for a while.'

Molly nodded, unable to speak, her eyes still on the illustration.

'You need to prepare yourself, my dear,' he continued. 'I really will be gone this time.'

Molly blinked, trying to staunch the flow and a wrenching sob escaped her. Peter reached out and she saw the tears coursing down his cheeks.

Beyond the glass, low sunbeams shone through the trees, showing the veins of leaves, transparent and reddening, as squirrels scuttered and ran, collecting their nut-hoards against the coming cold.

*

Tina lay back against the white pillows, exhausted. Her hair was still dishevelled, but she felt her face glow, as she luxuriated in her achievement. The dragging undertow of tiredness and relief couldn't diminish her boundless joy in the being she had produced.

'Felicity,' she said. 'It's Molly's middle name. It means happiness.'

'I thought you wanted Enid, for your Mum?' At the window, Carl was jiggling the new-born in his arms, entranced by her sleepy, short-sighted gaze. 'I can't get over how perfect she is. Look at her tiny finger nails. I bet everyone says that about babies.'

Tina appraised father and daughter, as if from afar. The baby's almond shaped eyes mirrored Carl's, as did a chin tending towards square, but her fluffy dark hair was far removed from his mousey brown.

'I did,' she answered, 'but then I reconsidered. It's not really a modern name, is it, Enid? It could be a burden.'

'Maybe.' Carl brought his daughter over to the bedside. He spoke in the high-pitched, tuneless lilt that adults use when speaking to the very young. 'Your clever Mummy's already thinking what's best for your future.' He handed the baby over and gently stroked Tina's cheek.

'Did you speak with the vicar about the christening?' Tina deflected his affection.

'Yes. He said we could join the harvest festival service, he's got a couple of others then and there'll be a full church. I – I'd expected him to be difficult, us not being churchgoers, but he wasn't.'

'Good.'

'Perhaps it's a good sign, the harvest thing. For her to be surrounded by plenty, all the fruit and crops.'"

'Fruit and crops? Tins of baked beans more like.' Tina declared. 'Though I'm glad it's the harvest service. Really.'

To her astonishment Carl bent and tenderly kissed her forehead. Tina blinked.

A voice called out from the central aisle of the ward. 'Congratulations!'

A huge bouquet tottered towards them along the central aisle of the ward, its bearer almost hidden beneath it.

'Molly! You shouldn't have!' Tina hugged her visitor, who smelled of French perfume and face powder.

'Nonsense! Although they'll only take them away you know. It's the pollen.' Molly perched on the bed, admiring the baby. Tina watched Carl wander off, as he so often did when Molly approached, taking the flowers with him.

'So this is little Enid?'

'No, in the end I couldn't do that to the child,' Tina grimaced. 'I thought, that is, we thought, Felicity, instead. If you don't mind?'

'Oh, no, of course I don't mind.' Molly was brusque, but her eyes sparkled. 'And how was the birth? She was very early.'

'Awful! Red walls of pain! If I had known what it would be like I don't think I'd have got pregnant. Why didn't you tell me?'

'You'll forget soon enough, we all do.' Molly answered. 'Nature's very clever.'

'Not that clever! The epidural couldn't some soon enough for me!'

'You'll get over it!' Molly smiled. Tina noticed that her skin looked grey and tired.

'And how's Peter?'

'He's fine.'

'Is there any improvement?'

'He's fine. When are they letting you out?'

'I'm to be kept in at least overnight,' Tina hesitated. 'To be honest, the thought of going home right now doesn't fill me with delight.'

'That's natural too.' Molly reassured. 'Here you're with people who are experiencing the same as you. At home it's just you and the baby.'

Tina was amused by Molly's casual dismissal of the father of the child, who was, at that very moment, returning, accompanied by a shaven headed young man of close physical resemblance, who clutched a bunch of roses.

Ian Thompson looked very ill at ease. Perhaps it was the milky womanliness of the maternity ward, Tina speculated, or perhaps it was because the last time he was at High Acres Hospital the police had been waiting to interview him following an incident on the by-pass.

'Look who's here! It's our Ian. And look what he's brought for me.' Carl brandished an enormous cigar. 'And this gorgeous creature...' he swept his arm, ceremoniously, towards the bed, 'is my wonderful new daughter.'

'Hi Ian.' Tina welcomed her brother-in-law.

'Hello Tina.' He stood, awkward. 'She looks lovely, what's her name?'

'Felicity.'

'Nice.'

Ian thrust out the flowers and Molly intercepted them. 'I'll go and add these to the others,' she said, withdrawing quickly. 'I'll come back later, when you've fewer visitors. I'm just across the garden.'

'Thanks Molly, it'd be good to see you later.' Tina called after the departing figure. 'Make sure you come back.'

'She didn't stay long,' Carl too watched Molly's retreat. 'But I suppose she's got a lot on her plate right now.'

'I'm not comfortable with letting her go off like that.' Tina tossed back the bed cover and carefully maneuvered around, legs dangling.

'What d'you think you're doing?'

'I'm fine. Women used to give birth in the fields and then carry on working.' Tina felt around for her slippers. 'Still do, probably, somewhere in the world.'

'But not here,' Carl stood over her. 'Not in this village, for centuries, I don't care how many old wives tales there are at the Ladies Society. You're staying in bed.'

Tina looked up at him, considering what to do next. She opened her mouth to respond but was distracted by Ian, who clicked his heels and raised his arm in fascist salute. Tina subsided, amid the laughter, too surprised to persist.

It wasn't long before Ian ran out of things to say. He resorted to taking photographs with his mobile from ever more obscure angles and Tina looked meaningfully at Carl, who offered to escort him back to reception. That way he wouldn't get lost and Carl could ensure that he stayed out of mischief. Tina waved them away.

Then, taking her chance, Tina stood into her slippers and shuffled along the ward, feeling a modicum of discomfort, but very little else. She found Molly, still in the ward kitchen, clad in a nurses' plastic apron and wearing rubber gloves. Molly was scrubbing and polishing with furious energy. The kitchen surfaces were pristine, the cupboard doors shone and the sink and taps gleamed. Mindful of Carl's imminent return, Tina spoke.

'Molly. Thanks so much for the flowers and for arranging them so beautifully.'

'Oh, I didn't see you there!' Molly spun round in alarm. 'Skulking in the corner!' She laughed, wringing out the cleaning cloths over the sink.

'How is Peter? And don't tell me he's fine.'

Molly folded and refolded the cloths.

'Molly?' Tina's voice caressed.

'I – it's the end. He's finally going.' Molly didn't turn around. 'We've known, for a while, that it would happen. We've made plans.... but it doesn't make it easier.'

'Oh, Molly,' Tina crossed the room to clumsily embrace the older woman. Molly's shoulders slumped and she laid her head on Tina's shoulder. Then, wiping her eyes with the heel of her hand, she gently held Tina away.

'And why are you out of bed? You should be resting. Resting and enjoying this day. Not worrying about me!' She picked up a cloth and resumed her polishing. 'You go back to bed. I'll just finish here and then I'll be on my way.'

'What are you doing, Molly?' Molly and Tina turned to see Amrita standing in the kitchen doorway, her family behind her.

'We employ cleaners, Mrs Morgan. You shouldn't be doing this.' Mandeep Dhaliwal peered over his wife's shoulder. He was a large, bearded and turbaned man, whose Bradford vowels, surviving all attempts at suppression, sounded comforting to many of his patients. He was still wearing his stethoscope. 'Though I think you clean better than they do.'

'Just sorting out the flowers,' Molly waved at the vases. She peeled off the gloves, smoothed her skirt and touched her hair. 'Tina's had so many. Look, make sure she goes back to her bed, will you. I must be off now. Goodbye.'

Molly bustled out just as Carl returned. Submerged under a torrent of good wishes, he had no time to remonstrate with Tina.

His hand was pumped by Mandeep. Amrita kissed his cheek. The children added polite greetings and all shambled slowly back along the ward towards Tina's bed, a gaggle of talk and felicitations.

As Tina climbed back between the sheets, she spotted Molly out of the window. 'There she goes.'

Below, Molly was striding across the garden which separated hospital from hospice.

'She was just scrubbing and rubbing, rubbing and scrubbing,' said Amrita.

Molly had got to the centre of the garden. She stopped dead, surrounded by blown roses. She looked round. A nurse and one of the hospice helpers were running towards her. Tina raised her hand, as Carl put his arm around her shoulders and she leant into him.

They heard the voices down below, faint but distinct.

'Molly! It's okay, Molly, he's still here. Come quickly, he's calling for you. There's not much time left.'

From the window in Maternity they observed the white-coated ones take Molly's arms, supporting her as they moved swiftly along the gravel path.

*

'At that point you all come up to the font, here,' the Reverend Jim Gardener indicated the area around the stone basin, just in case anyone was in any doubt. 'Then I ask you for your responses and you make your promises.'

The members of the small but attentive group nodded. Around them, preparations for the harvest service were at full throttle, the church bustling with activity.

'Any questions?'

'Yes, please.' Tina raised her hand, as if in school. 'One of Felicity's sponsors is making a statement, she'll make her promise in her own religion, but can her family join the service?'

'Of course. They won't take Communion, but giving thanks for the harvest is one of the oldest and most common festivals in all religions and in pagan tradition too, which, of course, is why non-believers can join in.' This prompted some shuffling of feet amongst the putative god-parents. 'Anything else? Well, if you think of anything, you can always give me a call, or text. Otherwise, I'll see you all on Sunday.'

Jim began to usher them all towards the exit. In the stone porch he noticed the Thompsons waiting for the others to leave.

'Reverend?' Tina asked, hesitantly. 'As you know, Molly Morgan has agreed to be a godparent to Felicity. But we aren't sure that she'll be able to attend the service. After Peter passed....'

'I think having Molly as godmother is a great idea, for lots of reasons,' Jim replied. 'And there are a few days to go, so she may feel able to join us. However, godparents are required to attend the baptismal service, it's when they become godparents.'

Tina and Carl exchanged glances.

'We don't know....' Carl began.

'If Molly really can't be here in person, there might be ways around it, but it would be unusual.' It was Jim's turn to hesitate. 'I read about a baptism in Australia that used a webcam to allow someone to participate.'

Both parents looked dubious and hopeful simultaneously.

'I'm visiting Molly tomorrow, do you want me to talk with her about it?'

'We don't want her to feel under pressure, she's....delicate enough right now.' Carl answered.

Jim nodded, gravely. Carl's sensitivity and concern for Molly surprised and gratified him, as Molly had never really bothered to hide her disdain of Carl, nor her disapproval. Maybe it's the maturity that goes with fatherhood, he thought.

Jim glanced at Tina, who was watching her husband as if beguiled. Jim suppressed a smile.

'Of course,' he said. 'Though maybe she could talk with me about it, without feeling that she's letting someone down.'

'Okay. But, have you seen Molly since Peter died?' Carl asked, tentatively.

'No, but I've spoken to her several times on the phone. Why?' What could have happened? Jim thought.

'We've called round. There's no response to the doorbell.' Carl shook his head, frowning.

'Nobody's seen her,' Tina interjected. 'She's not even been to visit Quentin.'

'That is worrying,' Jim's brows creased. 'She seemed alright. Just as well I'm going round tomorrow. I'll let you know how she is, what she says and what we can do.'

Jim waved the Thompsons away and returned to the church, brow furrowed.

Molly wouldn't do anything stupid, he assured himself, as he turned back to the aisle. But he knew how determined she could be once she had resolved upon a plan.

'D'you want this in the usual place, Vicar?'

Jim looked up. The question appeared to come from a giant plaster corn sheaf. The Church Guild member carrying it peered round its side.

'What? Oh, yes, please.'

Jim watched the corn sheaf trundle on as he, absentmindedly, placed embroidered kneeling pads on to pew rails, fingering the insubstantial padding on the most ancient.

'I really must throw these out,' he vowed. 'But then, I said that at Easter.'

The Order of Service leaflets sat beside the kneelers on the rails. Jim picked one up and read through the liturgy. Long-standing Harvest tradition determined that time-honoured favourites would echo around the transept. The villagers would sing 'We plough the fields and scatter' with the gusto only to be expected in a rural parish where machines did both.

Jim surveyed his church. The corn sheaf was at a standstill before the Ladies Society display, where finishing touches were being added and all other activity in the vicinity had to wait. He ran his eye over the ancient cream and grey stone, the wood and wrought-iron rood screen and the worn steps of the pulpit.

It would be full on Sunday. The village always turned out for Harvest Festival. To give thanks for sufficiency ahead of winter, just as their ancestors did, even if a trip to the local supermarket would easily re-stock the freezer. A race memory perhaps, something older, even, than Christianity? They came for Harvest, Remembrance Sunday and Christmas, though not for Easter, he reflected, sadly, as he replaced the leaflet.

His mind turned to the specifics of the service. If Molly was unable to get through it, if she broke down, the whole village would be there to see it. It might be safer if....

Jim exhaled forcefully, refusing to speculate until he'd spoken with Molly. He went to try and find some less threadbare kneelers.

*

The churchyard was shrouded in soft mist when Jim opened up the heavy doors on Harvest Sunday morning. As if to order, a ripe sun dispersed the grey chill with its mellow light and, within the church, the stone glowed warmly as sunbeams shone, richly coloured and jewel-like, from the high stained glass windows. Jim nodded to the organist, who took his place behind the venerable instrument and pulled and slotted keys. Low chords sounded, sliding one into another. From the vestry Jim watched as St Agnes began to fill.

By the time the Thompson party arrived there was little room left. In a pale hat and a suit still department-store fresh, Tina led the way. She carried Felicity, swathed in a long, antique christening shawl, a gift from Molly. Carl followed close behind, smart in suit and matching tie. Ian, too, was besuited, although with a lot of wrist and ankle on display. Evidence, Jim thought, either of the age of his suit or the vigour of late teenage growth.

Molly wore lacy black and shafts of light caught in her flaming hair, as they did in the golden thread of Amrita's fine sari. There was a subtle variation in the hum of conversation as the two soon-to-be godmothers passed along the aisle to the front of the church, whether prompted by the presence of the recently bereaved or by someone of a different faith, Jim couldn't tell. Existing occupants of the front pew shuffled along to allow the Thompson group to sit. Jim hurried away to take up his position at the back of the church.

The introduction to 'All things bright and beautiful' reverberated from the organ loft and everyone stood. The pure voices of the choir leading the procession of clergy were overwhelmed as the congregation began to sing, only a beat behind. Walking forward, Jim caught Mandeep's eye. He was seated, with his children, near the back of the church looking uncomfortable. Jim nodded to him, with an encouraging grin. As he approached the altar rail he shot a covert glance at the front pew – Molly was holding up thus far.

His visit to Molly had been curiously uneventful. She'd looked gaunt, with a worrying, washed-out quality and she had been meek and acquiescent, which had quite put Jim off his stride. Nevertheless, she was vehement in assuring him that she would be at the service, no matter what. Molly may have lost some of her spirit, temporarily Jim hoped, but nothing was going to keep her away.

The service proceeded. The readers read, the children paraded, the choir sang and the sermon was delivered. Congregants rose and knelt, intoning responses, when known. Jim was pleasantly surprised when Ian Thompson correctly mumbled his way through the Lord's Prayer (though he was somewhat too loud).

Eventually Jim summoned the celebrants to the font. Three family groups, all in their Sunday best, stepped forward, lead by Carl and Tina. The babies and godparents were presented to the church. The first of the three babies to be christened was Felicity Thompson. Jim took the child, casting a surreptitious look at Molly. Her eyes were red-rimmed and watery and her hand shook when she handed over the prayer book.

Maybe this wasn't a good idea, he thought.

They reached the point at which each god-parent made their promises. Amrita was excused this and Jim didn't entirely trust Ian to respond as agreed, as the teenager was looking bored and might, Jim feared, become mischievous. But this meant that the full weight of expectation fell upon Molly's fragile shoulders. She would be the first to make her undertakings before the congregation.

'Molly Morgan, do you turn to Christ?'

Molly's answer was inaudible and there was a low muttering among the worshippers. Jim stared into the body of the church and it subsided. For the next question, he raised his voice, but did not shift his gaze.

'Do you repent of your sins?'

'I repent of my sins.' This time she could be heard.

'Do you renounce evil?' Jim addressed Molly directly.

'I renounce evil.'

This was a louder and more Molly-like response. Relieved, Jim moved on to Ian Thompson. The teenager followed Molly's lead without a murmur, which prompted an exchange of glances between Tina and Carl. Tina looked thankful, Carl looked superior. Jim conducted the ritual with oil and water and handed Felicity back to Tina. The babe had made hardly a murmur.

The ceremonies continued and the Thompson party looked smugly sympathetic when the other babies wailed at the water's touch. By the time the congregation stood to sing the final hymn everyone was back in their place, pleased to have come through without mishap.

Even Amrita looks more comfortable, Jim thought. She seemed lulled by the shared ritual of the service, ignorant as she was about its deficiencies. Jim flinched as the choir missed their organ cue yet again.

Smiling and happy, the christening parties shuffled along the aisle behind the regular congregation. Jim observed Molly looking around, quietly absorbing the church and its contents.

The verger opened the heavy church doors, wedging them against the fluted stonework. There was a melee about the porch, as parishioners waited to bid good morning to their vicar and pass comment upon the service and each other. So Jim didn't see the departure of the Thompsons, but he was soon to join them, along with friends and neighbours, at Molly's house.

*

Twenty minutes later and less splendidly clad than he had been, Jim rang Molly's doorbell.

"Come in, Vicar, come in," said Amrita, ushering him into the kitchen. A brimming pint pot of ale was thrust into his hand with which to wet the baby's head.

In the living room Molly was enthroned in a large, upright armchair by the window. She held Felicity, who was still in her christening shawl, while Daisy sat at her feet, playing with the cat, Tinks. All were bathed in late Summer sunshine.

The personification of the season, Jim decided, looking at Molly. All she needed was a golden robe and a few corn sheaves.

He perched upon the broad arm of her chair.

'So what did you think of our service, then?' he asked.

'I thought it rather lovely, though I don't usually like ritual and panoply.' Molly replied. 'Your church has good acoustics, it's a shame that your congregation can't sing.'

Jim laughed. 'That's why we have a choir!'

The door bell sounded and Jim heard Amrita welcoming yet more guests.

'It's kind of you to have the party here,' he said.

'The happy parents are a bit up-side-down at the moment and they don't have a lot of room at the best of times. This place has plenty, Tinks and I rattle around in it.' There was a crash from upstairs and Molly looked upwards. 'Oh!'

'Only me!' Ian Thompson shouted. Dragooned into storing people's coats and jackets, he was causing quite a lot of rattling of his own, as he thumped up and down the stairs.

'So,' Jim tasted his beer. 'Have you decided? What's it to be?'

'I have,' Molly replied. 'A remembrance service at St Agnes, if you please.'

'I'm sure we can accommodate you.'

'Don't be sure, I have some very specific requirements. Peter knew what he wanted and I intend to see that he gets it.'

Jim raised an eyebrow. He was gratified to find Molly's spark was returning, yet he didn't underestimate the difficulties that might follow.

'When?'

'Early next month. The cremation's on Wednesday.'

Jim nodded. He was not officiating, this being Molly's final private farewell to Peter.

'I'll pop round on Thursday, then, to talk about the service,' he said.

'Yes, that'll be fine.' Molly stroked the baby's soft black hair.

'We can't do dancing girls, you know.' He looked sideways at her.

'Dancing girls aren't on the agenda.' Molly's face never flickered.

'Well, that's all right then.'

The doorbell rang again. Neighbours appeared in the living room doorway and Jim moved aside, to allow them to pay court to the earth mother and her godchild.

He wandered over to the piano, where he studied the cluster of photographs upon it. Prominent amidst the pictures of celebrations and holidays was a fine portrait of Peter set within a black border of satin. Next to this stood the most recent addition, taken only that morning, of Felicity in her shawl.

Tina came to his side.

'Thank you, Vicar, for this morning.'

'My office and my pleasure,' Jim replied. 'And thank you.' He looked over to Molly, receiving newly arrived guests. 'I only hope....'

'Yes.' Tina put down her glass. 'Come with me.'

They made their way into the crowded kitchen and over to the fridge.

'Look.' Tina pointed to the Page-a-Week calendar, which had entries on every page and a 'To Do' list marked 'library'.

'I guess she's going to be alright,' he concluded, with a silent prayer of thanks. 'She'll keep on keeping on.'

11.

The Fourth Estate

The last person Nicola Shah expected to walk into her little office at Herald Newspapers was PC William Ford. Nicola had known Bill since nursery days in the village, but she hadn't seen him since moving away several years before.

'Hello, Billy. What a surprise! What can I do for you?'

'Hi there Nicky, I'm here to see your boss, Mr Lovejoy.'

'What's he been up to then?' She checked Max's calendar. There was meeting with the police scheduled for two thirty. 'I'll let him know you're here. Take a seat.'

The policeman sat on a low sofa, his long legs bent, knees pointing upwards and large feet almost touching Nicola's desk. He clasped and unclasped his large hands as he looked around at the framed Herald front pages that adorned the walls. Nicola remembered this habit from school days. Billy did this when he was going over something in his head.

'What's going on, Billy?'

'Ah, er, I'm not really at liberty to say,' PC Ford looked sheepish. 'It's police business.'

'Oh.' Nicola sat back and raised an eyebrow. A chubby tomboy as a teenager, she was now an elegant, angular young woman. The sharp points of her hair swung about her jaw-line as she turned her head on her long neck. She abandoning attempts to continue working and gave Bill her full attention. She knew exactly what the meeting was about.

'How's Mo keeping these days?' the PC asked after Nicola's husband. 'Still teaching at St Jerry's?'

'He's well, thanks. Yes, he's still at the sines and co-sines.' Nicola and William exchanged knowing glances. Neither had been good at maths at school and both had found something mystical in Mohammed's early and startling proficiency. 'He's applying for the deputy head of department post.'

'A step up and more money, I suppose. Wish him the best from me.'

'I will.' The out-dated intercom on her desk buzzed. 'You're summoned. Good luck," she said. "And don't take any nonsense, Billy. We can't afford to alienate any part of our readership, what with the recession and falling revenues. I know what this meeting's about, as Max's PA I organise all his appointments. Remember, there's a fine line between being protectionist and incitement.'

PC Ford's grin took Nicola straight back to the fifth form. 'That's good - you always did have a way with words, Nicky, you should be writing the stuff.'

'If only.....I've been working here for five years just waiting for a chance.'

Nicola ushered the policeman into the editor's office, which was a larger version of the ante room, with a grander desk. From behind it Max Lovejoy rose and reached out a hand.

'Constable.' Max was a tall and florid man with a greying mane of hair flowing back from his forehead. He signalled to Nicola. 'Can you take notes please,' his voice was rich and theatrical. 'I think it might be useful to have a record of our discussions.'

Max remained standing. Using his height to overawe was a tactic Nicola had seen him employ before. But, in this instance, he gained no advantage, for the PC was over six foot himself and immune to attempts to physically intimidate.

'Sorry to keep you waiting. What can I do for you?' He indicated a low seat opposite as he sat, leaning back in his chair.

'I'm here to discuss your paper's recent coverage of the influx of Eastern European workers,' the policeman began.

'Let me just stop you there.' The editor smiled. 'How is it the business of the police to comment upon press coverage?'

'As I was about to make clear, there have been formal complaints.....'

'So? We get them all the time.'

'If you would allow me to finish, sir,' the policeman persisted, calmly. 'The complaints are that your newspaper published material likely to cause harassment, alarm or distress to persons because of their race. This is subject to the Public Order Act, 1986, as amended by the Racial & Religious Hatred Act, 2006. Councillors Framley and Kumar have also been involved.'

'Yes, I've spoken with them both. There are very few prosecutions under that statute, as you may know, constable,' Lovejoy waved his hand, dismissively.

'My colleagues in the CPS are aware, sir, that this is being looked into,' the policeman ploughed on. 'It may be advantageous to all parties if a prosecution is unnecessary, which, I believe, is the usual way forward in these cases. Nonetheless, this is a potential offence, so we are looking into it.'

*

'Prosecution my arse!'

Max fulminated loudly at the bar of Willow Meads country club where he liked to unwind after a long day at The Herald. 'What we need is a thorough-going, principled defence of press freedom.' He banged his heavy whisky tumbler down onto the bar. 'It might even get some Fleet Street attention, you never know.'

'You'll need legal advice,' said Andrew Wells, currently in residence at the club while his former home was being sold. He was legal advisor to Max and to Herald Newspapers. 'And you had better keep your voice down.'

214

The room was empty, but for a couple of fellow members along the bar. Max glared at Andrew but said nothing.

'So, who's made the complaint?' Andrew asked.

'Several people, I am told, though we don't yet know who they are.' Max spoke with contempt. 'Concerned citizens. If they're so concerned let them use their names.'

'At least one of them will have to if they want to bring a case, Max. Don't worry.'

Further along the bar, Gus King took his two pints and joined his son at a side table.

'What's that all about?' the younger man asked.

'It seems our local newspaperman has received a visit from the police. Questions about some of its recent reporting, 'inciting racial hatred'.'

'Eh? Well, The Herald's never been a liberal paper and some of their stuff is offensive, but no-one's pursued it before. Why now?'

'Search me, but old Maxie'll have to watch his back. His Board isn't going to like the negative publicity, especially as the group couldn't declare a dividend this quarter. Time that Max got his comeuppance, perhaps.' Gus sipped his pint. 'How about a game of snooker?'

The Kings padded through to the snooker table in the conservatory. Max watched them walk passed, his eyes narrow. Formerly an affable contemporary, Gus hadn't spoken to Max since the debacle at that summer's village Summer Fete.

'So, what are you being asked to do? Pay? Apologise?' Andrew asked. 'Max?'

Max turned back to Andrew and the matter in hand.

'What? Oh, an apology. But we can't libel a whole group of people, so we can't be sued. I know my libel law.'

'This isn't libel Max. It's more complicated than that and there are plenty of people who would like to see a test case in this area. If The Herald contests such a case, or even appears in one, you'll lose advertisers and funding.'

Max gave Andrew a black stare.

'And damages? Surely that doesn't apply?' he asked, only partly cowed.

'The Herald would be open to civil claims.'

'Phew!' Max expelled air in a gust. 'We're financially tight enough as it is and it would open the floodgates. But what about the principle of the thing, the freedom of the press, the right to free speech?'

'As I said, it's complicated. So what do you want me to do?'

'Talk. See what they really want. I'll have to raise this at our next board meeting, which isn't going to be easy, so I'll need a legal analysis by then.'

'Okay.' Andrew looked into his glass and then flicked his gaze to his friend's face. 'You were pretty near the knuckle over the summer, Max,' he said. 'Discretion might be...'

'Discretion! How can you talk about discretion? You've hardly been discreet. Carrying on all over the countryside! Is your soon-to-be-ex-wife well, by the way?'

'That's hardly the same thing,' Andrew protested. 'I've already explained. I fell in love with someone else, someone who wasn't my wife. These things happen. I should never have married Diane, we were totally unsuited.'

Max started to retort, but he looked at the worry lines etched deep into Andrew's face. His friend's aquiline good looks were becoming raddled. Max held his peace. 'No, you're right. Sorry.'

'And now it seems she might not be divorcing her husband after all. Those bloody children -,' Andrew clamped his mouth closed.

'We'll talk about the case tomorrow, okay?'

'Sure,' Andrew raised his glass. 'See you tomorrow.'

'Keep your chin up.'

Max made his way out to the car park, directing a studied glare in the direction of the conservatory where the Kings were still at the snooker table.

*

The young man opened the door, the laden tray balanced, precariously, on his left arm. He was supposed to slip in discreetly with coffee and place it on the small table at the end of the room.

The board room, a relic of the hot metal print days, was panelled in honeyed maple and contained a large polished oval table ringed by chairs. It was located on the top floor of the office block formerly filled by Herald Newspapers, but now mostly rented out. The view across the roofscape of the town was spectacular. Today, only half of the chairs around the table were occupied.

Nicola sat opposite the door, taking notes, and she caught the young man's eye, indicating the table to his left. She watched intently, waiting for the crash, but the informal meeting of the board of Herald Newspapers continued without mishap and the young man unburdened himself and left.

'What I want to know is how this action, if it comes to court, is likely to impact on profits?' The speaker was Phillip Runcible, a non-executive director, on the board by virtue of his Fund's shareholding.

'Aside from legal costs, which could be considerable, claims for damages would follow,' the Finance Director replied. 'I refer you to the paper on in-year reserves, number...what's the number Nicola?'

'Thirteen.' Nicola held up a copy. 'Tabled for discussion immediately after lunch.'

'Give me a rough estimate.' Runcible persisted, his gaze unwavering.

'I'm proposing that we reserve £2.5 million.' A tremor ran around the oval board table. "Assuming half a million in costs and a subsequent claim for damages.'

'Bear in mind,' Max intervened. 'That is in case we lose. If we win we pay nothing.'

'But might still lose substantial advertising,' the chairman stated.

'Temporarily, maybe.'

'The level of financial risk concerns me.' Runcible continued. 'Two and a half million pounds is a dent in the profits of the whole group, which would probably mean no dividend later in the year. I'm sure the board needs no reminding that shareholders are already aggrieved at the absence of a dividend in the second quarter.'

'What are the chances of our losing if this goes to court?' Someone else asked.

All heads turned to the company solicitor.

'It's difficult to say,' he replied, nervously. 'Few prosecutions take place under this legislation, but that depends, to an extent, on the determination of the complainants. The solicitor engaged by the opposition is Tanya Towers.'

There was a shared sharp intake of breath. The civil liberties lawyer was a public figure and had recently won a high profile case against a national newspaper.

'Would she be involved unless she thought there was something worth pursuit?' said Runcible. 'Are there any civil liberties or anti-racist organisations backing this?'

'Not as far as we know,' the company solicitor replied. 'Although, unusually, we do not yet know the identity of our opponent, or opponents. They can't take a case anonymously, of course, but only an apology is sought at this stage.'

'Tomorrow's editorial, perhaps,' Max suggested. '"The nameless bullies", to follow up all the recent cyber-bullying stories.'

There was a hub-bub around the table and various voices sought to dissuade.

'Now Max....'

'I really don't think....'

'May I remind the Board that it does not determine editorial policy,' said Max, semi-seriously. 'And our policy has remained the same for twenty years. We report on local events and raise the issues that concern our readers. The influx of European migrants has repercussions for the people of this area, not just out in the villages but also here in town. We show that we are on their side. And this fits with our general anti−EU stance. This is all within the purview of the editor.'

'But if the editorial policy creates costs of up to £2.5 million,' Runcible countered, with a thin-lipped smile. 'That may lose the editor his job - as the individual responsible....'

'Gentlemen, please.' The chairman intervened, raising both his hands, palms outwards. 'I, for one, would like to look through The Herald's reports on the issue. Nicola, could you get them together for us before lunchtime?'

'I'll arrange it for after coffee.'

'Even better. Now Max, I know you control editorial policy,' the cultured voice of the chairman continued. 'But you're asking us to support you at considerable potential cost. We need to understand the risk and we can only make a judgement if we know what The Herald said and why it could be considered defamatory.... inciteful... whatever the term is.'

'There is also the important principle of press freedom,' Max began.

'Indeed....' The chairman interrupted. 'I propose we break for coffee now, for fifteen minutes. Then we take ten minutes to read the new material and re-commence discussion. Thank you.' He rose and the others followed suit. 'Max, if I could have a word please.'

Nicola hurried to fetch the papers from her desk, which she had prepared beforehand, even though Max had insisted they would not need them. The chairman and Max slipped past her into the editor's office.

She looked at the intercom.

Hesitating for only a moment, she depressed the button. She hated eavesdropping − nothing good could come of it, her father always said − but this was her job at stake. The voices were distinct and she lowered the volume.

'What is your fall-back position?' The chairman asked. 'If you can't carry the board.'

'Do you mean, am I prepared to resign?'

'No, I meant exactly what I said, what is your fall-back position?' His words were clipped and impatient.

'To negotiate a carefully worded statement, expressing regret for any unintended distress caused.'

'Good, I suggest you prepare a draft. Look Max, I want this handled properly, or I will be looking for a resignation. And it won't be mine! Now, I need the Gents before we resume.'

Nicola just had time to turn off the intercom before the chairman strode out of Max's office.

Max came to the doorway, his face red. 'Get me Andrew Wells, now!' He barked, then slammed his door.

Within minutes Max was speaking with his friend on the telephone. Nicola monitored the call from her desk.

'Not a backbone among them.' Max cursed. 'The Herald and its Editor can sink, as long as the shareholders get their cash. Phillip Runcible screwed me over good and proper.'

'So, what's next?'

'We... negotiate.' Max almost spat the word.

'With a view to what?'

'Best case, they back down. Second best, we make some sort of expression of regret and make an ex gratia payment in full settlement, if absolutely necessary.'

'The expression to come from the board or from the editor?'

'Use the non-specific 'we', I'll sign it. Make no promises about the future, our editorial policy remains the same.'

'Okay, I'll fix up a meeting.' There was a pause. 'Have you considered that they may not want to settle? They may want their day in court? Towers is a campaigning lawyer.'

'Yes, that's been made plain.' Max sounded thoughtful. 'But I don't think the folk behind this are activists. It irks me that I don't know who they are. Perhaps I'll get Nicola on to it.'

Nicola almost exclaimed aloud.

She had almost given up pestering Max for an opportunity to write a story, having dreamed, since schooldays, of being a journalist, but she didn't want to do this. The villagers were her father's friends and neighbours. She had grown up with many of them, even if she now lived elsewhere. This would mean spying on them, betraying their trust. She wasn't sure she could do that.

Max had continued speaking.

'That village is where she's from. Her father keeps a newsagents shop on the green there. She's always saying that she wants to be a reporter. Well, let's see just how much.'

'That might not be the wisest course Max, especially if this goes to court. Investigating the plaintiffs isn't sensible. It could be considered to be intimidation and would prejudice any judge in their favour.'

'How can I investigate them, if I don't know who they are? Well, I'll think about it.' Max sounded as if his spirits were sinking even lower. 'We'll speak later.'

'Okay. 'Bye.'

Nicola quickly put the telephone handset back in its cradle and picked up her bag, hoping to make a swift exit.

*

Several hours later Nicola zapped her car lock and crossed, hesitantly, to St Agnes Church Hall. Night had fallen in the village, but the gothic tracery in the stone windows formed a filigree of light upon the tarmac around the cenotaph.

Despite her best efforts Max had cornered her after the board meeting. She hadn't moved quickly enough.

'Nicola,' he'd begun, after summoning her into his office. 'You want to be a journalist?'

'Max, you know I do,' she sighed.

'Are you sure you're up for it?'

'I think I am.'

'As things stand, of course, neither you nor I might still be at The Herald in a few months time. Where will you get your opportunity then?'

'Max, you know I've been waiting for a chance....'

'Yes, well, I think you've waited long enough and you're uniquely well suited to the story I have in mind for you. Your job will be to ferret out exactly what's happening in that village. I need to know which villagers have complained about The Herald. Okay?'

Nicola sighed. 'Okay. But I don't want anyone....'

'Exposed? But that's what investigative reporters do, Nicola. They expose people. Are you sure you've got the temperament for this?'

'I'll do some investigating,' she said, trying to negotiate a middle course. 'But I'm not going to write anything which hurts the village. My father has to live there.'

'We'll see about the story once you've got the information,' was all Max would say.

So this evening she was attending a meeting of the village Ladies Society and, if she learned nothing tonight, there was the Young Farmers Club tomorrow. It was typical of Max to use her in this way, she thought, as she crossed to the Church Hall, highly manipulative and very effective. If she wanted to keep her job and fulfil her ambitions, she had to agree to spy on the villagers.

She rapped on the heavy oak door. It was opened by Carol Pendleton.

'Nicola Shah of The Herald.' She proffered her card. 'Here to report on the latest good works of the Ladies Society.'

'Hello Nicky, I was talking to your Dad only this morning. He said you were doing a story.' Carol opened the door wide. 'Come in.'

Inside the hall was brightly lit, large metal lamps hung from the high ceiling. Serried ranks of metal framed chairs sat before a raised dais at the far end where people were setting up a presentation. Closer to hand, women of varying ages and sizes were chatting around a table laden with tea, coffee and homemade cakes. A few faces were, briefly, turned towards Nicola and Carol.

'Now, what is it that you want to do?' Carol asked. 'Tonight is just an ordinary meeting, nothing special.'

'That's okay. If I could have a look at a few agendas?' Nicola produced her notebook and phone. 'For interviews,' she explained, nervously.

'Oh we don't have formal agendas, unless the president attends.'

'Sorry, who is the president now?'

'Mrs Jane King.' Carol watched Nicola write in her notebook. 'Can I interest you in a cup of tea? Then perhaps you'd like to mingle, you already know most of our members?'

Nicola was easily absorbed into the group. She greeted Lynda Marshall, congratulated Tina Thompson and avoided the gimlet eyed Winnie Fortune and her silver-haired companion. Everyone was happy to talk about the Society and Nicola soon had enough information for such a story, although it was not the one she wanted.

The bustle was interrupted by Carol, who announced that the formal part of the evening was about to begin. Cups and plates were abandoned as women took their seats. Polite applause heralded the start of the first presentation.

By the end of the evening, after a talk that raised funds for Syrian Refugee Relief and a demonstration of clerical vestments, Nicola was gasping for a drink of a different sort, so she accompanied Carol across the churchyard to The Lion. She had learned little, other than how to dress a priest.

The lounge bar was quiet and Nicola studied the newer photographs on the walls, sipping her drink and recalling that this was where the ring leaders of the summer's riot were apprehended. She had been served by a black-haired young woman, unknown to her, who appeared in several of the photographs.

'Haven't you seen those before, Nicola?' Carol entered and the girl left.

'No, but then it's been a while since I've been in here. This was the famous show down was it? Dad told me all about it.'

'It got a lot more attention than it deserved,' said Carol. 'Just because there were press folk in the room when it happened.'

'I heard that your Len was quite the hero,' Nicola teased. 'And as for Billy Ford....I'm surprised he hasn't been tempted into a more glamorous line of work – that photograph was everywhere. He looked quite the poster boy, rugged chin and feathery eye lashes.'

'Yes, poor Bill,' Carol grinned. She began cleaning the bar.

'Are there any of the eastern Europeans still around?'

'No, most moved out or were moved on. Vali's still here, she's our Romanian bar-maid, you just met her, but she had nothing to do with it. We made sure her name was kept out of the press reports. Len heads off enquiries if the press call.'

'So she wouldn't have complained then?' Nicola finished her drink. 'About The Herald's coverage, for example?'

Carol stopped polishing and gave Nicola a shrewd look. 'Is that why you're here?'

'Yes and no,' Nicola responded.

'Well you'll get nothing out of me, I don't know anything. If someone's complained, good luck to them, I say. Your paper was fomenting things best left alone, in my opinion.'

'We don't tell people how to behave.'

'No, but you don't paint a balanced picture either! I'm surprised at you, Nicola Shah,' Carol emphasised the surname. 'You ask your in-laws about The Herald's reporting and what it's stirred up in the past.'

'I know. They've told me. But I just want to be a journalist and The Herald's the only newspaper in town.'

'It's not a popular one in this village, even aside from the migrant thing. There was that business at the Summer Fete. Not that we know what really happened, even now.'

'What? I missed the Fete this year, Mo and I were on holiday. Dad didn't mention anything.'

'Well, there were some strange goings on. Gus King stepped down as chairman of the Fete Committee, at least for a while and there were accusations of blackmail. The Herald was involved somehow, which Len and I found odd, seeing as how Gus is friendly with one of the board members.'

Nicola frowned. There had been nothing across Max's desk about blackmail, she was certain. Unless he had kept it quiet?

'Who is Gus's friend?'

'Somebody called Runciman.'

'Runcible?'

'Aye, that's it. "The Owl and the Pussycat".'

Nicola gathered up her handbag and took out her car keys. Her mind was buzzing.

'Thanks for this evening Carol, the Ladies Society meeting will make part of a human interest piece. I enjoyed talking to people, it was a bit like old times. Not tomorrow night – it's the Young Farmers.' She grimaced at the thought of the energetic ale-swigging for which the club was notorious. Nicola suspected that she might be tomorrow night's guest of honour and it wouldn't be for professional reasons. She would have to keep her wits about her.

'Best of luck with that,' Carol laughed, never ill-humoured for long.

Nicola chose not to brave walking across the darkened churchyard alone, but took the longer route back to her car, thinking.

So Gus King was friends with Philip Runcible and, it seemed, had reason to dislike The Herald. Gus wasn't a man to forget a slight. But going to law wouldn't be his way of getting even. The legal approach was too open, too self-righteous and moral, too prim. Influencing the board would be more his style, Nicola thought. But that brought her no closer to finding out who had made the complaint.

She looked across at the Vicarage, where a porch light still shone. Perhaps she had been going about this the wrong way? If anyone in the village wanted to do the right thing and take The Herald to task, who would that person talk to? Surely a concerned citizen wouldn't want to go it alone? Nicola decided to return to the village rather earlier tomorrow than she had originally anticipated. She would try to speak with the Vicar.

*

When she arrived at The Herald the following morning, Max was already in his office. She had barely time to hang up her coat before he was sitting on the side of her desk asking questions.

'So, what did you find out?' His face was thrust forwards.

'Little or nothing, so far,' she replied. She wasn't going to share her thoughts, about Valentina the bar-maid, for example, quite yet.

Max swore. He rose and began to pace around the small room, arms folded across his chest.

'But I'm going back this evening, to speak to some farmers,' Nicola said. 'They might have more information about the transient workers they employ for the harvest. Who's moved on, who, if anyone, has stayed.'

'Let's hope they do.'

Max was ill tempered and short with her all day and Nicola was glad when it was time for her to leave for the village. She arrived on the church car park just as dusk was turning to dark.

The red Alfa Romeo sports car parked by the cenotaph was a surprise, but Nicola pulled alongside it. Taking a deep breath, she walked over to the Vicarage front door, which she found already ajar. When no-one responded to her gentle tap, she stepped inside into the darkened hall. There were voices coming from the well-lit parlour.

'So you'll open discussions with The Herald's lawyers?'

Nicola stifled a gasp. It was Reverend Jim and he was talking about the case.

He went on. 'And let's hope that they will publish an apology. Their reporting made matters here much worse than they need have been.'

'The editor will probably want to avoid litigation at all costs,' a female voice replied. 'It'll scare off his advertisers and he'll be thinking of potential claims for damages.'

'Which is why we will waive any right to claim if a full apology is forthcoming and published prominently,' Jim continued.

'I strongly advise against that. You can't take up these cases if you're going to back down, or use half-measures.'

Nicola inched forwards. She could see the Reverend in the large over-mantle mirror. He was talking with a sharp-faced, be-suited woman. About forty years old, she had the bright-eyed, confident demeanour of the successful professional. This must be...

'Ms Towers,' Jim almost pleaded. "We don't want any money.'

"That's not the point,' said Tanya Towers. 'The point is to make them pay it! Then they'll be less likely to do it again.'

The Reverend sighed.

'I'm very grateful for your help, all the villagers in our little group are, but this is a very new experience for us, in any area of law, let alone this one.'

'You're making a principled stand, there should be no back-sliding.' Tanya Towers' face took on an even more trenchant look, if that was possible. 'And there are plenty of important people watching how this case plays out. If you back down now...'

'There is another issue,' Jim's tone was tentative, but Nicola could hear the determination in his voice. 'How would it affect our chances if we don't have an individual prepared to complain?'

'What do you mean?'

'Most of the foreigners involved have gone. Some have been deported or they've moved on in search of work. Don't we need an individual who has been harassed or distressed in some way?'

'Of course.' Tanya Towers looked astonished. 'It's a bit late to tell me this now! What about the barmaid you spoke of?'

'No, she's not interested.'

'Let me talk to her.'

'No.' Jim spoke firmly. 'That's not possible.'

Nicola thought back to the previous evening's conversation with Carol. Len would never allow Valentina to become a pawn in a legal case.

So was that it then? Case collapsed? She felt a wave of relief.

'There's not a lot to be done then,' Tanya Towers sounded very annoyed. Nicola craned forward as the woman rose and began to pace.

'So that's it then?' Jim asked. 'All over?'

'Quite. You said that there were individuals who would make a formal complaint,' Tanya Towers responded, angrily.

'But we've made the complaint now.' Jim's voice sounded plaintive.

Nicola heard a deep sigh.

'Well, I suppose we could play this out. But my advice is to withdraw right away.'

'We can't do that. We're in the right.' Jim said.

'And what has morality to do with the law?' Tanya Towers answered quickly.

'So we're going for an apology and will waive the right to any damages?' Jim pressed on. 'And you'll represent us, as agreed?'

'Very well.' Tanya Towers snapped. 'But our opening position must be that we want a prosecution. I will not go into negotiations with my hands tied. If we show weakness we will be ignored.'

A hall-floor board creaked.

'Er, hello!' Nicola called.

Jim poked his head around the parlour door and switched on the hall light.

'Nicola, I didn't expect to see you here.' He entered the hall.

'Er, no. I was just...'

'Is someone eavesdropping?' Tanya Towers followed, her eyes hard. 'This is a confidential conversation, Miss..?'

'It's all right, Nicola's from the village,' Jim assured her. 'It is all right Nicky, isn't it?'

Nicola flushed and lowered her eyes.

'Oh.' Jim pursed his lips. He strode to the front door and closed it. 'I always leave it on the latch,' he explained. 'In case a parishioner needs to speak with me urgently.'

Nicola swallowed hard.

'You know I work for The Herald, Reverend Gardener...'
she began.

'What!' Tanya's eyebrows leapt upwards. 'Spying on
privileged client counsel discussions.'

'Hold on a minute....'Jim turned to her.

'You realise that Miss Nicky here has just heard our case?'

'Did you?' Jim asked.

'Yes.'

'Did Max Lovejoy send you?'

'Yes, but...'

'So you were spying!' Jim's mouth fell open. He closed it,
frowned and slowly shook his head.

'Yes, but that's not the point.' Nicola answered. Jim was
looking at her, dismayed and saddened. She had to explain.

'Then what is, exactly?' Tanya Towers added sharply.

'The point is, what am I going to do with the information
I've inadvertently overheard?'

She had their complete attention now. Jim regarded her
with horrified curiosity, Tanya with ill-disguised hostility, but
both waited for her to speak.

Nicola took a deep breath.

'Max asked me to do an investigative story on this issue,
knowing that I would be more likely to find out just what's
going on than anyone else,' she began. 'I didn't want to do it,
but I'll lose my job if I don't. So I am. That doesn't mean that
I'll report back on everything I learn.'

When she paused for breath Tanya jumped in quickly. 'You have to be on one side or the other, you can't sit on the fence.'

'I'm beginning to realise that.' Nicola replied in a flat voice.

She knew that she would have to choose. She glanced at each of her listeners in turn. Tanya's mouth was a thin line. Jim looked pained. Yet he was the one with right on his side, she thought. He and the other villagers had tried to do the right thing, not realising what they were getting into. When it came down to it, she couldn't betray them.

'I won't report what I've heard,' she said.

Jim exhaled in relief and Tanya gave a grim nod.

'And I'll tell you this for nothing — they're going to propose a meeting at the end of the week, at The Herald's offices. So you don't have much time.'

'Nicola, you know that if Max finds out...' Jim spoke slowly and with care.

'I know, but then, it's possible that I'll lose my job anyway. And now I'm going to go. I don't want to hear anything more.'

With that Nicola turned and left.

When she got back to her car she lay against it, feeling weak and washed out. The bell of St Agnes chimed the quarter hour.

'Just time to pop in and see Carol Pendleton again,' she thought. 'Before the Young Farmers.'

*

In the boardroom, Andrew sat, alert and business-like, at one end of the oval table, his junior at his side. Behind them Nicola sat, trying to disguise her nerves. She was there to take minutes of the meeting.

Andrew rose as Tanya and Jim were ushered in. Tanya took the chair furthest away from him. Jim gave a friendly smile.

Andrew opened the discussions. 'We're here to try and resolve this with the least difficulty and cost. And, may I say, this would mean avoiding a court case if possible. Do you agree?'

Jim nodded enthusiastically.

'If a satisfactory settlement is reached,' Tanya replied.

'Naturally.'

'We require a full apology, prominently placed on The Herald's front page and signed by the editor," she demanded. 'Where is Mr Lovejoy, by the way? I'd expected him to be here.'

'The editor is busy,' Andrew replied. 'He's delegated full authority to me for negotiations.'

'Even in regard to the question of payment?'

Jim shifted in his seat.

'I'm authorised to negotiate,' Andrew repeated. 'In order to do so, however, I must know the identity of the putative damaged party or parties. How many people are we talking about here? Several hundred foreign workers were in the Vale over summer.'

'We were thinking a nominal sum only.' Jim jumped in.

'Yes, about half a million should suffice.' Tanya ignored both Jim's fidgets and the question from Andrew.

'My clients won't be paying anything, if there's no case to answer,' Andrew responded.

'The Herald's xenophobic and rabble-rousing reporting is a matter of record.'

'It is well known to take an entirely respectable anti-European Union stance. But, that aside, who exactly is claiming to have been threatened or distressed by it?'

'As you say, there were several hundred workers in the Vale over summer. I'd imagine quite a number were distressed by editorial comment that obliquely likened people to vermin. Reminiscent of Nazi propaganda, in my view, one that I'm sure any judge would share.'

Jim and the junior winced, but Andrew's face did not flicker.

'Without a victim, there's no pay-out,' was all he said. 'Produce your injured party.'

'Actually, there are a number of injured parties, I think,' Jim began Tanya glared at him, but he ignored her. 'Aside from the foreign workers there are British people who felt insulted by the reporting, residents of eastern European origin, whose families settled here after world war two.'

'Ms Towers, would you please explain to your client...?'

'Gladly....' Tanya turned to Jim.

'But my point is, we really think the apology is the most important thing.' Jim persisted, ignoring his lawyer's fierce glower. Nicola lips formed a silent 'o'. 'As long as that is forthcoming and suitably prominent, the injured parties won't pursue damages.'

'No damages?'

Jim could hear the ticking of the boardroom clock. Andrew's lip began to curl.

'You don't have a case.'

'Oh we do, I assure you. And we'll pursue it if an apology is not forthcoming.' Jim back-pedalled furiously.

Too late, thought Nicola. He'd let the cat out of the bag.

'One moment please, I wish to confer with my colleague.' Andrew was distracted by his increasingly exercised junior. He turned away from the table for a quick conference.

'We only checked out migrants, not residents.' Nicola heard the young man whisper. 'And he's right, a number of people of Slavic or Polish extraction live in the village.'

'Hmmm.' Andrew was still. 'Well, I'm inclined to force the issue. They've got to put up or shut up. And if they can't, well, we need to make an example of them.' He turned back to Jim and Tanya.

'I'm sorry, this was a genuine attempt to reach resolution,' he said. 'I must, however, ask you to name your plaintiff if you wish to continue. Please contact me with the information within the week, otherwise my clients must consider their position, including the pursuit of damages, given vexatious and unsubstantiated complaints to the police. The reputation of The Herald has been impugned. The secretary will show you out.' Andrew signalled to Nicola to do so.

'Good morning.' Jim said as he stood. He looked as though he knew that they were in real trouble and that much of it was his fault. Tanya said nothing, but her back was rigid as she preceded Nicola to the door. Jim's shoulders slumped. Nicola shot him a look of sympathy as she handed them over to the secretary. Unbidden, she returned to the board table, wanting to find out what would happen next.

'So, the ball's in their court,' Andrew said. He laughed and sat back in satisfaction. 'I doubt they can come up with anything. Yes, do you want to clear up?' He spoke to Nicola without looking at her and began to collect up the coffee cups. 'Given the church's involvement, a counter claim could mean big money. Max might like it. He could spin it as fighting the forces of reaction.' Andrew rubbed his hands together in gleeful anticipation. 'And it won't do my reputation any harm if I bring down a campaigner like Tanya Towers. Oh yes, they'll regret that they ever got into this.'

Nicola looked at him, horrified. It would mean humiliation for the Reverend and the villagers. She sat down at the table, placing her hands in front of her. Nicola didn't speak immediately, though she had been planning what she might say during the meeting. Now she had made up her mind.

'You seem to think that that went well?'

Andrew looked baffled by her question and her manner. 'Yes, of course, now...' He stood, but Nicola remained where she was, sitting at the table.

'I think you might want to hear what I have to say....'

*

'So why'd they back down?' Bill Ford was intrigued.

The text from Nicola had been a pleasant surprise and he readily agreed to meet her at a coffee shop in town. Even more surprising, and equally as gratifying, was the full page apology that appeared on the draft front page of The Herald which she had just handed him. 'I didn't expect Lovejoy to capitulate so easily. There has to be more to this than meets the eye.'

'Billy, we go back a long way, don't we?' Nicola played with a sachet of sugar as she looked at him. 'Long before I married Mo.'

'Schooldays, yeah. But...?'

'So I trust you not to tell anyone what I'm about to tell you.'

'Okay.' The plot thickened.

'What was my name when we were at school?'

'Nicola. Oh!' The policeman smiled, broadly. 'Nicola Piestrak.'

'Exactly.' She looked into her cup. 'Though I've never thought of myself as being half Polish.'

'So you complained? About your own employer?'

'Not right away,' she shook her head. 'I had nothing to do with the original complaint. That was the villagers.'

Bill nodded, he was aware of who had been involved.

'At first, all that reporting over the Summer seemed like the usual *Herald* Little Englander rubbish,' Nicola continued. 'My in-laws remember what sort of atmosphere that created years ago. No one ever challenged it. Then you turned up to speak to Max about the villagers' complaint and I thought 'At last, someone's doing something!' It didn't occur to me that I could complain.'

'But Nicky, what about your job? It'll be impossible to work there after this, even if they'd let you.' Bill leaned forward, concerned.

'Well, Mo and I have been planning to start a family for some time,' Nicola smiled. 'He got the promotion and it seemed like the right time. Then I saw Andrew Wells salivating at the thought of humiliating the vicar and the others. I couldn't let that happen.'

'He got the job then, that's great!' Bill was pleased, but was still worried about Nicola's future. How would she get another job? 'What about references for you, you'll be wanting to go back to work at some point?'

'The chairman's given me a glowing report and says that I can refer any prospective employer to him,' Nicola grinned shyly. 'And I've already got another job. It's less money, but I'll be writing, for a regional press blog and I can work from home.'

Bill was open mouthed.

'And Lovejoy...?'

'Max is still spitting blood, but as far as the board's concerned, the problem's gone away, so that's that. Some of them quite liked seeing Max eat humble pie. And after the way he tried to use me, I've no sympathy for him. Though he doesn't know it was me yet. The chairman told Andrew Wells to keep that quiet until after I'd gone.'

'Do the villagers know about your intervention? The Reverend and the others?'

'No and I'm not going to tell them. They did what was right. What someone should have done a long time ago. Let them have the credit. Justice has been done. She might wear a blindfold, but there's nothing wrong with her hearing. Oh, and the board made a private ex gratia payment, towards the church re-roofing fund.'

'Nicky, that's amazing! Nemesis, as well as justice. What does Mo think about it all?'

'Mo thinks it's amazing too.' She twinkled with pleasure. 'You must come round, he'd really like to see you. May be we can fix you up with somebody, especially now that you're famous.'

Bill's face contorted. The last thing he wanted was his friend organising his love life. 'Oh no, you don't, I've had enough unsolicited attention. But it'd be good to see Mo.'

'Right, so what about next Saturday night?'

*

So something of a reunion dinner took place at the Shahs on the following Saturday.

That same evening, in The Lion, another celebration took place. Villagers met in the snug, to conclude their brief flirtation with the law. There was quite a lot of rubbing of hands and being certain after the fact. Jim felt obliged to counsel reconciliation and humility, until someone pointed out that the only financial benefit from the whole case had, in fact, gone to the church.

In both locations, and with varying degrees of inebriation involved, a toast was raised in honour of the fourth estate.

12.

In the salon

On a wet Wednesday afternoon a darkening sky suggested more rain to come. The blue neon scissors sign above the salon window glowed brighter in the murk and car headlights dazzled as vehicles swished past. Within, all was light and warmth, a damp fug of smells natural and chemical. The local radio station sounded above the driers' constant thrum and the buzz of chatter.

Chatter, news and gossip, Jane King reflected, listening to the babble of voices as she sat in a styling chair, a damp towel about her shoulders. The common currency of the salon. No reputation is safe and everyone's fair game for speculation.

There was always something worthy of discussion, it was an article of faith with the Salon's staff and clientele, to provide distraction and entertainment for an hour on a dull afternoon.

'So I said "That's all very well, but I'm the one doing all the work".' Robert stopped, elegant long hands poised and scissors open above Jane's wet curls. 'You did say take off more? That will be much shorter, you know? You are sure?'

'I did. Don't worry Robert, that'll be fine.'

Jane studied her reflection in the large mirror before her. She saw a not unattractive woman, but one beginning to look decidedly middle aged. Jane wanted a change, she felt herself stagnating. She glanced down at the dark whorls that had already fallen like long question marks about their feet and smiled at Robert in the mirror. 'So what's going to happen to the salon?'

'I'm not sure.' Robert's scissors flashed and clicked. 'She's thinking about it. To be honest I don't care how long she takes to make a decision, as long as I get to buy it.'

Beth Castle, whom Jane had not seen since the summer, was considering selling the salon. Their paths were unlikely to cross now, since the Castles had sold their house and moved closer to Scott's work in town. When first the couple arrived in the village they had seemed a welcome addition to village society, being young, energetic and clever, but events at the Summer Fete had shown them to be highly unsatisfactory. Indeed, if it wasn't for Robert's popularity, Beth's salon might already have gone out of business, so pronounced had been the village's reaction to events at the Summer Fete.

The shop bell jangled and cold, damp wind gusted in with the latest customer. Carol Pendleton nodded in greeting to Jane and the others as she hung her sodden mackintosh on the coat stand.

Robert called out. 'Ellen, could you shampoo please.'

Ellen Fisher, his apprentice, ushered the new arrival towards the wash basins.

Robert turned back to Jane. 'Now, I hear that our latest arrival in the village, Mrs Wells, is having a lot of renovations done over at her new place.'

This wasn't news to Jane, who regularly took coffee with Diane Wells and knew that she had received a substantial, though as yet partial, divorce settlement, following the sale of the former marital home. This had funded both the purchase of the Castles' old house and the changes to it.

'I don't think Diane shares the previous owners' taste,' Jane suggested.

'I always rather liked it myself,' Robert smirked as he combed Jane's hair this way and that. 'Victorian bordello meets The Hamptons. No doubt, Diane will want to put her own stamp on things. Though I confess I was surprised when I heard that she was moving here.'

Jane didn't respond. It was common knowledge that Diane's husband had deceived her, in cruel fashion, with a village woman.

'I suppose it's more convenient for her work, being only five minutes from the school,' Robert said. 'And I heard that

Yvonne and Steve Young are moving too, going back to Norfolk.'

This was news to almost everyone. Glances were exchanged and lips were pursed. When were they moving? Had the Youngs put their house on the market? What about their children, weren't they at Priory Road School?

Robert spent several minutes confirming what details he knew, then had to do it all again for those clients who, seeing the hiatus, had emerged from beneath the hairdryers. Robert pressed on.

'I heard that Diane Wells met Yvonne Young at a country pub to discuss the situation.' Robert continued.

The salon gave a collective gasp.

'The wife and the mistress out together…?'

'I'll bet Wells was furious.'

Robert was exceptionally well-informed, for Jane knew this to be true. Diane had told her how she had grown weary of her husband's falsehoods, so she had telephoned Yvonne Young. She and Yvonne subsequently spent an evening checking what each had been told by Andrew. Both had discovered discrepancies in his stories.

'Yes, Diane's had a tough time and she's turned things around,' said Robert. 'Though,' he adding with a twinkle, "she's got Ray Marshall round at her place all hours, I'm told.'

Jane smiled. Robert could never resist the taste of gossip, even about a potential new customer. She tried to deflect any suggestion of misbehaviour. 'Isn't Ray doing a lot of the alterations work?'

This only played into Robert's hands. He cocked his head to one side and raised an eyebrow. 'Yes, hard at it all through the night, I'll be bound – giving comfort to the deserted wife.'

The salon was amused. One of the pleasures afforded its regular clientele was Robert's salacious embroidery of local gossip. He seemed to hear everything and exercised his wicked sense of humour at the expense of the foolish or indiscreet.

Jane studied her magazine with pointed detachment. She would mention this to Diane. There was nothing untoward afoot, she was certain, for Diane had only recently begun to achieve a state approximating to normality and Ray was a devoted family man, but matters could be misinterpreted.

First impressions were so important, especially in a small village. Diane shouldn't start on the wrong foot. And the Marshalls wouldn't want to be the subject of such speculation either. After all, who knew what went on within a marriage? How many devoted family men turned out not to be that devoted at all, when the wife finally found out?

Indeed, how did one really know with any certainty?

She and Gus had been married for over thirty years, but money and power were strong aphrodisiacs and Gus had plenty of both. Over Summer Jane had wondered, briefly, about Hari Mistry. Gus had been seeing a lot of her at committee meetings and Jane felt that something was awry. He didn't usually keep things from her, yet he had only told her about the Castles and what they had done once it was out in the open. Jane had set aside her suspicion as demeaning. She decided to do so again.

Robert teased out several side strands of Jane's hair, checking for length.

'There, I think that's that. Ellen, can you dry for me please?' Ellen unwound the dryer's flex and positioned herself behind Jane, taking Robert's place.

'Usual Mrs P?' Robert asked, as he moved on to his next customer.

'Yes please Robert, just a trim.' Carol responded, putting down a glossy magazine.

Robert combed and snipped. He looked back at Jane, as she was being dried, and considered, then launched another topic of interest.

'Anyway, did you hear about Max Lovejoy? Our esteemed local newspaper editor got thrown out of Willow Meads country club the other evening?'

This rich new seam of scandal was mined for some time. Speculation over what prompted the argument between Max and Gus King, which eventually got out of hand, provided entertainment for what remained of the afternoon. There was much faulty recollection of events at the Summer Fete earlier in the year and Jane protested that it was all a storm in a teacup, but this didn't prevent the habitués of the salon from dissecting all the known evidence (and some that was not) in attempts to learn more.

More than ready now to leave, Jane punched numbers into the card reader at the front desk. A disembodied voice floated towards her on the froth of sound.

'If this Mrs Wells is a home wrecker, she won't find a welcome in our village!'

Anxious to hear no more, Jane ventured out into what had become a wild November evening, her carefully constructed coiffure destined for immediate demolition.

*

Back inside, Robert's final customer of the day had been seated beneath a hairdryer for almost an hour. Winnie Fortune's newly darkened curls retained their stiffness even after the rollers were removed. Once a week she availed herself of Robert's half-price pensioners' discount and was accustomed to making way for those paying the full price, waiting until Robert or Ellen had a moment to spare. She liked to listen to the talk.

'Well, Winnie, how'd you want me to dress it?' Robert asked solicitously (he often forgot that she was there). She crossed to the mirrors and settled into a styling chair as Ellen bought her a cup of tea.

'Off the forehead, please Robert, a widow's peak,' Winnie took a sip. 'And,' she lowered her voice, 'you can tell me more about what's going on at Mrs Wells's house.'

*

Jane hadn't been prepared for the scale of the work at Diane's new home. The whole of the ground floor was being remodelled, so the two women were banished to the chilly conservatory, where a gas heater on maximum was misting up the glass.

'Ray's doing a terrific job, don't you think?' Diane cradled her warm coffee cup and wrapped her cardigan closer about her.

'I'm amazed at how much he's done,' said Jane. 'Isn't it rather expensive?'

'He's very reasonably priced.'

Since her divorce, Diane seemed much more aware of the cost of things, Jane had noticed and just how far money would stretch. She supposed that Diane's school teacher's salary wouldn't support the lifestyle to which she had been accustomed, so retrenchment would have to begin. There was no evidence of it as yet.

'We've found some interesting relics down in the cellar,' said Diane, as she crossed to a cupboard. 'Look.'

She drew out a laden tray with a flourish. On it sat a collection of small items, rusted metal implements and clouded opaline phials. 'This house was once a doctor's surgery. I wonder what some of these were used for?' She examined a hooked instrument and some leather strapping. 'This looks decidedly unpleasant.'

'Vicious and nasty,' said Jane. 'Somewhat like the house's previous owners.'

Diane began to laugh.

'Beth Castle may be selling her salon, you know.' Jane added, thankful fr the opening. 'That place is a real rumour mill, it's surprising what you hear there.'

'I don't doubt it,' Diane replied. She looked closely at her friend. 'That sounds like you're leading up to something?'

'Yes.' Jane inhaled deeply. 'Look, I know you've taught at Priory Road for years, but you've only recently moved to live in the village. And you know what this place is like. You're a source of interest and gossip to people here, especially given the circumstances. People are curious about you.'

'Mmm.'

'So, you need to consider how things might appear. How they might be interpreted by a mischievous mind.'

'You have something specific in mind?'

'All I'm saying is that sometimes having an eye to village gossip could save a lot of unpleasantness. There are rumours that you and Ray....that he's been spending nights here.'

'That's ridiculous!' Diane gave a mirthless laugh. 'Do people really say that? I'm mortified.'

Jane knew that Diane was especially sensitive to what people might be saying about her. Diane had imagined that Andrew's affair had been widely discussed behind her back, because she had been the last to know. This latest episode was an unpleasant reminder of her previous situation.

Leaping to her feet, Diane marched around the conservatory, gesticulating as she spoke. 'And Ray's hardly my type. A lovely man, no doubt and a fine human being but, I ask you — a builder!'

'Okay...' Jane also knew her friend to be acutely aware of social status, especially given her new circumstances. 'But few people here know you, other than as a school teacher.

They see a newly divorced woman – I know it was no fault of yours, but scandal breeds suspicion - with plenty of money and a will to spend it and Ray round here at all hours.'

'It's absurd! Ray's a happily married man with a young family and the whole village knows it.'

'Yes, but the village also loves its gossip.'

Diane checked. Jane heard the wall clock ticking as she watched her friend sit. Finally Diane grew calmer. 'For what do we live, but to make sport for our neighbours,' she said.

'Something like that.' Jane was relieved that the heat had gone out of the exchange. 'But it can't make Lynda Marshall feel any better. Gossip can be so destructive.'

'You're right. I know what that's like, being cast as the poor deluded spouse.' Diane frowned, then looked up. 'And Ray is going to have to work some more long days if he's to finish all this on time.'

'Which will only add fuel to the flames.'

'I know. There must be some way to squash it, but I really don't want to make matters worse by giving this thing credence. Let me think about it a while.'

With some misgivings, for it had not been her intention to provoke this reaction, Jane allowed the conversation to meander elsewhere.

*

'Mother, for the last time, will you shut up about Diane Wells!' Lynda banged the mugs down on the worktop, almost knocking over the sugar.

Lynda wasn't having a good Friday. Winnie had accompanied her to do the weekly shop and had been asking peculiar questions all day. In the car, pushing the supermarket trolley, Winnie had been like a dog worrying a bone. Now Lynda had had enough of her nonsense. With fierce, unwarranted concentration she filled the kettle and reached for the tea caddy. 'If I've told you once I've told you a dozen times, Ray is just doing some work for her!'

'By staying overnight?' Winnie persisted.

'He didn't stay overnight, he was just working late, that's all.'

'It's all over the village! And...' Winnie's chin jutted upwards as she delivered her coup de grace. 'It was discussed in the salon!'

'Oh, well, it must be true then.'

She slammed to the cupboard door, muttering under her breath.

'What did you say?' Winnie asked, pugnaciously.

Lynda glanced at her mother. 'I said Robert Santini is an incorrigible gossip. One of these days he'll go too far.'

'As if you haven't enjoyed his stories. You've laughed at other people, so you can't complain when it's you.' Winnie countered, her voice and intonation rising. 'But everybody seems to be talking about it.'

'If it's being talked about in the salon, everyone's heard it.' Lynda looked at Winnie sternly as she stirred the pot. 'Though it isn't me who gossips so enthusiastically with anyone who'll listen. I don't tittle-tattle There's more than one person in this village who'll see this as poetic justice, the biter being bit. That means you, Mother.'

Winnie and her cohorts (a group sometimes referred to as 'the coven' by people who ought to know better) were great blame-placers and vigorous condemners. Now her family's reputation would be tarnished at least until a suitably interesting explanation was widely disseminated, even if it wasn't entirely believed. She scowled at Lynda.

'You're just going to have to grin and bear it,' Lynda continued. 'Diane Wells is still picking up the pieces of her life, she's trying to start afresh. We ought to welcome her, not jump to conclusions and condemn.'

Winnie wouldn't yield. 'She's not denied the stories and she must have heard them by now. That might ease her way, but it won't do her reputation any good in the long term.'

'Only if people believe such stuff.' Lynda pushed her mug away. 'Look, I must go, I've to pick up Daisy after netball and I don't want her to start walking back in this weather.' The kitchen window panes were streaked with rivulets of water. 'It's pouring. Paul's due back soon from Stewie's and he'll be soaked. Make him dry himself properly when he comes in, especially his hair?'

Winnie gave a curt nod and poured more tea.

*

The rain was almost horizontal as Lynda drove out to Furzedown, peering through a windscreen barely cleared by the wipers. No-one was waiting at the school gates, for which she gave a silent prayer of thanks. She drew up to the visitors parking bays in front of the main school entrance. She turned off the engine and sat in the rain-pounded car.

'It's nonsense,' she told herself. 'Of course it's nonsense. I'm just being silly. Ray's simply feeling sorry for the woman.' She rested her arms on the steering wheel, flexing her tight shoulder muscles. She had been feeling tense and tired since she'd started working four days a week and she knew she was letting this get her down more than she ought to. 'It's just people being petty and Ray not thinking what others might make of things. He'd never do anything to harm this family and everybody knows that.'

There was no sign of Daisy under the wide porch, so she dashed across into the building. Inside a group of mothers were waiting for their respective daughters in the foyer, by the racks of coat hooks. Lynda recognised a number of faces and nodded a greeting.

'Aren't they finished yet?' she asked. 'I've been rushing, thinking I'd be late.'

'They're the late ones.' A woman looked at her watch.

Lynda craned to look over the coat hooks, down the wide corridor that flanked the assembly hall, towards the girls changing rooms. Gradually she became aware that she was the object of the others' attention. She heard her name amidst whispered mutterings and the repeated sibilant sound of 'Wells'. When she looked across faces were turned away.

She felt a rosy flush rising from her collar bone and her lips compressed. She had a good idea what they were talking about. Damned gossip. Damned salon.

"Ah, here they come.' A woman gestured towards a gaggle of approaching girls. 'Finally.'

Lynda saw Daisy's blonde hair amongst the little group. 'Come on,' she called. Lynda hustled her daughter through the gossips towards the exit. Her temper wasn't improved by the dowsing they received as they ran for the shelter of the car. Lynda zapped the door locks and they fell into the front seats.

'What's up Mum?' Daisy asked, stroking back her wet hair.

'Nothing love. It's just people being stupid.'

Daisy glanced sidelong at her mother, her face pinched and serious. Then she asked: 'What's for tea?'

*

The Lion was always full on a Friday night and Lynda zigzagged through the drinkers into the snug.

'Excuse me. Sorry. Thank you. Excuse me.'

She glimpsed Ray and Vince Luck seated in an alcove beyond the huge chimney breast, where a wood fire crackled and spat. Ray looked irritated and Vince was grinning, wolfishly. Lynda felt a spurt of compassion for her husband.

'So you didn't stay the night then?' She overheard Vince asking, in faux innocence as she inched through the crowd.

'No, I bloody didn't!'

'All right, calm down,' Vince soothed. 'Everybody's talking about it. People say that there's no smoke without fire, you know how it is.'

'It's spiteful gossip,' Ray was now huddled over his pint, looking hunted. 'What am I supposed to do? I can't just abandon the work, there's good money involved.'

Lynda stayed back, behind the chimney. They still hadn't seen her.

'Cheer up, mate,' Vince chivvied. Then he added, in a voice full of mischief. 'There are blokes who would be pleased to be thought capable of keeping two women happy...'

'Well, I'm not one of them!' Ray slammed his glass down on the table.

Lynda thought it an opportune moment to reveal her presence.

'Okay, okay.' Vince raised his hands in mock defence. 'Oh, er... look, it's your missus.' He stood, in ungainly fashion, as Lynda joined them. 'Hello, Lynda, let me get you a drink. Gin and tonic isn't it?' He scuttled off to the bar.

'Hello love.' Lynda settled on the bench seat next to Ray, giving him a peck on the cheek. 'I thought I'd best come and tell you, they've changed the time the coach leaves tomorrow. Paul's got to be at the school by eight o'clock.' It was the school trip to the England game at Wembley.

'Okay. I'm picking up Stewie too, on the way, so Paul better be ready to leave by half past seven.'

'And....' Lynda hesitated. She felt low. The episode at the school had upset her more than she had realised. She looked at Ray, wanting some reassurance. 'It's getting me down Ray, all this. When I went to collect Daisy I got some very funny looks from the other mothers at Furzedown. People are sniggering behind my back.'

Ray put his arm around her and massaged her shoulder. 'I know my love. I get it too, though it's worse for you. I don't know what to do about it?'

'Ray?'

'Mmmm.'

'There really isn't anything to it, is there? I mean... between you and Diane?'

'Of course there isn't.' Ray pulled back to look his wife squarely in the face. 'I swear there isn't. You know there isn't.'

'I do.' Lynda cast her eyes down. 'It's just, everybody...'

'Is talking a load of bollocks! Oh, thanks Vince.'

Vince returned and placed three drinks down on the table. He pulled up a stool.

'Looks like it's still pouring down.' He nodded towards recent arrivals with dripping umbrellas, shaking themselves like wet dogs. 'Ray, d'you know when you'll be finished at Diane Wells's place? Only I've a leak over at the Park House. It needs repairing before the rain makes it worse.'

'I promised I'd finish by Wednesday, though I don't know how I'm going to manage that. I could pop over and take a look tomorrow, if you like, see what needs doing?'

'Okay, what time?'

'About nine? I've got to put our Paul on to the coach to London at eight.'

'He's off to Wembley isn't he?' A look of fond remembrance crept over Vince's face. 'I remember going, when I was a kid.'

'So you'll be working late again next week?' Lynda asked.

'Yes, sorry love, I'm supposed to finish by mid-week. I might... I might have to do an all-nighter, to get it all done.'

Lynda stifled a retort. It wasn't Ray's fault. She shot a glare in Vince's direction, daring him to comment, but his eyes were fixed, unwavering, on the hunting print hung on the wall behind her.

*

'Morning!'

'Hello Ray,' Diane called, as she heard the front door open. It was Tuesday morning. 'Would you like a coffee?'

She poked her head around the door into the hall. At the foot of the stairs Ray was divesting himself of various tools and boxes, placing them on the plastic sheeting that covered the floor.

'No thanks, Mrs Wells, I'd like to get going straight away. Last day today – it's likely to be a long one.'

Diane entered the hall, still holding the coffee jar. Since when had he become so formal?

'Mrs Wells?' She said, her eyes narrowing.

Ray smiled, but she could see he was uncomfortable. He said nothing. Diane realised that it would be up to her to ease things along.

'I guess you've heard the rumours,' she began, in a matter-of-fact voice. 'So have I. It's amazing what people can concoct in little communities like this one. As if folk don't have enough to fill their days.'

Ray relaxed a little. 'Half of them don't, that's the trouble. I will have that coffee, after all, if you don't mind.'

'Good.'

Ray followed her through to the kitchen and Diane busied herself with kettle and crockery. Her briefcase lay ready for school and she set down a steaming mug next to it on the table.

'It's all nonsense,' she said. 'People will forget it as soon as they have something else to talk about.'

'Yes, but it's not pleasant, especially for my wife. Even Lynda's having her doubts....'

'No! Surely not.' But, all the same, Diane wondered what Lynda Marshall must be thinking.

'Lynda thinks she's being talked about everywhere she goes in the village and she's probably right,' Ray went on. 'People love to gossip.'

Of course. Diane nodded, her face grim.

'I hadn't noticed anything myself. But then, they're unlikely to gossip in front of me.'

'I feel so powerless – anything I do just makes it worse.' Ray's shoulders drooped, his forehead creased as he drew his brows together. He looked a picture of misery.

Diane felt so sorry for him. Such an honourable and honest man, brought low by the petty minded and thoughtless.

'It'll pass. Look, don't you worry,' she said, reaching over to give him a hug. 'Oh!'

Lynda Marshall was standing, her posture still and intense, in the kitchen doorway.

Diane dropped her arms and stepped away from Ray. She tried, desperately, to think of how she could explain.

'You forgot your sandwiches, Ray.' Lynda walked up to the table and deposited a plastic lunchbox on it. 'As well as your marriage vows, it seems.'

'No, no, no, no, no, no!' Diane hurried to block Lynda's exit. 'It's not at all what it seems. Really!'

Lynda hesitated.

'It's true, love,' Ray said, quietly. 'She was just being kind.'

Diane looked Lynda in the eye.

'That's right! I have absolutely no interest in your husband in that way. None!'

Diane watched suspicion, doubt and hopefulness pass across Lynda's countenance. She knew how Lynda must feel and made common cause with her.

'I've had my fill of being whispered about, I know what it's like. All I want to do now is start again on my own.' She briefly paused for breath. 'Ray told me how miserable all this talk was making him... because you doubted him.'

Ray started to speak, but stopped as Diane continued. 'He looked so... hang dog... It was just a hug.'

Lynda looked at Ray.

'We've been through all this,' he said, his eyes tired. 'It's a load of rubbish.'

'But...'

Ray shook his head. 'She was just being kind.'

Lynda's stance softened, the tension left her.

'It looked...'

'Yes, I can understand how it looked.' Diane exhaled, forcibly. The crisis had been averted. 'Given the rumours.'

'Which seem to be following me around like my own tail.' Lynda looked exhausted.

'Come here.' Ray opened his arms and Lynda settled into his embrace.

Diane pulled on her waxed jacket. 'Lynda, please feel free to stay for as long as you want, to be reassured. But I'm afraid I have to go.' She picked up her briefcase. 'I'm probably already late for Assembly. But let me say, for the avoidance of doubt, that there is nothing – I repeat, nothing – going on between myself and your husband.'

With that she made her exit, hoping that the couple would kiss and make up, but not take too long about it, for there was still a lot of work to be done on the house.

*

The following afternoon the shop-bell jangled and Diane entered the salon. The events of previous day had convinced her that the issue must be addressed. It was time to go to the source of the trouble.

'Good afternoon, how can I help you?' Robert came forward, his long body slightly inclined towards the unknown newcomer.

Diane saw him notice her expensive mackintosh, her well-preserved skin and her Italian leather handbag. Evidently a man of some discernment, she inferred, if only in material things.

'Hello, I wonder if you could fit me in for a cut and blow dry?' Diane asked.

'Oh, yes, I think so,' Robert dried his hands on a fluffy towel. 'Now?'

'If you have time?'

'Certainly.' Robert turned to a fair-haired girl who was sweeping the salon floor. 'Ellen, we're out of sparkling mineral water. Could you go to Piestrak's and get some, just to be going on with, please.'

Ellen plucked her pink mackintosh and umbrella from the coat stand and the bell sounded again as the door closed behind her.

'Please.' Robert was already eyeing Diane's light brown shoulder-length bob as he ushered her to a chair beside the mirrors. 'How would you like it cut? As before or something different?'

'Keep the general shape, please. But I'd like a change too, I was thinking of a fringe.'

'Yes, I think that would work.' Robert ran his hands through her hair. 'Come over to the basins please.'

He swathed her shoulders in a towel and, when she was seated, tipped her backwards until all she could see was the ceiling spotlights.

'Is that too hot?' Robert's voice was solicitous, as he ran the water.

'No that's fine,' Diane replied.

'I don't think I've seen you here before?' Robert's strong fingers expertly massaged her skull. 'Are you from the village?'

'No, not until recently. But I understand that the salon is at its heart, the place to hear about everything.'

Robert didn't reply. Diane felt water gushing over her head. Once it stopped the hum of the driers was all she could hear. There was no longer a buzz of talk and someone had silenced the radio.

He doesn't know who I am, Diane thought. But others in here do.

She felt a tension in the air.

'We're right at the heart of the village, it's true,' Robert's voice intruded on her thoughts. 'Who told you about us?'

'A friend of mine, Jane King.'

'Ah, Jane, yes.'

The water stopped flowing. Diane sat up. Robert patted her damp hair dry with the towel and pulled it up into a turban.

'If you'd come over to the mirrors, please?' With a graceful gesture Robert indicated a chair.

Diane noticed him glance around the salon, smiling. But eyes were averted into the pages of magazines or the screens of mobile phones.

Not the response he expected.

Diane sat in the proferred seat and watched Robert in the looking glass, through her bedraggled hair. He seemed uncomfortable, glancing at his other customers, perhaps sensing that something was awry, as he combed through her hair.

The shop bell sounded and the cold swept in with the returning Ellen, who fought with her tangled brolly. She deposited two large bottles of water on the counter and began to remove her dripping coat.

'You'll never guess what I've heard,' she began. 'Ray Marshall was over at Diane Wells's house until the early hours of this morning.'

This set the salon aflutter, as its clientele conferred in low tones. Heads were shaken and there was a general murmuring of disapproval, not the expected, avid interest. Ellen looked perplexed. Diane hid a smile. It was an ideal opportunity to intervene.

'Ray was there until about midnight, actually.' Diane looked around at a succession of stunned faces. She waited, allowing silence to fall (Robert's latest customer was slow to catch on), before continuing. 'He worked really hard to finish on time.'

One of the water bottles on the counter crashed to the floor, the plastic bouncing as it rolled beneath the dryer chairs. Ellen bent to retrieve the bottle as Diane continued.

'Lynda, Ray's wife, came to collect him, he was so tired. You know Lynda Marshall, of course, I believe she's a regular customer here too?'

'She is, yes.' Robert gave a weak smile, affecting nonchalance.

Meanwhile Ellen was staring at Diane open-mouthed and eyes wide.

Like one of those small rodents one sees on wildlife documentaries, thought Diane. Waiting for the scorpion to strike.

'I thought it prudent to invite her round for dinner last night,' Diane skewered Ellen with withering school teacher's condescension. 'I think, young lady, that you have been putting two and two together to make five. Though not without encouragement, I'm aware, from people who ought to know better.' She glanced at the man standing over her.

Robert's Adam's apple agitated violently. He looked sidelong at Diane, striking a wounded attitude. 'Mmm,' was all he said and focussed on cutting her hair, scissors clicking.

The radio blared back into life and clients turned to one another to resume their earlier conversations. The tension eased.

Robert continued to cut in silence. Finally, he asked: 'How would you like me to dress the front?'

'A wispy fringe, please. Not too long. I like to be able to see things clearly.'

Robert cut the hair falling over her brow.

'It was only harmless gossip.' He said.

'It was my reputation.'

'You didn't like the role of femme fatale?' Robert tilted his head and looked at Diane in the mirror through half closed eyes.

Diane pursed her lips, to strangle a smile.

Robert began to wield the hand dryer on full blast, precluding any further conversation and, for a while, the business of the salon proceeded. Diane was dried and styled and, eventually, made ready to depart.

Standing at the counter, she handed over her card. 'Thank you,' she said, admiring her new hairstyle in the looking glass over the desk at which Robert was sitting. 'You've created a new me.'

'Oh, I wouldn't say that,' Robert presented the machine to her, with a wry grin and a sparkle in his eye. 'I think you've had just as much to do with it. Shall we be seeing you again?'

'Yes, though I'll make an appointment next time.' Diane delivered her parting shot. 'How else would I get all the village gossip?'

He watched her go out into the blustery dusk, then turned back to the salon.

There was a cough from beneath one of the driers.

'Alright there, Winnie?' Robert checked the timer. 'Won't be too much longer now.'

13.

Accident and Emergency

Frosty leaves crunched under foot as he made his way up Wyven Top, watched by curious, if curiously untroubled, woodland creatures. The recent changes in his outward appearance meant nothing to them. He was no longer grey-skinned, for the newspaper girl, Nicola, had insisted that he wash and he found that he now did so with regularity.

His hair was close cut, his shiny black overcoat had been replaced by a fleece-lined, long waxed jacket and he wore a hat made of leather. The meagre income from his writing, first for The Herald and then for various nature blogs, allowed him to rent a room for the winter in a house beside the churchyard, so he no longer dwelt among the untrodden ways. Yet every day Sid Calley, Nature Correspondent, for that was his chosen by-line, walked the countryside as he had always done, only now he could call it research.

Wyven Top was the highest point in Calley Wood, with panoramic views. The horizon was brown and spiky, life having retreated beneath soil and bark. Regeneration would begin in earnest after the solstice, but, for now, the land lay quiet. A shuddering boom drew Sid's attention eastwards, towards the by-pass.

Several vehicles were skewed off the road. As he watched, the engine of an overturned double tanker burst into flames. But the fire didn't grow, it drew back into itself. Birds rose, shrieking, from fields and trees and headed towards the Top, as a pale mist formed around the accident site. Sid's instinct was to offer assistance, but he didn't move. The day was still, but the dense vapour flowed into the rills and hollows close to the road. Sid sniffed the clear air of the Top. There was a westerly wind coming, but not yet. What was the unnatural looking rolling mist? He turned through half a circle and looked down at Furzedown School.

There were children out on the playing fields, though it was still too early for the mid-morning break. If the mist kept moving at its current rate, without the wind to disperse it, it would soon reach the school. He had to warn them. Sid reached for his mobile and, as he spoke, the birds settled in the bare trees around him. Snapping shut his phone he strode west, down towards the forest's edge.

*

In the village's single squad car PC Ford received a call from HQ and took a deep breath. Already a team had been despatched to the by-pass, to identify and, if possible, contain, the spillage and Furzedown and St Jerome's schools were being informed. The policeman turned the squad car around to return to the two roomed police station on the green. He would have to activate civil emergency plans and evacuate the village.

He only wished they had tested the plans sooner.

*

Out on the football pitch Paul Marshall and his teammates cheered as the ball slid between the opposing goalie's legs. Surely this meant victory, for the games lesson was almost over. As the cheers subsided he heard other shouts. Beyond the fields, up on the edge of Calley Wood, a man stood, waving and shouting. Paul and his teammates stopped to look. The man was waving his arms, signalling towards the school.

'What's the matter with him, Sir?' Paul asked the referee.

'I'm not sure,' the games teacher replied. 'He seems to be urging us to go inside.' He looked at his watch. 'It's time, anyway.' He gave two loud blasts on his whistle and indicated that the game was over. Boys gathered into groups as they trudged back towards the school.

'He's jumping up and down now,' Paul said.

The man was gesticulating more wildly, shouting and waving towards the school, pointing to the foot of the playing field.

Then Paul noticed.

The stream at the edge of the playing fields was shrouded in white mist.

'Sir! Sir!' Paul yelled, but the referee was now far ahead, almost back at the school and out of hearing. Behind Paul kids were still out on the pitch, enjoying their stolen moments, having a kick-about. Oblivious to the mist.

'Hey! Come in! Get out of there!' Against all his instincts, Paul gritted his teeth and ran towards the boys and the mist, as the encroaching cloud crept forward.

*

On the other side of the village, Sylvia Luck waited, impatiently, at the kerb outside her house, canvas shopping trolley at the ready. Her heavy gabardine was buttoned up to the neck and she wore a woollen scarf around her neck to ward off the cold. She checked her watch again.

Vince was supposed to collect her and take her to the supermarket. He was very late. Sylvia missed her grandson, Matt and their thrilling rides on his motor bike, but Matt had been away at university since the Autumn. She had to admit, the teenager had been more reliable than his uncle. Sylvia tried Vince's mobile number again, but there was still no reply. With a sigh she resigned herself to having to catch the bus and began the walk along Cowslip Lane, pulling her shopping trolley behind her.

*

In a large-windowed room, on a campus outside a city, Susan Pendleton tried to contact her parents, Leonard and Carol, but there was no reply from The Lion. She'd tried their mobiles too, but there was no service. Valentina wasn't replying either. She switched from news channel to news channel on her laptop. She'd been told that her village had featured, briefly, on the TV at midday. This all suggested disaster to Susan.

Susan had stayed in touch with Greg since their meeting last August. Now she dialled the number of his press agency. She knew that Greg was abroad, beyond the reach of a mobile signal, but someone there might remember her and be able to give her some information.

'Hello, Sagittarius Press.'

'Oh hi, could you put me through to...' she flicked through her paper diary. 'Zoe Black, please.' This was the young reporter who had accompanied Greg to the village. 'Hi Zoe. I don't know if you recall meeting me? I'm Greg Layton's daughter.'

'Susan, yes of course. What can I do for you, Greg's in...'

'Pakistan, I know. I wondered if you could do me a favour? I was told that my village was on the news and now I can't get hold of my parents, or anyone else I know there. Can you check the news feeds for me? I'm at my wits end.'

'Sure. Hold on.'

Susan heard indistinct voices.

'The only thing on the wire is an accident nearby, a pile-up on the bypass. No further details, I'm afraid.'

'Okay, thanks. That doesn't explain why my parents' phones aren't working. Unless they're involved....' Susan suddenly felt faint.

'The networks could be down,' Zoe suggested. 'Too many people trying to call.'

'Yes, of course, that'll be it.' Susan exhaled in relief, but her anxiety remained. 'Thanks Zoe. I'll keep looking, 'bye.'

Susan tossed her phone on to the bed and returned to her laptop.

*

'Prep for theatre, please.'

The white-coated Dr Hari Mistry directed the porters to wheel the bloodied body onwards, out of the Accident and Emergency reception. In the white tiled room, rows of seated patients, some coughing, some weeping, waited to be seen by a doctor. Most were children, which was why Hari was there. She raised her voice above the general mayhem of competing sound as she addressed a dishevelled man wearing a fabric sling. 'Would you sit over there, please, Sir, someone will be over to take a look soon.'

Hari hadn't expected there to be such a crowd. She was beginning to feel over-whelmed, as well as frustrated by not knowing exactly what she was dealing with. The authorities didn't know what the gas was, the tanker's markings being unintelligible after the accident. At the back of her mind gnawed the possibility that whatever it was might somehow contaminate the medical staff. As the influx of newcomers ceased, temporarily, Hari was able to turn her attention to individuals.

Within a curtained cubicle a boy sat, spluttering, high upon a trolley. His eyes and nose were streaming mucus. She checked his wrist tag. 'Stewart Fisher, from Furzedown School? You were outside, I understand, when the mist arrived?'

Stewie nodded. 'Blaying football.'

'Okay, now turn around for me and take a deep breath.' Hari applied her stethoscope to the boy's back, just as the curtain was drawn aside. The solid form of Mandeep Dhaliwal was revealed, emergency beeper in hand. He was removing his jacket and putting on a white coat

'What's going on?'

'Major accident on the by-pass. Two fatalities, a number injured, some seriously, you'll be needed in theatre. Also, respiratory trauma from a chemical spill, gaseous, agent as yet unknown, though a public safety hazard indicated.'

'Right.' Mandeep scanned the waiting patients. He turned back to Hari. 'The village is being evacuated. Is there anything you want from your flat, I could ask Amrita to pick it up?'

'No, thanks.' Hari replied. She didn't want Amrita nosing around her flat. 'Though she could check on Molly Morgan.'

Over-hearing their exchange a trolley-wheeling orderly reminded them, 'Molly's here, it's Wednesday.'

Molly had been enjoying her usual cup of tea in Accident and Emergency when the first casualties arrived. She tried to distract and calm the youngest children, who were distressed rather tha physically affected by the mist, by reading stories to them and giving them picture books. Daisy Marshall, who had somehow managed to find her way in, despite being unaffected by the gas, was helping her.

The large room was slowly becoming more and more crowded as further patients arrived. Uniformed teenagers clustered together, their faces pale, while younger children fretted and whimpered, their eyes streaming. Teachers soothed and calmed, plucking out those most badly affected and sending them to the front of the queue. The volume of noise rose, chatter mixed with the sounds of distress.

'We need more help here,' Hari said to the receptionist. 'Get the manager to contact all the other hospitals in the region and call in all the standby staff. We mustn't let these kids become hysterical, they've enough difficulty breathing as it is.'

*

In Calley Wood Sid's breath froze in airy plumes as he clambered over the fallen oak. He'd spent so much time trying to warn the schoolchildren that the mist had almost caught up with him, but the wild things had warned him. He grimaced as he slithered down the tangle of tree roots. He had to find the policeman and tell him that the wind was coming.

It had been the pale-haired boy who had seen him and had run to warn his fellows. The boy who, back in Spring, had found the hare. Sid hoped that he and the others would be all right. But, for now, there was nothing to be done about them. Along the path and over the stile, Sid started off down Priory Road.

*

Hari ran a hand through her hair as she gazed at the crowd. All the chairs in Accident and Emergency were taken, including those bought from elsewhere in the hospital. Now there were people standing against the walls. They needed comfort and support, but Hari took a deep breath and did what she'd been trained for, entering the next cubicle. Daisy was sitting by the trolley's side, holding her supine brother's hand. She didn't let go.

'It's Paul and Daisy isn't it?' Daisy nodded. 'Was your brother outside when the mist arrived, do you know?'

'That's what the others said.'

Hari carried out all the routine checks. Paul's air passages seemed clear enough, if a little clogged, but his breathing was very shallow and his lips had lost colour. She pulled out the stethoscope ear-pieces and spoke to Daisy.

'Okay, now listen. I'm going to take Paul onto one of our emergency wards, just to make sure that he gets enough oxygen, because he isn't breathing well.'

Daisy's eyes grew wide and liquid.

Hari turned away, pulling back the curtains, summoning porters and giving instructions.

'Daisy!' Hari heard a sharp voice calling out from the entrance. 'What are you doing here?" It was Lynda Marshall.

Hari didn't have a chance to explain the situation to Lynda before the woman caught sight of the trolley and its passenger. She saw the colour drain from Lynda's face as she hurried over, weaving between groups of children.

'Mrs Marshall, Lynda,' Hari began while Lynda hugged Daisy. 'It's nothing to worry about. You can come and see him once he's settled.' The trolley disappeared through the swing doors, Lynda looking after it.

'What are you doing here?' she repeated, to her daughter.

'I came to look for Paul,' said Daisy. 'I thought you'd be coming.'

'We could do with some help,' Hari suggested. 'Contacting parents and families. If you're here in a professional capacity?'

'Okay,' Lynda replied. 'I'll talk with the manager and start collecting names and numbers.' She turned to her daughter, 'You...'

Molly appeared at Lynda's shoulder. 'She can stay with me,' she said. 'Help with the little ones.'

Lynda looked reluctant to let Daisy go, but she relinquished her hold and strode over to the reception desk. More trolleys came through, as another ambulance arrived.

'Gangway, mind your backs!'

Hari came forward, yet again, to decide who needed immediate attention and who could wait.

*

Outside the small police station on the green, PC Ford was handing out maps and rosters to the group of uniformed police and support officers who had been detailed to deal with the emergency. All held portable breathing gear. A small phalanx of cars and vans sat in the parking bays at the side of the green.

'Jag, can you and Moira take the outlier roads?' PC Ford gestured towards two PCs from the neighbouring Bridge station. 'They're marked in turquoise. Car Two, the Flowers Estate please, it's green. Car Three, the farms and single dwellings please. In red.'

An ambulance hurtled past, siren wailing. It was heading to The Elms, in answer to an emergency call. Behind it, coming along much more slowly, was a wooden-framed estate car with a fluted metal tannoy trumpet attached to its roof.

'Hey, Bill where'd you dig that up from?' Jag asked, his eyebrows raised. 'It looks like something out of a museum.'

'World War II model,' his colleague added.

'As long as it gets the message out, I don't care what it looks like,' PC Ford replied. He spoke to the support officer who sat behind the wheel of the extraordinary vehicle, a grey haired woman with a no nonsense expression. 'Rosie, can you circle through the village and broadcast the standard message? All residents are to evacuate, quickly but safely, to the emergency reception centre, otherwise known as the Secretarial College. Mini-buses are available, for those without transport, at St Agnes car park, here at the Green and at the car-park of the Queens Arms on Flowers.' He turned to his other colleagues. 'Once you've done your sweep, rendezvous at the College. Right, everybody clear? Off you go!'

The group of police dispersed and PC Ford returned to the police station. Behind the desk sat a Support Officer, who had been using the village's e-mail list to inform everyone of what the car tannoy would be telling them in rather older technology.

'You'd best get yourself off to the Reception Centre too,' said PC Ford. He pressed a key on his walkie-talkie and brought it to his ear as he walked outside again.

'Reverend? It's Bill. How many have you got so far? Over.'

'Thirteen, so far. Er.. over.' Reverend Jim's voice reverberated from the hand set.

'Roger that. Wait for a while longer, then give me a call. It'll arrive here before it reaches you. Over.' He terminated the call.

*

On the green a forlorn band of villagers was forming a queue by the police mini-bus, as Ray drove the Marshall & Son van by. Minutes later he parked as close to his mother-in-law's house as he could get, running the car up onto the pavement. In the window, a lace curtain fell back into place and the front door opened a crack. Then Winnie emerged, manhandling an enormous suitcase.

'You're not going for a month! It's just overnight, I hope,' Ray exclaimed, but he knew better than to argue and hauled the case down the path, through the picket gate to the car.

Winnie closed and locked the front door behind her, clutching a holdall almost as big as she was. She clambered into the car.

'Supplies,' she said, staring down Ray's enquiring look. Ray started the engine. He had another call to make on the Flowers Estate.

Ray tooted his horn as he drove by the Queens Arms, where bags were being loaded into the pub's mini-bus. He saw Dev Patel with a laptop, trying to find a Wi-fi signal as his squabbling siblings fought around him and Mrs Patel, being soothed by an ancient neighbour, who looked as if she could remember being evacuated in earlier days.

The streets were unnaturally quiet. No children were playing on the wide grass verges, there were no people walking or cars driving. In Cowslip Lane Sylvia Luck stood at the kerb, still in her heavy gabardine, with a wheeled suitcase beside her.

'Okay Sylvia. In you get.' Ray hurried round to pick up the case, which was heavier than he expected. 'Even more supplies, I suppose' he murmured under his breath.

'You haven't seen our Vince, have you?' Sylvia asked as she climbed into the car. 'He left as usual this morning and I haven't heard from him since.'

'He's probably outside the cordon,' Ray replied. 'He may already be at the reception centre, waiting for us.' He put the car into gear and pulled away.

*

'And now we go over to a local news blogger at the scene,' the newsreader said.

Susan turned up the volume on her laptop. The head and shoulders of Nicola Shah appeared, in front of High Acres hospital main building.

'Hello, Hugh, not quite at the scene, thankfully,' Nicola began. 'That's about three miles north west of here, where there was a major road accident earlier this morning. This involved a large chemical tanker carrying hazardous material, though we don't, at this time, know what those materials are. Apparently the markings indicating the contents of the tanker were destroyed in the accident.' She paused as a siren wailed. 'An area within a two mile radius of the accident has been closed off and evacuation is under way right now in the village nearby, so this would suggest an airborne hazard. Casualties have been arriving here all morning. Many are children from a local school, located about half a mile from the incident.'

'And have you been able to speak with any of the victims or the hospital staff?'

'No. As you can see,' pictures of ambulances arriving at the hospital were shown as the report continued. Susan recognised one or two faces. 'There has been a lot of activity here during the last few hours, but as yet no-one has been released for us to talk to.'

'Thanks Nicola.' The picture cut to the studio. 'We'll bring you more when we have it. Now, today's speech by the Governor of the bank of England...'

Susan pressed the laptop's mute button. Carol had telephoned from The Lion to say that she, Len and Vali, along with the rest of the village, were being temporarily removed. Carol couldn't tell Susan more, other than it was to do with an accident on the by-pass, but said she would ring again when she could. Susan had tried her parents' mobile numbers several times since, without success.

Her laptop trilled. A face appeared on the screen, it belonged to her friend, Matt Hare, who was studying at Manchester University.

'Hello Sue. Are you watching the news?'

'Yep, not that it told us much. I got a call from Mum before they left the village. Have you heard from anyone?'

'Yes. They're all being taken to some sort of temporary accommodation.'

'What are we going to do?'

'There's no point in going home,' Matt answered, shaking his head. 'But I want to find out more. I've been trying to reach Dev. You know Dev Patel, he was in our year?'

Susan didn't remember him but was too polite to say so.

Matt continued. 'He's at home and studying locally. I'll try Ellen as well and I'll get back to you if I get through.'

'Okay, thanks. Oh, Matt, can you give me Dev's number too?' She scribbled it down and waved, just as Matt's face disappeared. She switched back to the news.

*

'I can't do that right now, Lynda.' Hari was signing off patients for referral, initialling forms on a clip board as she stood. 'There's just too much to do here.'

'But he seems to have got worse. His breathing...' Lynda Marshall was standing in front of her, strained and anxious. She had returned to A & E from Archer Ward, where Paul had been taken and was trying to persuade the harassed paediatrician to take another look at him. She followed Hari through the swing doors. 'The nurses say that they have to wait for you.'

Hari could see that Lynda was worried, but then, so was everyone. She closed her eyes and leaned against the wall, giving a deep sigh. 'I can't be in two places at once, though heaven knows I'm trying.'

'Help!' A high pitched cry came from A & E, followed by a fresh bout of wailing. Hari hurried back through the swing doors, with Lynda in close attendance.

On the floor, a middle-aged man was lying, gasping for breath. It was Howard Goodman. The Furzedown science teacher and his colleagues had supervised the evacuation wearing laboratory masks, shepherding children onto the coaches which had arrived to take them away. He had given the newer masks to others.

A pupil, whose calls had attracted help, was shaking his shoulder. Orderlies lifted him from the floor onto a stretcher trolley and pushed him through the swing doors into relative quiet. Hari made to follow. She turned to Lynda.

'Lynda, I can't come now! Don't you see? The nurses will keep an eye on your son. I have to treat the patients.'

Leaving Lynda standing in the doorway, Hari followed the stretcher.

*

Sid finally reached the village green and stopped, awed by the frantic, but controlled activity before him. Community centre staff were helping aged or infirm villagers towards and into mini-buses, having ferried them from their outlying homes. They were given breathing masks as they climbed aboard.

'What's this?' Sid heard Alf Harkiss exclaim, as a mask was thrust into his hands. 'Mustard gas attack?'

Several of the buses were setting off. Sid spotted PC Ford outside the little police station and strode across.

'Sid.' The policeman greeted him. They were known to each other, PC Ford sometimes having had occasion to move the other on, before Sid attained his recent, more settled, status − living in the village and writing for a living. 'I understand that it was you who raised the alarm. I'm grateful and the whole village will be, when everyone finds out.'

'Wasn't nothing,' Sid replied. 'Needed doin'. You should know, there's a wind comin'.'

'A wind? From which direction and how fast? What will it do to the cloud?'

'It's a westerly, but it's not here yet,' Sid's nostrils flexed. 'Should've blown the mist out be now. Do we know what it is?'

'Tankers should display that information,' the policeman replied. 'But the accident damaged this one so badly that nothing's readable. HQ is tracking back to the haulage company.' He grimaced. 'I think you're right, what breeze there is moves the mist along the ground, but there just isn't enough wind to disperse it.'

'We need to be somewhere up high.' St Agnes bell-tower caught Sid's eye. He and PC Ford exchanged looks and they both started out towards the church.

*

On the outskirts of a nearby town the Queens Arms mini-bus, which had left the pub car park about forty minutes before, turned through the gates of a college. This was the designated emergency reception centre.

Dev recognised many of the vehicles already in its car park, some still disgorging passengers familiar to him.

Once out of the mini-bus Dev and his group joined a long line of people going to the sports complex. Inside staff took their names and personal details and directed them to the areas allocated for assembly.

This was the college gymnasium. It was thronging with people, their voices echoing beneath the high ceiling. Stacks of chairs lined one wall, to which people helped themselves. Family groups sat on them, or on the wooden floor, while children ran around or played on the wall bars. Clusters of people stood, discussing.

In a corner, Dev was finally able to get on-line. His screen resolved into an anxious female face.

'Hello? Hello, is that Dev Patel? I'm Susan Pendleton. You mightn't remember me, but I was in your year at Furzedown. Matt Hare gave me your number. Where are you now?'

'Er, hello, Susan.' Dev frowned, nonplussed by this development. 'They've set up an emergency reception centre. It's a college. We're in the gym – so is half the village."

On screen Susan asked. 'Do you know if my parents are there? Len and Carol, they keep...'

'The Lion, I know. Hold on, I'll have to see.' Dev climbed onto a chair to take a look around the huge hall full of people, colour and noise. In the centre of the melee he spotted Len and Carol Pendleton and the bar-maid, Valentina, standing in a small group. Like everyone else they were looking around, waiting for someone to come and tell them what was going on. 'Yes, they're here,' he said. 'Everyone's here. I'll tell them to call you.'

Dev caught sight of Ellen, with her boss and some women with wet hair and curlers. He recognised Mr de Silva with the Priory Road kids and Mrs Wells. Over by the small stage the Vicar was getting a group of pensioners seated, helped by the Thompson brothers. Mrs Thompson and her baby were already sitting.

'Did you speak to Matt?' he asked Susan.

'Yes,' she replied. 'I'll call and let him know you're on line.'

Dev became aware of a small sea of anxious faces peering up at him as a crowd formed around him. Folk had seen him standing on the chair, laptop in hand.

'I've suddenly become very popular,' he said. 'I'll have to go....'

In another corner of the gym Winnie dispensed tea from her thermos, laced with something stronger. She and Sylvia were perched upon a stack of rubber gym mats, their suitcases and other baggage making a narrow moat around their feet. Sylvia couldn't settle, she was becoming more and more anxious.

'I still can't see our Vincent.'

'If he's here, Ray'll find him, don't you worry,' said Winnie, giving her a reassuring pat.

Ray frowned. Vince's name hadn't been registered at the reception desk, so he hadn't arrived at the centre. When Ray called his phone it went straight to voicemail, yet the networks were functioning again. But Ray had more pressing worries than tracking down a recalcitrant Vince. Lynda had phoned to tell him about Paul. He kept the news to himself. There was already enough to scare the old ladies and all might turn out well, but the uncertainty worried at him as he paced back and forth.

Anything could be happening and he wasn't at his family's side. Ray wanted only to go to the hospital, to where Paul lay. He looked at Winnie and Sylvia. Both were grey-faced. He shook his head – he couldn't tell them about Paul and he couldn't leave them either. He would just have to stay where he was. There was nothing to do but sit and wait.

*

Back in the village the air was still untainted, but it was becoming increasingly deserted. On the roof of St Agnes bell tower PC Ford and Sid could see the occasional police car or emergency vehicle, cruising around empty roads. But nothing else was moving.

Sid looked towards Calley Wood, brown and spiky on its rise. 'I hope the wild things knows enough to get up high,' he said.

The police radio crackled into life.

'Flowers Estate is clear Bill. We're taking the last of them over to the reception centre. Over.'

'Thanks, Darren.' PC Ford pressed buttons. 'PC Ranu, come in please. Are you there Jag? Over.'

'Hello Bill. Plough Lane, Coppice Row and Canal Road are clear. We're going to swing around Larkhall and Weir House and then we'll be heading back to base. Over.'

'Thanks.' The radio in PC Ford's hand went silent. 'Well, that looks like it. We'll keep the patrols going for as long as possible, in case anyone comes out of the woodwork and to deter looters, but otherwise... evacuation complete.'

'S'just as well.' Sid nodded, his face grim.

The policeman followed Sid's gaze. At the far edge of the village, the mist had just arrived on their side of Calley Wood. The wood was being marooned, an island in a sea of white vapour.

'Come on. We'd better get going ourselves.' PC Ford was careful in leading the way down the twisting stone stairs. At the bottom, he closed the old wooden door and turned the iron key. The two men hurried across the church lawn and climbed, not without haste, into the police four by four. PC

Ford helped Sid with his seat belt. He put the car into gear and they drove away.

*

At the reception centre Ray was leaving yet another urgent message for Vince to call, when he spotted PC Ford entering the gym. He found himself part of a small scrum, moving towards the policeman, who headed for a makeshift dais at the far end of the huge room. PC Ford climbed onto it and faced the crowd of vilagers.

'Hello, everyone. I'll answer questions in a moment, but first I'd like to let you know what's happening.' Hush descended as he spoke. 'The village has been successfully evacuated, although patrol cars are still driving round, just in case. As far as we know there are no fatalities, though the hospital isn't releasing anyone until the nature of the gas is known. I'll be posting lists of names of those at the hospital around the room in a moment, though I expect you know about your own friends and relatives already.'

The policeman looked around the crowd. 'I don't know how long you'll have to stay here. We have to ensure that the gas has been sufficiently dispersed before letting you all go home. However, there is hot food being prepared and lunch will be available shortly. Now, are there any questions?'

Basil de Silva spoke up. 'What happens if we have to stay away over night? Do I close the school tomorrow?'

'We won't know about tha until later,' PC Ford replied. 'Though people here have already been volunteering to put up folk for the night if there aren't enough hotel rooms.'

'Hotel rooms!' A strangled cry from one corner diminished to a low whisper. 'Who's going to pay for hotel rooms?'

'Some of you may prefer to stay with a local family and there is some, limited, accommodation here on campus. Please speak to reception. If you have preferences they'll try to take them into account. Right,' he received a signal from the door. 'I believe that lunch is now being served in the canteen and, before anyone asks, there is no charge. Thank you for listening.'

He jumped down and was surprised by a smattering of applause, as the villagers began to shuffle towards the exit.

*

In the children's ward of the hospital, already swathed in glossy streamers and inflated Santas, Paul Marshall opened his eyes.

'Mum!'

Daisy shrieked, leaning over his bed. Lynda jerked up from reading the newspaper and came to his side.

'Paul. Are you all right?' She clutched him to her body, an embrace which he was quite content to endure. 'How are you feeling? Do you want me to get the doctor? What about a nurse?'

When Lynda's frantic questions finally stuttered to a halt, Paul interjected, lying back on the pillows.

'I'm okay, Mum. I can't breathe very well, but I'm okay, I think.' He struggled to sit up, but fell back. 'What happened? I can't remember coming here.'

'The ambulance bought you.' Daisy explained. 'You collapsed.' She looked sideways at him. 'They say you ran into the mist to warn the others and breathed it in. They say you were very brave, but I didn't see it.'

'You ran into the mist!' Lynda looked horrified, but a little bit proud too. 'That was a brave thing to do.'

'It didn't seem like it, it seemed obvious.'

'Your Dad will be very proud of you. Just wait 'til he knows.'

Daisy stood up. 'I'll go back and help Molly now, Mum.'

'No, wait.' Lynda tried to catch her daughter's sleeve, but Daisy was already out of reach. She seemed to relent.

Anyway, thought Paul, what was the fuss? The crisis seemed to be passed.

'Oh all right then,' Lynda said. 'But tell Dr Mistry that Paul's all right."

*

The westerly wind predicted by Sid finally arrived in force and began to disperse the heavy mist. A second, very different, migration got under way from the college and villagers streamed from the gym, anxious to return home. They reloaded vehicles and, smiling, started for home, car horns honking. It sounded like the entire village was setting out on holiday.

Ray explained about Paul, very gently, to Winnie and they headed for the hospital. It took time to find a parking space, for lots of vehicles had preceded them from the college and there were also the usual hospital visitors. The facade of the building was illuminated by the setting sun. Ray glanced up with trepidation as the trio slowly made its way towards reception. This place figured in far too many of his memories.

They were directed to Archer, the children's ward. Half way along, against the left-hand wall, they saw Lynda sitting at the bed-side of a chalk-faced Paul. Winnie swallowed hard and Sylvia put an arm around her friend's shoulders as they followed behind the long striding Ray.

'Oh, Ray, I'm so glad...' Lynda stood and Ray held her. Then he embraced his son.

'Where's Daisy?' He asked.

'Gone to help Dr Mistry and Molly. She's all right.'

'Good,' Ray nodded, with a thin smile. 'What's the prognosis?'

Lynda smiled, nervously, in response. 'He should be fine. He was outside when the gas got there.' She explained what had happened.

Ray listened carefully, his face grave. He turned to his son.

'You ran into the mist? Weren't you scared?'

'Well, yes, of course, but. I only ran towards it.'

'Good lad!' Ray swelled with pride. 'That was a courageous thing to do.'

Chairs were fetched and the family grouped around the bed, a cage of brushed aluminium. Only then was Sylvia's absence noticed.

'Well, where did she go?' Winnie was perplexed at her friend's disappearance.

Ray stood, saying − 'I'll go and look for her. She might be searching for Vince.'

'But...'

Ray shot Lynda a look and she bit back her objection.

*

As Ray reached reception he heard his name called.

'Ray, Ray Marshall! I'm glad you're here. Please.' It was Dr Mandeep Dhaliwal, looking stern. What could the doctor want to speak to him for? Ray began to conjure all sorts of possibilities. Was Paul worse than he'd imagined?

Mandeep steered Ray into a room no bigger than a large cupboard.

'Your son is fine,' he said, seeing the frightened look on Ray's face. 'But I wanted to tell you about Mrs Sylvia Luck.'

'Sylvia?' said Ray.

Mandeep sat and motioned Ray to do likewise. He spoke carefully and slowly. Ray wondered what was going on. Whatever it was, it was serious.

'Mrs Luck is in our bereavement suite, with the Reverend Gardener.'

'What?' Ray didn't understand. Who was bereaved?

'Her son, and your friend, I understand, Mr Vincent Luck...?'

Vince? Ray's mouth dropped open.

'He was fatally injured this morning, in the road accident which began all this. His body was brought in once it had been freed and is presentable now. Mrs Luck has asked to see it. Him.' He corrected himself. 'I was going to take her in

294

myself, then learned that you were here. It might be better if she was with someone she knew well. I've left a message for her daughter, but... with all the chaos....'

'Yes, of course.' Ray nodded again. He understood the words Mandeep was saying to him, but couldn't absorb their meaning.

Mandeep lead the way out into the corridor, then through what seemed like a labyrinth. They arrived before a plain door. Ray felt numb. If something happened to Lynda and the children, he couldn't imagine living without them. He remembered his grandmother's suffering.

Mandeep paused with his hand on the door handle. He was waiting for Ray's signal.

'Okay,' Ray said.

The room was quiet and comfortable. Its uncurtained window was a black rectangle. Sylvia was sitting in a corner. Jim Gardener rose from the seat next to her, drew close to Ray and gripped his arm as he left.

Mandeep crouched down before Sylvia, he took her hands in his and looked up into her face.

'Mrs Luck. Mrs Luck.'

She seemed to return from far away. Sylvia focussed on the medic and gave the briefest of nods.

'I've brought Ray to be with us,' Mandeep spoke softly. 'When we go to see Vincent.'

She gripped Mandeep's hands and tears rolled down her cheeks without a sound.

Ray knelt on the floor beside Mandeep. 'I'm here, Sylvia,' he said. 'If you need me.'

A raw and feral sound issued from Sylvia's throat. She slid forward, the will that held her upright had deserted her. Ray caught the frail body and held her in his arms. Wrenching sobs shook her with a different cadence. Salt tears soaked Ray's shirt. He carried on soothing, rocking her as he rocked Paul and Daisy when they were distressed or in pain. Eventually the dreadful keening cries ceased. Sylvia seemed exhausted.

'I don't think she ought...' said Ray.

'No, nor do I.' Mandeep agreed.

'I want to see him!' Sylvia summoned up a wiry strength and disengaged from Ray, heaving herself upright. 'I'm his mother. It's my right!'

Ray and Mandeep exchanged glances, but neither considered that they had the moral authority to gainsay her and prevent it. So they all stood and the two men helped Sylvia through the unmarked door to the basement.

In the hospital morgue there was a smell of formaldehyde and white spirit. Vince's body lay on a shiny steel table, covered by a white sheet. Ray held Sylvia as Mandeep drew back the cotton to reveal Vince's sandy hair and freckled face.

*

Outside the bereavement suite window, in the rose garden, white lights hovered and danced and muted laughter sounded. Hospital staff, released from more important duties, were putting Christmas decorations on the pergolas by torch-light, festooning them with coloured faery lights. Within the hospital other staff were doing similarly. In reception two nurses were pulling the silver tree into position. Tomorrow those young patients who were able, or could be enabled, would decorate the tree with baubles and gifts.

In the children's ward lights had been dimmed and Paul snoozed, his breathing shallow, but steady. Even Winnie dozed in her chair.

Daisy made her way along the ward towards the bed. Molly had sent her to be with her family. The sight of her youngest child, returning red-eyed and yawning, prompted Lynda to prepare to leave. She looked around for Ray, who had been gone for what seemed like a long time.

'Come on,' Lynda whispered to her daughter. 'Time to go. It's been a long day. Text your Dad, tell him we're going home.'

Lynda leaned across Winnie and took her shoulders in her hands to awaken her.

Winnie chuntered, opening her eyes. She heaved herself to her feet, wincing, for her arthritic knees were complaining at the sudden movement. She pulled on her coat and placed Daisy's woollen hat upon the girl's head. Lynda gathered up bags and rucksack from the floor. She glanced at Paul, his chest rising and falling in a gentle rhythm. She hesitated to wake him and it fell to Daisy to reach across to kiss his forehead.

'Mum. Mum!' Daisy's high, tremulous voice cut sharply through the hush. 'He's stopped breathing! Mum!'

Lynda turned back, leaned over the bedside cabinet and slapped the emergency button, again and again. Daisy clung to Winnie's coat, looking on in terror.

The emergency medical team was there in seconds, gently but firmly moving the trio away. Curtains were pulled around Paul's bed and a nurse rushed in a trolley of equipment. Lynda, Daisy and Winnie waited on the outside, stunned and silent.

*

In the bereavement suite, Sylvia's daughter finally arrived. Ray greeted her, not knowing what to say.

I'm muttering platitudes, he thought. Is that what people do at times like this? Shaken, he excused himself and started back to the children's ward. His phone shuddered.

'Hello, Lynda.'

'It's Paul, oh Ray, it's Paul.' Ray heard the panic in his wife's voice. 'He's relapsed.

'What? When?' Ray looked about him. How quickly could he get to the children's ward? Was there a sign? There.

'Just now, we were about to leave…'

'So what's happening?' Ray lengthened his stride.

'The emergency team's here. They've pulled the curtains around. Oh Ray…'

His limbs seemed to turn to water and shiver.

'I'm coming,' he said. 'I'm on my way.'

Ray snapped shut his phone and broke into a loping run, dodging staff and patients. He barely saw the people, wheelchairs and trolleys as he ran, heart pounding and afraid to his marrow. The short journey seemed interminable, as the corridors twisted and turned. At some point he became aware of the small figure of Dr Mistry running alongside him and realised that they were nearing the children's ward. They clattered through its doors. Half way along, on the left, curtains were drawn around a bed.

Dr Mistry turned to Ray and ordered in a commanding voice. 'Stay!' She disappeared beyond the curtains. There were low voices and murmured consultations.

Outside the curtains his family waited. Lynda eyes beseeched him to make things right. Daisy looked lost and had been crying. Winnie seemed crushed and old. He wanted to embrace them all and make it better.

Out of breath, he reached for Lynda and Daisy.

'What's happening?'

'He wasn't breathing. He'd stopped breathing. Daisy saw. I didn't. Why didn't I look more closely?' Lynda's fist was at her mouth, even as she stood in his arms.

'How long? For how long wasn't he breathing?'

'Not long, Dad.' Daisy's face was tear-streaked and puffy. 'He was breathing and then, suddenly, he wasn't.'

'That's good, that you noticed it straight away.' Ray crushed her shoulder.

There was a muted whimper from Winnie.

'Did you find Sylvia?' she asked.

'Yeah.' Ray blinked.

And?'

'Her daughter came to collect her. She's on her way back to Bluebell Road by now.'

Winnie nodded, eyes fixed on the patterned curtain.

The four of them stared at the pattern as the minutes went by. Ray thought that he couldn't bear the tension any longer when Dr Mistry pulled back the curtain. Behind her Paul was being carefully lifted on to a stretcher trolley. She gave a weak smile.

'He's still with us. We think he's going to be all right, but we're taking him to intensive care where we can keep a closer eye on him'

Lynda crumpled against Ray and Daisy burst into relieved tears. Winnie clutched at the place where she thought her heart should be.

'What is it?' asked Ray. 'What happened? He was fine?'

Dr Mistry's eyes were smudged with dark shadows, her eyelids seeming so thin as to be almost translucent. 'His air tube blocked, just for an instant,' she said. 'We know what the gas is now, so we'll be able to treat him properly. You can come and visit him tomorrow and he'll probably be sitting up in bed. But go home now. Get some rest.'

'Thank you, doctor.'

'Yes, thank you.'

The Marshall family shuffled out of the ward, each of them watching Paul's trolley as it disappeared. Wrapped around each other they walked, in an unfeeling haze of release and fatigue, towards the car park.

Above the hospital the night sky was filled with cold and glittering stars. Their eldritch light illumined the countryside around. At Furzedown School a single beam of torchlight lit the janitor ensuring that the gates were firmly padlocked. Calley Wood was dark and silent.

In the village householders drew their curtains closed against the frosty dark. Children who were previously too excited for sleep now slumbered. People looked on their loved ones more mindful of their preciousness. Phone land lines were busy and the air was full of voices.

At St Agnes Reverend Gardener lit candles for Vince Luck and the unnamed tanker driver and gave thanks that these were the only fatalities. Len Pendleton opened The Lion's low wooden door, just in case anyone wanted to come in for warmth or comforting talk. Nearby PC Ford finished his report, spell-checked it and sent it off to HQ. Switching off his computer he decided to drop by The Lion on his way home.

In Marigold Road Winnie sat before her coal-fire, stroked Sylvia's dog and said little. She was exhausted. Nearby, upstairs in the Hare household, Sylvia slept a sedated sleep.

On the Marshall's sofa Daisy was curled up with her head in Ray's lap. Lynda, sitting alongside him, stroked her daughter's loosened hair. The Christmas decorations boxes were stacked in the corner.

'I tell you what,' Ray began. 'Let's put up the tree and all the decorations tomorrow morning. So everything's magical when Paul comes home at the weekend.'

Daisy stirred. 'Will he be coming home by the weekend, Dad?'

Ray patted Daisy's shoulder. 'I don't know, but let's hope so.'

Lynda looked at Ray. 'Aren't you working tomorrow?'

'No, I think tomorrow's work can wait a day,' was Ray's reply.

'Okay Dad.'

'Okay.'

14.

Coda

We are almost back to the beginning.

It is Felicity's Thompson's first Christmas and her parents, Tina and Carl, are full of joy. It is the first Christmas for Molly since Peter's death. She celebrates with the Thompsons and with Tinks and takes Quentin his presents. Molly brings Carl all Peter's tools.

Sylvia is too raw and damaged for celebration. She spends Christmas at Bluebell Road with the Hares. She hasn't yet returned to Cowslip Lane. She visits Winnie and the Marshalls and goes, for the first time, to Midnight Mass.

Diane enjoys her new home and status, reflecting on the year gone by and how things change. She dresses the house and invites her neighbours and friends for drinks. Jane is surprised to see Robert Santini there. There are architects plans for a basement. Retrenchment has yet to begin.

The Games Room at the Queens Arms sees a reunion of newly legal drinkers. Ellen Fisher and Matt Hare are awkward and shy, but soon catch-up with each other's news. Matt is planning a trip to the Himalayas, in the footsteps of the great plant-hunters of the past, to search for new species. Dev Patel is dating a girl from college, whom his mother hasn't met. They plan to move on to the Lion, to meet with Susan Pendleton and Vali Bubcek.

Like Vali, Greg Layton has been co-opted into the Pendleton family, a loose arrangement whereby he visits when he's in the UK. He finds himself serving behind the lounge bar on Christmas Eve, when the Lion is full, but celebrations are more muted than is usual. He ships out to Australia on Boxing Day. This time he will, to the envy of more than half the Lion's clientele, be photographing cricket. Vali's parents arrive the day after.

The Reverend Jim Gardener is busy, as is to be expected. Midnight Mass is well attended, despite the cold, and the ancient kneelers come out of store once more. St Agnes is always beautiful when filled with song and the presence of a police squad car on the church car park deters the rowdier element. On Christmas Day he visits the hospital where Hari Mistry is taking the unpopular shift. She is happy to do so.

Mandeep and Amrita Dhaliwal and family celebrate the birthday of Guru Gobind Singh at temple and return home to a feast of turkey, before visiting across the village, bearing traditional gifts.

In the Marshall house, amity and the season of goodwill has given way to the usual squabbles. Ray and Lynda insist that both their off-spring accompany them to visit Sylvia Luck's ninety-four year old cousin in her care home in Bridge.

Nature takes its course. The horse chestnuts around the park stand massive and leafless. Ferns grow in between their twisting roots. The line of trees marches up the hill to meet the ancient woodland, where life is already stirring, 'though it will not be evident for many weeks to come. The wild wood is waiting for the longer, lighter days, as the turning world continues its course around the heavens, amid the wheeling constellations.

ACKNOWLEDGEMENTS

I wish to thank all those who have encouraged and supported me in my writing. In particular, thanks to Myfanwy Garth, for patiently reading and re-reading these tales from the start, giving constructive and useful advice (and remaining my friend throughout). Similar thanks to Annette Souter for her positive encouragement and unstinting help and support. They are mid-wives to these stories. Thanks also to Victoria Mixon, Stuart Wakefield and Roz Morris. And to my patient husband, who copes with my disappearances into the world of the village without reproach and creates wonderful oriental food to tempt me back.

WRITE A REVIEW

If you enjoyed this book, or just want to comment on it, please write a review on Amazon.com